THE SCHOOL OF ANECDOTAL MEDICINE

STORIES

JACOB M. APPEL

These stories first appeared in the following publications:

"Natural Selection" — *Gulf Stream*
"Enoch Arden's One-Night Stands" — *Beloit Fiction Journal*
"The Ataturk of the Outer Boroughs" — *Raritan*
"Exposure" — *Sycamore Review*
"The Magic Laundry" — *Columbia Journal*
"The House Call" — *Shenandoah*
"The Empress of Charcoal" — *Harpur Palate*
"Animal Control" — *Potomac Review*
"Cavitation" — *Opossum Magazine*
"In Sickness and in Health" — *Southwest Review*
"Flotsam Conundrum" — *Portland Review*
"The Price of Storks" — *Western Humanities Review*
"Emus Forever" — *McNeese Review*

The first eight stories were also previously collected in book form under the title *The Magic Laundry* (Snake Nation Press, 2015).

The final story, "The School of Anecdotal Medicine," is published here for the first time.

Set in Mrs Eaves with LaTeX.

ISBN: 978-1-963846-36-2 (paperback)
ISBN: 978-1-963846-37-9 (ebook)
Library of Congress Control Number: 2025936661

Sagging Meniscus Press
Montclair, New Jersey
saggingmeniscus.com

For Rosalie and Kaely

Contents

THE SCHOOL OF ANECDOTAL MEDICINE

NATURAL SELECTION

HE STOLEN BABOON. On the evening news, she's an irrelevancy—a simian mug shot tucked between National Hairball Awareness Day and an interview with the Boston Strangler's children. Six hours later, she's lounging on the sofa in our living room, smacking together her protruded lips, scratching her back on the damask. Suburban Tampa is apparently far more fun than a lab cage in Atlanta. At Emory, they didn't have a baby-grand piano to pound with her toes. Or curtains to swing from until the rods collapse. Or a cornucopia of plastic fruit. Pears. Bananas. Pineapple. She pelts these at me, one after another. When the fruit bowl runs dry, she lobs coffee table books, a bouquet of irises crafted from Matsuno beads. Her deep-set eyes look curious and playful; her rhythmic grunting sounds friendly, even gentle. But I am in no mood for games. The occasion calls for composure. Damage Control. Later, after Mrs. Bonzo has been returned to sender, there will be time to wring my daughter's neck.

"This is just unacceptable," I say. "You've crossed a line."

Tabitha sits with her chin braced on the back of a dining room chair. She is munching on sunflower seeds. Her eyes wander impatiently. I imagine she acts no differently from any other college sophomore, home for spring break, being chewed out by a beleaguered father. Her look is new since Christmas: a torn T-shirt, too large, screen-printed with an iconic Che Guevara. Rope sandals. Matted auburn hair. It strikes me that there is a slight sag to her breasts, a definition to her nipples—my daughter has abandoned her brassiere. All that is fine, of course. I'm a child of the sixties. I've described my own father, a professor of jurisprudence, as "well-intentioned" and "hopelessly bourgeois." If anybody can sympathize with a bit of youthful idealism, it should be me. But this is different. This is a federal crime. According to the legal commentator on channel seven, this may qualify as terrorism.

"Good God, Tabby," I say. "What were you thinking?"

"Do you know what they were going to do to her?" demands Tabitha. "They were going to cut her spinal cord. Intentionally. On the off chance they might be able to reattach it later."

"So you had to steal her?"

"Liberate her," retorts Tabitha. "How would you feel if somebody paralyzed you for their own amusement?"

I recognize the matter is far more complex than this—that the research at Emory, whatever its drawbacks, is not being conducted whimsically. They say the experiments may help quadriplegics walk again. I'm a conservation biologist. I have no way of knowing whether they are correct. Nor is this a matter I want to get into while a stolen baboon is beating the stuffing from my pillows.

"So you *appropriated* her," I say, neutrally. "You had to bring her home?"

"Her name's Kidogo. It means 'little one' in Swahili."

The baboon, as though on cue, sweeps across the coffee table and topples the stand of fire pokers. She appears to be grinning.

I ignore the mounting damage as best I can. I feel like the musicians performing with equanimity as the *Titanic* goes under.

"Couldn't one of your friends take her home?" I ask, desperately.

"They took the rabbits and the rats."

"Of course," I say. "The rabbits and the rats."

"It was a big operation," explains Tabitha. "We had only one chance." A big operation—I picture them sporting ski masks, secretly stockpiling rabbit feed and carambolas. "The Great Train Robbery" meets *Watership Down*.

I'm not sure how to respond to all this. Tabitha has always been a good girl, studious, top of her class. Pretty, too, like her mother was. Large eyes. Delicate chin. The truth is—at some point even a widowed father of an only daughter must admit this—boys like her. They want her. Enough to send roses, unsolicited letters. They throw pebbles at her bedroom window, beg short strolls to bare their hearts. I suspect some are luckier than others. That's her business. I've never asked. But then something like this happens, a case study in calamitous judgment, and you question how you've been so lax. At fifty-eight, I find it hard to understand why a popular, apolitical girl suddenly risks her future for the welfare of a gelada baboon.

"I could lose my job for this," I say. "We could go to jail."

Kidogo finds this amusing. She yanks a photograph from the wall, one of the prints I shot while rafting the Amazon. The picture sails over our heads. Its glass frame shatters against the mahogany sideboard.

Tabitha is now sobbing. She's driven straight through the night—she must be exhausted to the bone. Her bags are still in the Plymouth.

"I'm sorry, Dad," she says. "You don't understand. I had to."

"I know," I say, soothingly. "I'm sure you did."

Not certain is why Charles Robert Darwin, my relative and namesake, started scribbling the journal entries that would become *The Origin of Species*. I was pondering this very question—a matter central to my manuscript—when Tabitha, who happens to be his great-great-grand niece, arrived with the baboon.

A bit about my book: it will be entitled *Darwin on Darwin*. It is part of a series. They've already put out Clement Freud on his grand-father, and the anthropologist Selma Einstein-Loewenthal on her cousin, Albert. The volume wasn't my idea. I am writing at the urging of Francine Garvey, who teaches with me in the department of biology. Francine is the planet's foremost authority on ivory-billed woodpeckers. She searches for them, every spring, in Cuba's Sierra Maestra. There is a strong possibility that the birds—last sighted in 1987—have gone extinct. There is also a possibility that Francine is Tabitha's future stepmother. *This last part,* Tabitha doesn't know. Nor, though she carries his genes, has "Uncle Charlie" ever drawn my daughter's interest.

Back to Darwin. One theory contends that he suffered, after the age of thirty-five, from a panic disorder. The naturalist experienced "uncomfortable palpitations of the heart," also a fear he was "going mad." He shunned social engagements—preferring, instead, to read Thomas Malthus and to correspond with authorities on animal husbandry. The recent Cambridge graduate who boarded the *HMS Beagle* in 1831 was a gregarious dandy distinguished by his passion for hunting, shooting and cards. By 1845, he was somber and reclusive. According to psychiatric authorities, an acute shock or stress often precedes the onset of such chronic, debilitating anxiety. A chief suspect in this case: the death of Darwin's daughter, Mary Eleanor.

Tabitha falls asleep in the living room and I carry her upstairs. It's been at least a decade since I cradled my daughter's body like this, a lifetime since I tucked the flannel blanket around her delicate shoulders. Her heft surprises me. She's added pounds since grade school, a "freshman fifteen" on top of her "adolescent fifty." Sleeping, she seems to weigh extra—like a lifeless kitten. I adjust the pillows under her head, drawing the knotted bangs from her eyes. I kiss her on the forehead. Downstairs, I hear Kidogo barking sharply. I can also hear the television: an inopportune rerun, the late Marlin Perkins introducing *Mutual of Omaha's Wild Kingdom.* Our baboon is no lucky monkey. She's tuned to "Leopards of the Serengeti." Now she's terrified, flipping her black lips, emitting high-pitched wails. Serves her right, I think.

My next step is baboon-proofing the house. For this, there's no twelve-step program, no *Primate Management for Dummies*. You have to learn on the job, build sequentially like Robinson Crusoe or Swiss Family Robinson. It's part science, part art—for both of us. We discover she's too heavy to use the chandeliers as vines, gifted at finger-painting with feces. Initially, I'd kept her off the enclosed terrace, afraid her clamor might draw attention from the neighbors. That was a mistake, I see now. Keeping her in the living room, even overnight, is impossible. Kidogo's temporary home will have to be the side porch, though this means replacing the screens with storm windows. The job takes two hours—including twenty minutes icing the thumb I've crushed in the stepladder. Around dawn, I nail a heavy chenille bedspread over the glass. This will keep Kidogo hidden from view. (Unfortunately, it will also keep out the light—everything except for a glimmer of day at the edges of the cloth. There's no choice. I cannot risk Kidogo alone with electric cords, lightbulbs.) It takes nearly another hour, and a dozen frozen grapes, to lure the baboon onto the darkened veranda.

When I wake up around noon, Tabitha is already gone. She's left a plate of toast crusts and a quarter glass of milk on the kitchen table. She's also left a note:

GONE TO LUNCH AND A MOVIE.

PLEASE TAKE CARE OF KIDOGO.

LUV U. TAB

PS: CAN YOU GET HER CUCUMBERS & GRASSHOPPERS?

The baboon, mercifully, is still asleep. She's managed to topple the vintage telephone cabinet we inherited from my mother-in-law, and she's cuddled against its side, her head propped on an aquamarine vinyl hatbox. I tiptoe back into the kitchen, sliding shut the porch door behind me. Still in my bathrobe and slippers, I retrieve the morning paper from the front yard. It's cool for April. There's a breeze blowing off the Gulf. The frangipani have unfurled their tri-colors, dancing over an ocean of white gardenias. This should be an afternoon spent in the flower beds, transplanting day lilies, pruning tea roses. Unfortunately, the lead headline in *Tribune* reads, FBI: NO MONKEY BUSINESS IN LAB HEIST. Kidogo is also the top story on public radio, the midday TV news. A combination of national politics and human interest. Fortified, of course, by images of cuddly animals. The Berkeley-based "Animals First" has claimed responsibility. They've offered to barter Kidogo for a testing moratorium. The Attorney General has derided the perpetrators as "a fifth column of the Eco-Taliban."

Kidogo raps on the porch door. When I draw open the glass, she vaults from the folding table onto my shoulder; another jump lands her atop the refrigerator. She inspects me closely as I go about my business. We are out of instant coffee. Also cucumbers, grasshoppers. "You'll have to settle for bananas and water," I say. Kidogo pokes her nose forward and clutches the air with her hands. I suddenly feel guilty, as though I'm running a primate penitentiary. "Okay, okay," I say. "I'll go get you something. But you're going to wait on the porch." It's not that easy, of course. I don't want to draw suspicion, so I can't buy too many supplies at one location. By the time I return—my Saturn loaded with unbreakable mirrors, miniature tires, commercial primate food—Tabitha's Plymouth is already parked in the driveway.

My daughter's crouched on the porch, slapping around a ball with the baboon. It's a lightweight, rainbow beachball. She's dressed Kidogo in one of my cotton T-shirts. The shirt has DARWIN FAMILY REUNION emblazoned across the chest. I imagine my daughter finds this amusing.

"You had no business going out like that," I say.

"What was I supposed to do? It was the first day of spring break. Don't you think my friends would have gotten suspicious?"

I hadn't thought of it this way. "That's not the point."

Tabitha claps the baboons hands together several times; afterwards, Kidogo repeats the clapping gesture unassisted. "She's very smart," says Tabitha.

"We can't go on like this," I warn her. "This is an untenable situation."

Tabitha looks up, pleading. "We'll keep her hidden. Nobody will know."

"Sweet Jesus, Tabby. She's practically destroyed the house. How am I supposed to invite people over?"

"You don't have people over anyway," she says.

"I do, sometimes," I insist. "Hasn't it even crossed your mind that I might be dating again? That I might have a girlfriend?"

Tabitha hugs the beachball to her chest. "No," she answers. "It hasn't."

This isn't an objection, I understand—simply an observation. And the truth is that I'm not dating, that I haven't dated in the eight years since Annie drowned. Francine Garvey isn't a girlfriend. She's merely a prospect. "There's a nationwide monkey hunt going on, Tabby. Do you understand how serious this is? You have to take her back."

"I *do* understand how serious this is," she answers.

Kidogo raises herself on her hind legs, sniffing. Tabitha tosses her a piece of sliced mango.

"Maybe we could leave her somewhere," I suggest. "After all this attention, they won't dare hurt her."

"You don't know the first thing about baboons, do you?" retorts Tabitha. She says this as though it's the most degrading putdown. "She'll find her way back."

"To Atlanta?"

"To here, Dad. Baboons have homing instincts, sort of like pigeons. Anywhere you take her, she'll lead the F.B.I. right to your door."

"You've got to be kidding," I say. "We can't be stuck with her forever."

I frown at the baboon. She responds by squeezing the mango slice in her fist, letting the juice ooze between her fingers. Then—without warning—she jumps into my arms. Her nose is only inches from mine. She apparently wants to rub them together. Her long fingers grab at my face, leaving a fruity thumbprint on my glasses. I am suddenly nervous, overwhelmed. I recognize this feeling. I've known it before. It is being the parent of a young child. Against my better judgment, I rock Kidogo in my arms.

"What do you know about an organization called Animals First?" I ask Tabitha.

She shrugs. "Never heard of them."

"I didn't think so," I say.

I keep rocking. The baboon gurgles like a baby.

My great-granduncle's forty-three-year marriage to his first cousin, Emma Wedgwood, was repeatedly marred by tragedy. Only seven of their ten children survived to adulthood. Mary Eleanor, as I've mentioned, died of diphtheria in 1842. Her death coincided with her father's retreat from Victorian society. During the next seven years, the naturalist expanded his trove of display beetles, at its time the most impressive entomological collection in Europe, and penned an obscure treatise about barnacles. His ideas on natural selection remained private. They were heretical, after all. Unlawful. Moreover, Darwin was a communicant of the Church of England. He'd studied theology at Christ's Church. A publicity-shy ex-divinity student, particularly one dependant on a government fellowship, wasn't a good candidate to radicalize "the species problem." But then his daughter, ten-year-old Anne Elizabeth, succumbed to tuberculosis. Annie's death drove her father to atheism. His notes on natural selection rapidly became the most widely kept secret in England.

Darwin argued for gradual evolution. In recent years, a competing school of thought led by the late Harvard geologist Stephen Jay

Gould has championed 'punctuated equilibrium'—the theory that change occurs in sudden bursts. That has certainly been the case for me. Tabitha's birth catapulted me into adulthood. My own Annie's death—dragged off by a riptide at forty-seven—reordered my priorities. Ballet recitals and trick-or-treating rose in the pecking order; botany expeditions fell off the map. And now a third transformation. Kidogo. I watch her playing dress-up with Tabitha. They are working through my daughter's childhood wardrobe. This afternoon, the baboon's decked out in a blue dress with anchors embroidered on the shoulders. A red neck bandanna. A sailor's cap. She looks a bit like Ethel Merman in *Anything Goes*. Tabitha holds the mirror for her, letting her poke at her reflection with long, pointy fingers. I haven't seen my daughter so happy since Annie's death. I've been watching her all week. I've accomplished nothing on my manuscript. I haven't even returned Francine's phone calls. Six days ago, my future looked as clear as the horizon: writing, gardening, excursions on the Gulf in Francine's speedboat. Now, who knows? I try not to think about what we'll do with the baboon when Tabitha returns to school.

In one way, Darwin had it right. I'd die for Tabitha. I'd kill for Tabitha. It's impossible for me to understand surviving the loss of a child. Maybe that is why writing about my great-granduncle brings me to tears. He did not attend the reading of his seminal paper, *The Origin of Species*, at the Linnean Society on July 1, 1858. His favorite son, Charles Waring, had died of scarlet fever three days before.

I read the headlines on the Sunday *Tribune* with relief. Every morning we've been the lead story: NO LIGHT ON MONKEYSHINES; ALL POINTS BANANAS IN BABOON HUNT. Fortunately, there's been an apocalyptic earthquake in Peru over the weekend, and the governor of Florida's confessed to cross-dressing, so we're out of the paper. That's how it works on the Gulf Coast. Either you're page one, or you're yesterday's news. The rest is all sports, obits, crime blotter. That's usually frustrating. Today, it's a gift from the gods. I shuffle back into the house, feeling as though I've knocked the scythe from death's arms. "You may be home free yet, you dumb baboon," I announce. "Papayas on the house! What do you say to that?"

Tabitha stumbles down the stairs, rubbing her eyes. It is early afternoon. Caring for a two-year-old baboon has addled our sleep cycles. "What's going on?"

I hand her the newspaper. "Our fifteen minutes of fame are over," I say. I've already done a calculus in my head: it took them eighteen years to catch the Unabomber, twenty-one to nab the Jackal. The Zodiac Killer is still on the lamb. Comparatively, we're small potatoes. To celebrate, I peel the skin off a cucumber. That's when I'm struck by the silence from the porch. No pounding. No wailing. Not so much as one guttural moan. I slide open the screen door, still carrying the cucumber.

"Kidogo!" I shout. "What the hell——?"

She's gone, of course. The hatbox stands atop the ironing board, an improvised stepstool, and the bedspread has been torn from its perch. During the night, Kidogo has managed to unscrew one of the storm windows. They don't call baboons "mimic monkeys" for nothing. All those hours watching me work with the phillips head, she was bound to pick up the basics of carpentry. Outside, a soft breeze flutters the magnolias. A pair of purple gallinules cavort beside the canal. In the distance loom the shore-front highrises, hostile concrete watchtowers. Tracking a baboon around Tampa Bay would be both foolhardy and futile.

I sit down at the kitchen table, unnerved. Tabitha combs the porch, peeking behind lawn chairs and under stacks of plywood. "Maybe she's just hiding," she pleads. "Maybe she's playing a game." Her eyes are glazed, slightly bloodshot. Pillow stuffing hangs in her hair. My daughter looks as though her home has just been blown away by an unexpected hurricane. "Kidogo!" she cries. "Kidogo!"

"Don't. The neighbors will hear."

Tabitha kicks aside two badminton rackets. "Who the hell cares?"

I cross the kitchen and hug my daughter; she practically collapses into my arms. And then the buzzer sounds. Twice. A pause. Three times. I gently push Tabitha back onto her feet. Through the living room curtains, I see two state troopers standing in the portico. One is short with a small nose, protruding ears. His tall, broad companion boasts a chiseled jaw and an overhung brow. They look like toy soldiers plucked off different rungs of the evolutionary ladder. Both men have orange blossoms, the Florida state flower, pinned to their lapels. Uneasily, I inch open the door.

"Good morning, officers," I say. I sense Tabitha behind me in the shadows. My instinct is to obstruct the entryway, to shield her from view.

"Sorry to bother you," says the shorter trooper. He bears a striking resemblance, I realize, to a marmoset. "We're looking for a missing baboon."

What a coincidence, I think. I can feel the blood in my temples. "We've had several sightings this morning," continued Officer Marmoset. "You haven't seen anything, have you?" He passes me a photograph of the wanted animal—as though to distinguish Kidogo from other baboons afoot in Southwest Florida.

Officer Gorilla looks bored. He tests the strength of the porch swing, pokes at the wasp nest above the drainpipe with a stick.

I shrug at the photo. "I'd remember that face," I say.

Marmoset nods agreeably. "Well, if you see anything."

"Of course, of course." We're in the clear. At least for the moment. I flash a plastic smile, gradually inching shut the door. That's when Gorilla takes a sudden wasp sting on the thumb.

"Fuck!" shouts Gorilla. "Fuck! Fuck! Fuck!" The trooper wrings his oversized hand, trying to shake away the pain. As the initial throb recedes, he grins sheepishly. "Sorry about that," he apologizes. "Think I could use your john?"

I have no choice. I direct Gorilla to the downstairs bathroom. Marmoset stands in the foyer, examining the broken chandelier and the overturned hat rack. "You redecorating?" he asks.

"We had a bit of a row," I answer. "All over now."

"I've got the world's worst temper," adds Tabitha.

Marmoset ambles to the cherrywood letter table. He picks up a partially peeled banana and examines it suspiciously. I realize I am still brandishing the vegetable knife and the naked cucumber. The trooper turns to Tabitha. "You in school?" he asks.

She nods.

I'm afraid he'll ask where. Emory is ground zero in the baboon saga. Instead, he says: "Funny time to leave bananas out, isn't it? With a wild monkey on the loose."

It seems he's toying with us. Now's the time, I know, to shout for Tabitha to flee. It's two against one. If I take Marmoset by surprise— tackle him from the side—she might make it. But my daughter's in no condition to escape. She's wearing thin cotton pajamas dappled with miniature teddy bears. These make her look girlish, innocent. Not the outfit I want my daughter displaying for the neighbors. Or even Florida's Finest. That's when I realize Officer Marmoset isn't playing detective. He's flirting with my daughter.

Marmoset grins at his banana remark. "That was a joke," he explains.

"I hope your partner's okay," I say. "I feel dreadful."

I hear Gorilla shut off the bathroom faucet. He returns, his thumb wrapped in toilet tissue. "What's with the primate food?" he asks.

I've realize I've left the feed sack under the sink.

"I'm on a diet," I say. "Anti-Atkins." I pat my stomach for effect.

Gorilla frowns. "Mind if we look around a bit?" he asks.

I try to conceal the knife and cucumber behind my back. "We're actually on our way out," I stammer. "Maybe later."

"Maybe later," echoes Gorilla. "Maybe we'll bring a warrant."

He gives the foyer a once-over as he departs. Marmoset follows, offering Tabitha an apologetic smile. "I guess we'll see you later," he says.

I push shut the door. Nausea is building in my throat. With our narrow escape comes a violent recognition of my own stupidity. How could I possibly hope to conceal a stolen baboon on my veranda? How could I take such risks with Tabitha's future? Kidogo's disappearance—any way you look at it—is a blessing. "Let's clean this place up," I say. "Before they come back."

Tabitha's teeth are chattering. "What's that?" she asks.

There's no mistaking it. A hard knock at the back door. How could I have underestimated Marmoset and Gorilla? Surprise is on their side.

I'm ready to fess up and beg for mercy. I'll plead guilty, if they'll drop the charges against Tabitha. That seems fair. It's unnecessary, of course. Marmoset and Gorilla are not on the back steps. It's Kidogo. Returned. Offering me a hug and a sprig of orange blossoms.

Many philosophers before Darwin had noted the brutality of the natural world, the struggle between the lion and the lamb. What made Darwin's work so original was his focus on conflict within a single species. He wrote about finches competing with finches, relative mating advantages among crabs. Survival of the fittest. The most cynical of all biological theories. A direct contrast to Lamarck's optimistic claim that animals' traits reflect "inner longings" for perfection. One cannot help wondering what set the man's thinking down this pessimistic path.

Two recent biographies emphasize the death of Darwin's mother, Susannah, when the naturalist was only eight. The boy may have developed the seeds of his theory while watching his five siblings, and numerous cousins, compete for the attentions of his widowed father. Interestingly, several studies link genius with the early death of a parent. Newton, Dante and Copernicus all lost parents before the age of seven. This childhood tragedy may also be advantageous from an evolutionary viewpoint. Such a death forces the other parent to be more careful, take fewer risks. I've found that to be the case with me since Annie died. I've quit smoking. I won't go up with Francine in her Cessna. I refuse to collect specimens in the Colombian Cordillera. What choice do I have? Tabitha needs me. The death of a second parent, from the perspective of an individual organism, is an evolutionary calamity.

Our window of opportunity is narrow. The monkey squad may return at any moment, armed with a warrant and a tranquilizer gun. I recognize that the situation demands parenting of the unpopular, bullet-biting sort.

"I've made a decision," I say. Tabitha is cheerful again, bathing Kidogo's soft black fur in the kitchen sink. We've learned the hard way that baboons need regular washing, particularly their rumps and the coarse tufts at the tips of their tails. They cannot be toilet-trained and possess a knack for peeling off diapers. "Please, Tabby. Hear me out."

Tabitha wipes the baboon's nape with a washcloth. "I'm not taking her back," she says, sharply. "I'd rather go to jail."

"Nobody is asking you to take her back," I say. "But she can't stay. You know that. You have to go to school and I have to go back to work. If those cops find her here, it will ruin our lives." My daughter eyes me apprehensively. Kidogo splashes suds onto the countertop.

"I have a colleague," I explain. "She owns a speedboat. She's willing to run the baboon down the coast into Cuba. Or to give it a shot, at least."

"When?"

"Tonight." I'm clenching my fists behind my back, hoping this works. "She'll let her loose on the coast. Near Puerto Esperanza. What do you say?"

"I love her," says Tabitha. "It's not fair."

She's already lost her mother. It tears me apart to watch her go through this again. "I can't see any other way, honey. Trust me."

※

Tabitha slumps into a kitchen chair, cupping her coffee mug in both palms. She pours chocolate syrup into the coffee. I watch as the syrup oozes glacially from the jar and as my daughter stirs the concoction, then licks off the spoon. "What if I say yes?" she finally asks.

"That's the end of it," I say. "I take her down to the marina and tomorrow morning she wakes up across the water. Baboons can't swim, can they?" Tabitha doesn't smile at this jest, so I add: "Francine knows people in Cuba. I'm sure she'll be looked after. Safer than risking recapture around here."

"I guess," says Tabitha. "Can I come with you to the boat?"

I shake my head. "Best not," I say. "Someone has to straighten this place up before the return of the monkey wardens." I'm not thrilled about leaving Tabitha alone with Officer Marmoset, particularly with Gorilla as chaperone—but the alternative is leaving a trail of coconut shells and citrus rinds that leads straight to Alcatraz. Or Guantanamo. Or wherever they torture monkeynappers. "And Tabby," I say, "put on some real clothes before they come back."

"Yes, Dad." Tabitha's tone is sarcastic. She's unused to being parented.

I smile and squeeze my daughter's hand. "Now say your goodbyes."

Kidogo has been churning up a storm in the sink. She's already made projectiles of the paper towel dispenser and the plastic drain board, and now she's applauding by smacking two Brillo pads together. The baboon snorts merrily. Tabitha lift her out of the sink by the armpits.

"Should I pack some toys for her?" asks Tabitha.

"They have toys in Cuba."

"Just a few," says Tabitha. "For the trip."

My daughter darts to the porch. She returns with several fluorescent rings, a rubber pumpkin, a stringy velvet orangutan. Meanwhile, I retrieve my own supplies: my spare gardening gloves, a handful of mangoes, a bottle of valium. I use one of the mangoes to lure the baboon down to the garage and into the trunk of the Saturn.

"It'll just be for few minutes," I apologize. "She'll have plenty of air." Tabitha leans into the trunk. She rubs noses with Kidogo, scratches the sensitive skin behind her ears.

"I'll love you always," she says. "I promise." My daughter draws back her head. I slam the trunk lid like a guillotine.

We stand inches apart in the hot stillness of the garage. Around us rest the relics of Tabitha's childhood: a warped ping-pong table folded on its side, a pogo stick, an iron cabinet stocked with board games, the husks of several cardboard dioramas. There are also dented metal trashcans, Annie's easel. The air smells of mulch. And now a three-year-old Saturn sedan with a baboon locked in its trunk. Until I drive away. I guess that's what happens to all childhoods. They're carted away, piece by piece, until nothing remains.

"One thing," I say. "About your companions in crime. Rabbits and rats. They won't break down and confess, will they?"

Tabitha cast her eyes toward the floor. She shakes her head. "You sure, Tabby?"

"I didn't have any companions," she says. Her voice is hardly audible. "I let the rabbits and rats out in the park. It was the best I could do."

"You mean you did this on your own?"

"I read about the experiments on-line. I had to do something."

"On your own," I say again.

"You're going to kill me, aren't you?"

I place my thumb under her chin and raise her head. "I love you, Tabby," I say. "Far more than you love that baboon. Never forget that."

"Make sure she's safe."

"I will," I promise. "Now clean up the house. We'll have plenty of time later to discuss your life of crime."

Tabby smiles.

I press the garage door opener, flooding us with sunlight. I wave at my daughter as I pull the Saturn down the driveway. I've never been so proud of her in my life.

It's around 4:30 pm when I arrive at the Pelican Cove Marina. The attendant, Ike, is a jovial retiree with a full white beard. He knows me well. Several years ago, I helped get his granddaughter admitted to the state university at Gainesville, so when he hears that I've planned a romantic surprise for Francine—an unqualified fabrication—he's delighted to loan me the spare keys to her speedboat. So far, so good. I pull the *King Woody II* out into the channel. A shirtless teenager is feeding mackerel to the cormorants on a nearby jetty. The fat birds squawk and tussle over fish. Already, the sun is dipping toward a pink horizon, playing cat-and-mouse with a bank of innocent clouds. When I clear the harbor, I open the throttle and hug the mangroves until I reach a thoroughly secluded patch of sand. It's an abandoned loading dock at the end of a lane of ground seashells. That's where I've left the Saturn. That's where Kidogo waits for me.

I pop the trunk. The baboon peers tentatively over the side, her eyes adjusting to the blinding light. When she sees me approaching, she bellows a series of high-pitched chirps. This is a good sign. The equivalent of tail-wagging in dogs.

"None of that," I warn her. "We'll have to gag you."

She jumps into my arms and snuggles her nose against mine. Within minutes, we're out on the open water.

To the south lies Cuba. Three hundred miles. To the west is open water, the Dry Tortugas, Mexico. "I'm going to miss you, you dumb baboon."

My eyes are tearing up. Kidogo frowns in sympathy.

"You have to understand," I explain. "It's nothing personal." We are soon out of sight of the shoreline, cruising fast. "I have no choice," I add. *I don't have a choice.* I've thought it all through. Calling Francine isn't an option—I understand that now. She has her own priorities. She'd want no part of this. And Cuba? Far too much risk. I'd get caught. And how could I possibly explain smuggling this baboon out of Florida in a way that wouldn't implicate Tabitha? That wouldn't threaten her future?

"I'm not happy with my decision," I say. "But I can live with it." I feed Kidogo one final mango, slice by slice. I've taken care to embed a handful of valium in the fruit. She drifts off to sleep with the dusk. I slide my hands into my gardening gloves and firmly close them around her throat.

Gelada baboons are native to the Horn of Africa. Although Darwin discusses them in *The Origin of Species*, he relies upon first-hand observations of other naturalists. His own research focuses on finches, tortoises, and mockingbirds. These he gathers, week after week, while the Beagle island-hops through the Galapagos. He does not yet recognize that different species inhabited different islands. He stores his specimens together, unmarked, in one large bag. The significance of the finches' beaks, some blunt, some stout, some pointy, is, for the moment, entirely lost upon him. The winter the Beagle leaves London, Charles Darwin is only twenty.

That's my daughter's age. Years will pass before he figures out what's important.

ENOCH ARDEN'S ONE-NIGHT STANDS

THE PELICAN CITY Young Widows & Widowers Bereavement Circle met every Tuesday evening in the art/music/dance room of the Pelican Harbor Jewish Day School. The room itself was cluttered with the odd chaff of children's festivity: stacks of miniature xylophones, a pink tutu abandoned on an old gymnastics mat, finger paintings suspended along a line like laundry. Alex—who had arrived nearly an hour early—did not wish to be the first to cross the threshold. Instead he waited outside in the underlit corridor. Here the walls had been painted a cloying institutional yellow. Glass cases ran along both sides of the passageway, one documenting the history of the Holocaust through photography and the other relating local efforts to rehabilitate injured manatees, the parallel displays reflecting the heaped carcasses of Mauthausen and Ravensbrück onto newspaper images of beached aquatic fauna. Alex paced the length of the manatee exhibit, skimming the articles from the *Harbor Gazette* with nervous indifference, before suddenly latching onto the dangers of aiding sea mammals: that's how Karen had died, he decided. It was as promising a lie as any.

Although he'd had twenty-six months to decide precisely what had killed Karen, Alex had only given it meaningful thought in the five weeks since Big Mitch suggested a support group. "It's not just about what it's about, boss," the one-armed sous-chef had prodded him. "When I was in NA, nobody went to get clean. Half the women there were there for cock," he added. "And the other half were there for pussy." Maybe, thought Alex. But you couldn't show up for grief counseling if your spouse was still alive, he knew, so he imagined ways to kill her off: *My wife was devoured by alligators. My wife was kidnapped by pirates. My wife was vaporized by pioneers from the Andromeda Galaxy.* He strove to keep the scenarios as implausible as possible—to avoid all thought of serial rapists and ocean undertows—and in the end he was back at square zero. So why not death by sea cow? He'd say that Karen had detoured from her afternoon jog to comfort a stranded manatee, and the creature had dragged her off to Davey Jones' locker. He'd say . . .

Alex's eyes grew moist; he dared not wipe them. People passed behind him in the corridor—beneath the Israeli flag and into the room with the undersized chairs attached to undersized desks. Alex did not look up. His entire body rebelled against these first awkward moments of knowing nobody, enflaming his forehead, flushing the tips of his ears, so he did what he often did at weddings and parties: he focused all of his earthly attention on the first inanimate object to cross his gaze, which in this case happened to be the final glass panel in the manatee display. Staring back at him—all of her earthly attention focused on the Holocaust photographs to his rear—shone the petrified dark eyes of a young female reflection.

Causes of death, it turned out, played little role in group bereavement. The widows and widowers did not gather in a conclave and introduce themselves like alcoholics: *My name is John, I'm thirty-five, my wife toppled off a Ferris wheel; I'm Mary, forty-two, my husband skimped on second-rate fugu.* While the facilitator, Charlotte Ann, spoke at some length about the three drunk teenagers who'd shattered her husband's canoe with their speedboat, the other survivors—Will, Natalie, T.J., Tina, G-Man, Sammy B. and Joanna—steered clear of the morbid. They told stories of ski trips and tailgate parties; they complained about delinquent babysitters and the awkward prospect of introducing a new girlfriend to old in-laws. Alex grew anxious for each speaker. He wanted them to go over well—for their sakes. When it came time for the delicate, dark-eyed girl named Joanna to unburden herself, he thought of her reflection and how he had looked away too suddenly, and now he positively trembled. It was her first meeting too. She told of how her husband had once been clawed by a cat at his office on the afternoon before a charity dinner-dance, and how that evening when she accompanied him into the unisex restroom at the Cormorant Arms hotel to change the dressings on his wounds, the door jammed shut behind them. "So I manage to tear my gown practically in half, working on the lock," said Joanna. "And I'm shouting. And I'm crying. Help me! Let me out! The whole nine yards. When the security guy finally gets the door open, there I am with the front of my dress ripped open and Owen sitting on the toilet seat with his shirt off and scratch marks all over his chest and neck." The girl spoke very quickly, in desperate bursts. She couldn't have been more than twenty-five. When she finished her story, Alex realized that he was smiling directly at her.

Charlotte Ann thanked Joanna. Others murmured assent. "Anyone else?" asked the facilitator.

Everyone except for Alex had spoken. He looked down at the top of his miniature desk. A choppy hand had scrawled on the wood: *Why couldn't Helen Keller drive? Because she was a woman. Why couldn't Helen Keller read? Because she was from Alabama.* She'll adjourn the meeting, Alex thought, and I'll never come back. Nearby, the equine woman named Natalie reached for the jacket on the back of her chair.

"*That* man," chirped Joanna. "He hasn't had a chance." Alex suddenly found himself at stage center.

Charlotte Ann grinned. "Would *that man* like a chance?" she asked.

"Sure," lied Alex. "Why not?" And then he told the story of the night he'd proposed to Karen—when they were both only eighteen and living up north in Trenton, New Jersey. Her stepfather had owned a downtown bowling alley. Alex worked there as the manager on weekend evenings. During the pre-dawn darkness, the deserted Capital Lanes were an ideal setting for a lovers' tryst. Every Saturday night for nearly a year, Alex drove his future father-in-law home— and as soon as the old man entered the house, his daughter snuck out of the shrubbery for the return trip to the sofa in the bowlarama office. Until the March of their senior year. On the final day of that month, a Sunday, a mini-blizzard swept through Trenton after midnight. Its heavy, wet snow clung to the burgeoning leaves like webbing. When Alex and Karen arrived at the bowling alley for their rendezvous, a robust white oak had already plummeted through both the roof and the ceiling. Drifts rose waist-high on the lanes around the tree; frost seeped its way along the metal gutters like blood. The automatic pin setters had also gone haywire, toppling and replacing in a berserk game of chicken and egg. Alex was about to phone his employer when Karen's first snowball hit him smack between the eyes, and soon the two of them were on the slick floor of lane seven, groping and giggling, planning a wedding and a honeymoon in Florida. "I miss her," said Alex. "You know."

"Of course, honey," said Charlotte Ann. "We know."

Alex looked over at Joanna to see how his story had gone over, but she was diligently scribbling in a notebook. He tried to delay his own exit. He sat back down again and wrote on his desk: *Why couldn't Helen Keller find a husband?* Alex didn't know exactly why he was waiting, what he was waiting for. Soon he and the delicate girl were the only two people left in the room. When she shut her notebook, she appeared startled to find him still in his seat.

"Oh goodness," she said. "I'm so sorry. About before." Alex thought back to the reflection in the glass.

"You didn't want to say anything, did you? I realized that as soon as I said something. I'm stupid that way—I was just writing about it in my journal."

"No big deal," said Alex. He didn't like the expression *stupid that way*; he suddenly felt disappointed, almost betrayed.

"What you said was so romantic, though. All that snow reminded me of *Ethan Frome*."

Alex walked her to the elevator and they rode down the three stories in silence. It was only nine o'clock and the summer dusk greeted them on the boardwalk outside. Silhouettes of wood storks crisscrossed the horizon. Alex searched for words to continue the conversation.

"It's a book," said Joanna. "You're wondering about *Ethan Frome*. It's a book, not a movie."

"Okay."

"I'm an English teacher," added Joanna.

"Okay."

Alex focused on two small green lizards darting along the wooden planks. Across the school parking lot, a pickup truck churned dust in its wake.

"I need to unwind after that," said Joanna. "Do you know a good place to eat?"

The lizards ducked under the railing. "You're in luck," said Alex, smiling, relaxing. "I own a restaurant."

"Is it good?"

Nobody had ever asked that before. It was like asking if he was good in bed.

"Not without Karen," he answered, mechanically. "Not any more."

Alex revealed his secret over a sizzling platter of Apalachicola oysters and mussels marinière. They were ensconced at one of the corner booths in the Quarterdeck Room, swaddled by antique barometers and mollusk-draped rigging. The early bird crowd had long since departed, and through the swinging doors to the kitchen re-sounded the clash and clatter of the Captain's Mast readying for slumber. "A good restaurant needs beauty sleep, coddling," he said. "When we first bought this place from Karen's aunt and uncle, we tried to run it late into the night. We learned the hard way: the best bistros eat breakfast in bed." Alex refilled his wine glass, conscious of his tongue growing loose in his mouth. "I'm boring you to tears, aren't I?"

"No," answered the girl. "Not particularly."

Alex fumbled with his napkin ring. He regretted his vignette on the history of Oysters Rockefeller—but what else was he supposed to say? Seafood and Karen were the only two things he knew anything about.

A thin smile trailed across Joanna's lips, then faded. "That was supposed to be a joke," she said too quickly. "*The not particularly.*"

Alex nodded. "My wife's not dead."

He braced for anger—Karen's temper would have flared. Joanna merely dabbed her lips with her napkin and waited for more.

"She's missing," he said. "Vanished off the face of the earth."

Joanna toyed with her wedding ring; he wondered if this meant something.

"One day she went out jogging," he continued, "and she jogged straight off into oblivion. They had search teams combing the beach for weeks, but nothing. Not so much as a tennis shoe." When Joanna said nothing—just focused on him with her intense, sooty eyes—he let himself go. He spoke of the days squandered leafleting shopping malls, the exertions whose eventual purpose grew merely to fend off suspicion. And he spoke of the uncertainty, the frustrations, the second-guessing. How could he know whether she'd been carried away, gouging and clawing, or absconded fully of her own volition? How did he know if she'd show up again one day—at fifty? At eighty? He read in the paper about missing schoolgirls escaping from cults, amnesiacs stumbling upon long-lost spouses, Japanese kidnapees returning from North Korea. All this hope made his bed feel colder, his plight more desperate and urgent. "Every time I accept that she might be dead, something reminds me that she's still alive . . . But when I get to thinking she's coming back, death throws me a zinger." Alex tore the top off a pack of artificial sweetener and poured the grains into his water glass, watching them form a sheet of frost on the surface. "Sometimes I dream of footprints on sand," he said. "Shallow footprints filling with murky water."

Joanna reached forward as though to take his hand, but she stopped, tentatively, several inches short. "How awful. Like 'Enoch Arden.' "

Alex nodded. "You mentioned that earlier."

"Did I?" puzzled the delicate girl. "Oh, no. That was *Ethan Frome*. This is 'Enoch Arden.' It's a poem by Alfred Lord Tennyson."

"Next time around," said Alex, "I'll go to college."

"It's about this woman, Annie, whose husband is shipwrecked at sea," continued Joanna. "And presumed dead. Only he's actually not dead—and he comes back to find her married to a new man—"

"—named Enoch Arden—"

"—*named* Philip Ray. It's one of those popular misconceptions that the new husband is named Enoch Arden. The *old husband* was named Enoch Arden. Sort of like how some people think the one-armed man was The Fugitive."

Alex stirred the saccharine frosting in his water glass. "Okay," he agreed.

"But here's the important part," said Joanna—her face suddenly aglow like a schoolgirl with gossip. "Enoch doesn't reveal himself to Annie. He loves her too much to ruin her happiness, so he conceals himself in a boarding house and dies alone."

The room turned silent. From the kitchen came the sound of Big Mitch hurling profanities at the industrial dishwasher. "So you're saying that Karen's out there somewhere. Hiding."

The delicate girl wilted. "I don't know what I'm saying," she said, unmoored. "You should read it."

"If I should, then I will." He reached across the table to fill his wine glass one last time. The thought crossed his mind that he had revealed too much and she too little. Good clams enter the pot closed and exit open. His instincts told him that the same rule applied to women and dinner. "And what about you? What's your story?"

"My story?" The delicate girl flicked back her long sable hair. "My story," she announced with sudden decision, "is that it's nearly eleven thirty and I'm teaching *Anna Karenina* tomorrow at eight."

"That's a book," said Alex, grinning. "Not a person."

She stood up and walked briskly toward the door. "Next week," said Joanna.

Alex agreed—though he wasn't certain what he was agreeing to. "Next week."

That night he missed Karen more than he had in months. Her absence actually afflicted him as physical pain, as a jab somewhere deep within his skull. Ever since losing his wife, Alex had abandoned their queen-size bed. He slept on the moth-gnawed olive sofa in the living room—to hear the door chime, in case she returned in the dark without keys. The couch itself was a stunted little pallet that Karen had once tagged a love seat with ambitions. It didn't even let him stretch his legs. Yet now, for the first time, this constricted berth struck Alex as far too roomy, and he pitched about on the cushions for hours like a toy boat lost at sea. Shortly after three a.m., he retreated to the lanai. He sat at the end of a dew-soaked chaise longue. He wore only boxer shorts. The breeze off the ocean sent chills down his spine. In the pine barrens that rose beyond the bougainvillea hedge, scarlet ibises roosted like Christmas ornaments. So many of his nights with Karen had been spent in this little nook of paradise—

reveling in the shock of their own successes. He could still hear her boasting, her voice slurred with sherry, *"The fucking* American dream!" That was the bare-knuckles Karen speaking, the hardscrabble New Jersey schoolgirl. She was the cart that drove the horse. Alex could not imagine loving anybody different.

When dawn broke, Alex went to market. Karen's uncle had taught him to inspect each fish individually at the wholesalers—to hand-pick the largest pompano, the tilapia and grouper still flailing in the stalls. The work required sharp eyes, stamina. Sometimes a thick apron. Not surprisingly, his arrival at the two-room municipal library several hours later—his work boots and dungarees still lacquered in snook guts—drew the attention of the puffy, chinless young man behind the counter. The youth folded his stubby arms across his breast. "Need any help?"

"Just looking," muttered Alex. Libraries and bookstores generally made him feel self-conscious, and this attendant's polite offer stung like an accusation of shop-lifting. The problem was he'd forgotten the poet's name. He had no choice. He walked briskly to the main desk. "Do you have 'Enoch Arden'?"

The librarian looked up from a crossword puzzle. "Is that a book or an author?"

"It's a poem," retorted Alex. "I don't know who wrote it."

He waited for the librarian to snicker, but the young man merely smiled in sympathy. "That's hard, if you don't know the poet's name."

"It's a famous poem," said Alex.

The librarian scratched the pink flesh around his collar. "You know what I'll do," he said. "I'll phone my grandmother." The youth flicked open his cellular phone, adding in a more professional voice: "She reads a lot."

They finally found *Tennyson—Selected Poems* in the children's room; it had been propped against one of the windows to keep the air-conditioner from blowing open the drapes.

※

The delicate woman didn't show up the following week, or the next. Alex had arrived early both evenings in the hope of discussing Enoch and Philip and Annie Lee. He'd also tackled "In Memoriam" and "The Charge of the Light Brigade"—the idea of knowing something other than shellfish *did* appeal to him—but it was Arden's turmoil that he burned to explore. She'd said next week, hadn't she? A promise, a contract. What sort of person plays so fast and loose with her words? Alex understood that he had no legitimate gripe against the woman— she'd made an idle remark to a virtual stranger, nothing more—but he didn't care. So what if his anger was irrational? Anger wasn't rational. On the occasion of Joanna's second absence, Alex shared the Enoch Arden tale with the rest of the support group. Philip Ray, the second husband, sent Sammy B. into a dither. His own dead wife, it turned out, had been unfaithful. G-Man called Enoch a "chicken-shit bastard" who deserved what he got. When Tina stood up for the hapless fisherman—"it's just like on *The Days of Our Lives*," she insisted—the two went at each other's throats. Eventually, they both turned on Alex. He apologized: "It was stupid to bring up." For the remainder of the meeting, he kept silent. His attention drifted, and he counted the colored tags that labeled the walls, the windows, the chalkboard in both Hebrew and transliterated English. He read the wisdom on his desktop: *Abe Lincoln was Jewish. He was shot in the temple.* Also: *Lucy eats snotburgers, Chazz & Lindsay 4ever.* In response to *Why couldn't Helen Keller find a husband?* someone had inked *Because she was a lesbian.* Alex snuck a glance at his watch. At the Captain's Mast, Big Mitch would be rolling out the first of the key lime pie.

I'm not coming back, he decided. Enough is enough.

He did, of course. He arrived early again—planning to ask the facilitator if she knew the delicate woman's last name, seething with two week's pent up frustrations—to discover Joanna standing in the corridor and sipping coffee from a Styrofoam cup. She wore a low-cut cotton dress. The fine ridges of her collarbone danced with every breath. Alex examined her reflection in the glass display case—where a tribute to Israeli astronaut Ilan Ramon had replaced the manatee exhibit. Everything about her struck him as so fragile, almost ethereal: her slender shoulders, her perfect teeth aligned like small white tombstones. A contrast to his wife's substance, fullness—to Karen's fleshy thighs and the breasts he could palm like baby pumpkins. In the glass, he traced Joanna's fine features—superimposed upon a profile of the space shuttle at dawn, reflecting also the death chamber atrocities and swastika-emblazoned banners from the opposing glass case—to uncover his own reflection, and her eyes once again locked upon his. He shifted his gaze to the fringes of the Shuttle Columbia portrait and examined them with a sudden and ferocious intensity. She reeled to face him, leaving his eyes no escape.

"You're back," she said. "I'm so glad."

His anger—what was left of it—turned upon him. All of his past frustrations now seemed so unreasonable, so utterly overblown. "I read the poem," he said.

The threads of her eyebrows rose in uncertainty.

" 'Enoch Arden,' " said Alex. "I wanted to tell you how much I enjoyed it, but you weren't here."

"Oh, Tennyson," answered Joanna. "I'm so glad you liked it. Many people don't, you know."

Alex tucked his thumbs into the pockets of his slacks. It hadn't crossed his mind that G-Man and Sammy B. were in the majority—that *he* was the odd man out. "I don't know much about poems," he said. "All I know is what I like."

Joanna nodded. "Some people find 'Arden' a bit too . . . forced, maybe hackneyed. All that Victorian gloom and doom. I like to think Enoch must have had a mistress tucked away somewhere, maybe more than one."

The woman paused, bit her lip. She added disdainfully: "Tennyson would never tell us that, of course."

"Of course," echoed Alex.

He followed her into the meeting room. His entire understanding of the poem had suddenly come loose at the hinges—and all the questions he'd had for the delicate woman no longer seemed relevant. After Karen's disappearance, Alex had seriously wondered whether she might have been having an affair. How could he not? Yet if that were the case—and deep down he didn't accept it—then he'd always assumed the transgression and her absence to be linked. Either she'd run off with this unknown man, or he'd done to her the unspeakable. A third possibility now confronted him: maybe his wife had been unfaithful *independent* of her disappearance. Everybody had secrets, after all. One look around the circle at his grief-stricken companions—all of whom except Joanna and Charlotte Ann had already confessed to cheating—reminded him how easy it must be to become enmeshed in the tangled gossamer of infidelity.

Joanna told the circle about her trip with Owen to the Galapagos—of how they'd watched the mating dances of the blue-footed boobies and how her husband had tried to replicate them in their cabin. Alex didn't reveal anything. He waited for her at the end of the meeting, but the equine woman named Natalie had visited the ladies' room, and now shared their elevator ride. Natalie also had a connection to the Galapagos, having watched a Discovery Channel special. She peppered Joanna with inanities about giant tortoises and tropical penguins. Mercifully, the woman's ride awaited her at the curbside. Without warning, Alex and Joanna stood alone. The insect lamp drove their long shadows toward the cusp of oblivion.

"You weren't here last week," said Alex. Joanna held her hands clasped in front of her.

"I had a good time at dinner," she said. "I wasn't ready for that."

Alex rustled in his pocket for his keys. "The mussels were tender, weren't they?"

Joanna smiled. "Passable," she said.

She nodded in the direction of the beach—and they walked down the boardwalk, alongside the cast-iron benches and topiary shrubs. Beyond the grassy dunes, the distant surf murmured through the darkness. "Do you want to know?" she asked.

"I wouldn't have asked."

"Owen drove off the Cormorant Island causeway," she said.

"Intentionally?"

Joanna shrugged her frail shoulders. "Who knows? He was a pediatric dentist . . . One of the girls said things . . . said he did things."

"Oh Jesus," said Alex. "Was it . . . ?"

"How the hell should I know?" slashed Joanna. "She was goddam *thirteen.*"

She paused and drew in her breath; she made no effort to dampen her tears. "I'm sorry. You didn't deserve that." The young woman stretched her arms, opening her hands as though to cast away anger like feed grain. "Uncertainty," she said.

"You're telling me," answered Alex. "Dinner?"

Her nod was faint, fleeting—yet it was a nod. And over dinner they discussed lighter topics: the rare yellow lobster on display at the Tampa aquarium, the ongoing boycott of sea bass and bluefin tuna. Joanna had her own take on shellfish: she related how Cleopatra had dissolved a pearl earring in wine to prove Egypt's wealth to Marc Antony, how Chekhov had written of oysters, and later how the playwright's coffin had been transported from Germany to Moscow on a freight car labeled, "For Oysters Only." She also spoke of her interest in poetry. She'd arrived at literature "late in life"—she'd actually studied marine biology in college, but had killed time reading while waiting for "scientific magic" in the lab—and, at the end of the evening, she even recited Browning's "My Last Duchess" to the delight of the kitchen staff.

"Encore," demanded the one-armed sous-chef. "Encore!"

"Next week," she promised—to Alex, to Big Mitch, to the twin bus-girls Susana and Mariana. "You've worn me out."

She stopped Alex from walking her to her car: "Next week."

※

When he returned to the kitchen—half jubilant, half on-edge—Big Mitch cut the ground out from under him. "She isn't nothing like Karen," he said. "Not better or worse, you know. Just a different cut of meat."

"How do you break up with someone you're not dating?" Alex asked Big Mitch.

They were standing on either side of the seafood station, shucking oysters. Alex had already jabbed himself twice. A few stray shells lay in a puddle of bloody water on the countertop. Alex admired Big Mitch's dexterity. The sous-chef held each oyster in his one large hand—and carved it with a thick makeshift blade strapped to his thumb.

"Fucking depends," said Big Mitch. "You breaking up with her to start dating her? Or you breaking up to get rid of her?"

Alex stuck his knife into the wooden cutting board. He dabbed horseradish on a raw oyster and sucked the tiny body into his mouth. "Good flavor in these Olympias," he said. "Try one."

"Not in May," said the sous-chef. The conventional wisdom—long since trumped by commercial farming—warned against oysters in months whose names did not contain the letter "r". The sous-chef carried his cache of mollusks to the shellfish refrigerator. "Nothing romantic about getting the runs."

"I don't know what I want," said Alex. "She didn't show up again last week. That's four meetings out of the last seven."

The sous-chef returned and carried off Alex's store of oysters. "Why the fuck don't you just ask her out? Take her dancing or something?"

"Jesus Christ," said Alex. "I'm married."

The sous-chef shrugged his one good shoulder. "Don't stop most people," he said. "And if you're so married, boss, where's your wife at?"

The ceiling fan buzzed overhead like a helicopter. Big Mitch stepped into the alcove bathroom and left the door open; Alex heard his urine hitting the water. "You're way out of line," shouted Alex.

The toilet flushed; the faucet ran. "So fucking fire me," called the sous-chef. He returned with the fronds of his Hawaiian shirt poking through his fly.

They glared at each other: Alex's eyes flashed sharp and hot against Big Mitch's unflappable durability. The sous-chef's exposed stump—a birth defect, not a war injury—suggested courage, street smarts. Eventually, Alex looked away. His gaze settled on a shiny silver pot brimming with crushed ice.

"It's me I should fire," he said. "How about bowling?"

The enterprise proved far easier than Alex had anticipated. He offered; she accepted. That evening—after a raucous meeting in which Sammy B. publicly declared his love for an unsuspecting Tina—they braved a torrential Gulf Coast squall, which had flooded shut the interstate, and followed the mangrove-lined back roads to Sawgrass Bowling & Billiards. Joanna drove a beige Dodge Dart from the late 1970's that resembled a giant cigar on roller skates. The car's interior smelled of spearmint, of lemongrass, of woman's shampoo. Hand-knit hoods covered the seat backs; baby pink Mardi Gras beads dangled from the overhead light. Magazine clippings—cartoons, photographs—were scotch-taped to the face of the dashboard. Alex's father, a transmission specialist from Camden, always insisted that cars mirrored souls. That theory made Joanna spiritual, complicated. Alex's own pickup stank pungently of ocean musk—evaporated brine, mackerel viscera—which also struck him as an unfortunate confirmation of his father's hypothesis.

"When was the last time you went bowling?" asked Alex.

"You'll laugh," answered Joanna. "I've never been."

"Never?"

Joanna squinted through the sheets of rain. "Owen had a bad knee. He fell off a horse as a kid."

Something inchoate and feral cut across the road; Alex's foot reached for an imaginary brake. "It's amazing, you know, how people define each other. *Owen* had a bad knee, so *I* never went bowling."

"With Karen it was airplanes," said Alex. "Scared the living shit out of her."

His own use of the past tense caught him off guard. "I love flying," said Joanna. "It's like magic."

The glowing, low-slung form of the Sawgrass Lanes rose suddenly against the gray horizon. A sign out front flashed "OWL OWL OWL" in neon—the burned out "B" hunkered down against the storm. If Karen's father was running the place, thought Alex, he'd have me out there changing bulbs in a hurricane. But the old man was dead, of course. Diabetes. Renal failure. Too independent, too stubborn, for dialysis. Yet the interior of the Sawgrass Lanes—that septic junior high school stench, poorly lacquered over with cleanser and verbena—pricked at Alex's memory. A list of 300-game bowlers ran the height of one wall; a case of league trophies traversed the length of another. In the far corner, near a decapitated payphone, teenagers clustered around an arcade game. Somewhere out of view, Alex sensed, hid a manager's office with a sofa.

"What do we do first?" asked Joanna. "You've got to tell me what to do, you know. I don't want to mess up."

Alex steered them to the shoe-exchange counter. Thunder from outside melded with the crash of falling pins. "There's only one important rule in bowling," he said. "You want to make sure you keep the ball on your own lane."

"Like driving," said Joanna.

"You've got it," said Alex. "I've never thought of that."

Joanna examined her bowling shoes suspiciously; they were the smallest size. "You'll teach me step by step?" she asked.

"I promise. Just like swimming."

They were already through nine frames—with Alex leading 186 to 47—when the conversation rapidly veered away from bowling. It was all Alex's doing, though he wasn't sure what prompted him. Maybe the 50's music, maybe the college kids on a double date in the adjacent lane. "Those poets," he said, apropos of nothing. "Browning. Tennyson. Swinburne. They must have gotten lonely."

Joanna sat down beside him on the plastic aqua bench. She held her bowling ball between her legs, as though she'd just given birth to a boulder. "Swinburne?"

Alex had discovered Swinburne on his own; he now feared that he'd pronounced the poet's name incorrectly. "What I mean is—it must get lonely doing all that writing."

"I always think it's worse for the characters," answered Joanna. "They're stuck forever in the same bad relationships. Poor Hester, poor Anna. But sometimes I think it's all a pack of lies—that Emma Bovary was actually messing around with Homais the chemist."

"Yes," agreed Alex. "Or that Enoch Arden was having one-night stands."

Immediately they both realized that they were no longer talking about what they were talking about. Joanna fumbled with the gold bangles around her wrists; sometime since their first meeting, Alex realized, she'd removed her wedding band. He glanced nervously around the alley. Most of the other lanes stood empty. One of the college couples had departed early, while the other had given up bowling. The girl now sat on the guy's lap—and he clearly had his hand under her skirt. Women inside, Alex remembered, feel like squid.

"There's a scene in *Anna Karenina*," said the delicate woman in a wispy voice, "in which this learned intellectual named Sergey Ivanovitch and a poor relation named Varenka go out mushroom picking."

Alex's lower back had started to cramp—too much bending—but he dared not stretch. From the seat behind them came the desperate sounds of giggling or whimpering; he focused hard on Joanna.

". . . They have this moment," she continued. "Out in the forest. Where either he'll propose—where something will happen between them, or it will all be over forever."

Joanna looked up; a thin smile traced her trembling lips.

Alex felt his own body fluttering. He knew something was called for—statement, action. A charge of urgency swept through him, priming his senses, magnifying the odor of floor polish and the clatter of pins. But with his heightened emotions came the sudden tug of the past—flashing before him that lost moment of youthful enrapture on lane seven, the groping, the fumbling, Karen's long auburn hair dappled with frost. He could feel her snow-numb nose meeting his—like Eskimos. The memory reached for him like a hand reaching forth from the grave. Alex found his focus entirely derailed and he stared blankly at Joanna. Her eyes remained wide and hopeful. She was waiting for him to speak.

"*Anna Karenina*," Alex said finally. "I've never read it." He struggled for something further and added: "Is it good?"

Joanna opened her mouth to answer, but didn't. Across the alley came a ripple of plangent euphoria—someone had toppled his tenth straight strike. Alex watched the fellow high-fiving his buddies.

"Yes, of course," said Joanna sharply. "It's good."

She stood up and walked rapidly to the ladies' room. After that, they bowled out the last frame, speaking only when necessary, and she drove him home.

※

The storm worsened past midnight. The wind picked up something fierce, slashing palm branches against the siding of the bungalow. Alex sat on the edge of the threadbare couch in his boxer shorts. He wanted something to happen—he wanted the doorbell to ring. "Ring the goddam bell," he thought. "Just ring the goddam bell!" Whether he was speaking to his missing wife, or to the delicate woman, even he no longer knew. Around three a.m.—shortly after the power went dead—he lit a candle and read to himself the opening passages of "Enoch Arden." He grew drowsy. The words waltzed aimlessly under the lambent flame. Alex kept waiting, irrationally, for Enoch to reveal himself to his wife. He didn't of course. When the tears came to Alex's eyes, he folded shut the book and retreated to the master bedroom. He slammed shut the door behind him and slept with the thick down comforter pulled snug over his head. It was the deep, stony sleep of a man who'd died twice in one night.

THE ATATURK OF THE OUTER BOROUGHS

THIRTY-ONE-YEAR-OLD Onur Erdem was re-keying the tumblers on an antique strongbox when the pretty woman attorney arrived to carry off all that he owned. The Turkish locksmith greeted her warnings with a meditative silence: he gritted his molars down on his calabash pipe and fed a stack of blanks through the computerized code cutter. Twice already he had lost everything—once to the creditors who'd bankrolled his late father's gambling sprees, once to an electrical fire—so the prospect of dispossession, which in the past might have conjured up traumatic images of refugees pulling featherbeds with horse-carts, now merely vexed him like a minor rash. Transience was the price for breathing American air, for doing business in Jackson Heights, Queens. He could live with it. (That was why, in his personal affairs, he favored things British—test match cricket, Darjeeling tea from Taylors of Harrogate—anything that smacked of stability and empire.) Yet Onur enjoyed having the pretty woman attorney, whose name was Claudia Crane and whose sandy hair flaunted an un-lawyerly streak of fuchsia, sitting with her legs crossed on the cast iron mini-vault in his shop. Claudia wore a black skirt, stockings. Pink lacquered nails poked through the toes of her shoes. Onur noticed her wedding ring, but still had no desire to see her leave too quickly. "What did you call it?" he asked.

"Eminent domain," answered Claudia. "If they pay you fair market value, they can come take your property."

Onur nodded indifferently. He blew the tiny brass shavings from each of the processed keys, holding the finished products to the light one at a time. "I understand that," he said. "Why don't you stop them?"

Claudia breathed deeply—maybe to mask frustration. "That's what we're trying to do, but at this point it won't be easy. They already have an order of necessity."

"Why didn't you stop them sooner?" asked Onur. He fancied the way his visitor toyed with her crystal necklace.

"We didn't know. All the state has to do is run 'notice of intent' ads in the local papers, and that's like not doing anything at all. The whole process is completely Kafkaesque. What I mean is—-"

"I understand Kafkaesque," said Onur.

Claudia took another deep breath—this time pausing to exhale as though she'd been punched in the abdomen. "*Of course*, you do," she said. "What I wanted to emphasize was that if we don't take action soon, the bulldozers are going to roll over your business."

"And my home," interjected Onur. "I live upstairs."

"*And* your home. *And* my office. *And* the Whatever 4 Cafe. *And* everything else within six square blocks. All in the name of hockey. And minor league hockey at that. All so that a bunch of assholes can get piss drunk, shout obscenities and drive home."

The locksmith smiled thinly; he wished to conceal his jagged teeth. Although he had no interest in hockey, the prospect of a government buyout actually had its plusses: what better excuse to invest in cutting-edge equipment? Or he might expand into home security systems, maybe closed-circuit surveillance. Next year—when the hockey players rolled through—he'd be installing burglar alarms in the suburbs. His aunt might not like the move, but she'd get over it. Onur bit his tongue to keep from laughing, steeled his face. "Is that hockey on grass?" he asked. "Or hockey on ice?"

"Hockey on ice. An arena. Please, Mr. Erdem, we need you."

"Me? *I'm* so important?"

Claudia glanced toward the shop window. Her pale, slender neck shimmered like rose marble under the fluorescent light. "I'll be honest with you, Mr. Erdem," she said in a hushed voice. "We think it's very important for the committee to reflect the community . . . Different viewpoints, you know."

Onur wondered how many Gujarati *farsan* mongers and Senegalese hair beaders and Hmong green grocers the woman attorney had approached before finding him. He explored the stem of his pipe with his tongue, while running security keys across the electric buffer. "Did you know that the first locks were made of wood?" he asked.

The woman attorney smiled at him as though he'd walked in off the moon.

He looked straight into her eyes for the first time. He had a granduncle in Baltimore—also a locksmith—who'd once told him that the eyes were like keyholes into the palaces of royalty. He had been only a child; the uncle had been drinking. Now Onur wondered what regal secrets lurked behind the pretty woman's opaque gray irises. She struck him as a woman of significant complexity. "The first wooden locks adorned the imperial gates of Sargon of Persia in the eighth century before Christ."

"How interesting," said Claudia.

"I think so," said Onur. "You said you wanted diverse viewpoints. I'm offering you the viewpoint of a locksmith."

The woman attorney opened her mouth—but at first no words came out.

She finally asked, "Does that mean you'll do it?"

"Sure," he said. "I'll do it."

He shook her hand across the countertop. He did not appreciate the way that she held her arm straight out from her body; it was almost insulting. But her long, glabrous fingers were as cold and delicate as porcelain. Outside, a taxicab honked. Onur relinquished the exquisite tiny hand. His body shivered at the burst of chill air as the woman attorney exited the shop.

On the counter stood a coffee cup. It bore the inscription: "Small keys open large doors"—a present to his late father from a friend. Onur picked up the stack of newly minted keys and dropped them into the cup, one by one. The polished metal clinked on glass like coins upon the stones in a fountain.

❋

"You're running out on me for *that*?" asked Jude Basso.

The twenty-six-year old elevator technician leaned over the chessboard; his beefy forearms rested atop his thighs. Onur had competed against Basso on the Internet for months before discovering that the Italian lived in nearby Flushing. Now the two men played in Onur's sitting room, as they did every Wednesday evening, surrounded by the scents of turmeric and toasted caraway. Mama Fairuza, Onur's maiden aunt, had cleared the tea service moments earlier.

"Trust me," said Onur. He used his palms to mime the shape of the woman attorney's chest. "Like the Himalayas."

Basso shifted his queen's bishop the full length of the chessboard with the assurance of a surgeon wielding a scalpel. "Has her husband invited you mountain climbing?" he asked.

"Come and see for yourself, my friend," said Onur. From the kitchen rose the crunch of Mama Fairuza grinding coriander for Harissa sauce. The locksmith removed Basso's bishop and replaced it with his king's knight. "Checkmate."

"I'm no politician," said Basso. He stared at the chessboard in wonder—as though attempting to Monday morning quarterback a shell game.

"And *I'm* a politician? It's all about business."

Onur explained his calculus to the Italian. If the activists de-
feated the hockey arena, his stature in the community would rise
considerably—and that could only be good for the shop. If the devel-
opers prevailed, of course, he'd pocket his "fair market value" and
upgrade to a security outfit on the Island. Neither way could he lose.
"So I'll pay lip service to property rights and John Locke and Jeffer-
son," he told the bewildered Italian, "but what I'm *really* doing is mar-
keting *me*."

Basso grinned. "I bet you want to pay lip service."

"We'll tell them you live in my building," said Onur. "It's not like
you're doing anything else tonight."

Onur settled the chessboard onto its perch atop the piano. He
threw on his black cashmere coat and led Basso down the two flights
of steep wooden stairs into the bitter gelid night. They walked
quickly, the wind at their backs. The gusts hooked sandwich wrap-
pers around car antennas and sandblasted the traffic signs. It was
too cold to speak. When they finally arrived at the offices of Tooth
Fairy Orthodontics, where the steering committee conducted its
biweekly meetings, tears frosted the corners of Onur's eye sockets.
Fifteen people had already crowded into the lobby. He recognized
the orthodontist, Dr. Gussoff, from his subway advertisements; Gussoff's rodentine features instilled even less confidence in person.
The pretty woman attorney was also present, speaking with the elderly Ismaili Muslim who owned the flower shop at the corner of
Jackson Avenue and St. James. All the rest were male and strangers.

"Looks like you've got competition," whispered Basso. The locksmith stood in the doorway defrosting, watching the florist demon-
strate a dance move to the female attorney.

"Piss off," answered Onur.

He wove his way through the sea of bodies. The woman attorney
had traded her business outfit for tight acid-washed jeans, glossy
maroon boots and a skimpy scarlet top. She flashed her smile in
his direction—and he was about to call out her name—when a ro-

bust older man emerged from the crowd to peck her on the lips. The newcomer wore a thick mustache and had eyebrows like hedgerows. Onur heard Claudia introduce him to the Ismaili. "Mr. Kurji. My husband, Eric."

Onur stepped into their conversation. He did not like that the woman attorney had any husband other than him. "Ms. Crane," he said.

"Ah, Mr. Erdem," said Claudia. "Mr. Kurji was just showing me a traditional Tajik folk dance."

"The dance of the eagle," said the florist. "It is usually accompanied by flutes."

The locksmith did not know any traditional Turkish dances. At the state university, he'd won the intercollegiate waltz competition three years running.

"Who has time for dancing?" asked Onur. "We have a neighborhood to save, don't we?"

He had intended no offense—but the crestfallen Ismaili mumbled apologies, his hands jammed into his trouser pockets and his gaze down at the floor.

"I don't see it that way at all," said Claudia. "I agree with the anarchist Emma Goldman: if I can't have dancing—traditional dancing, folk dancing—I don't want your revolution." The woman attorney added all too quickly: "But I am glad you've come, Mr. Erdem. We need enthusiasm like yours."

At that moment, the orthodontist rose on a plastic milk crate—like a false muezzin on an ersatz minaret—and called the meeting to order. The woman attorney took her place at Gussoff's side, affording Onur no opportunity to say anything further. The locksmith retreated to the back wall. He tried to feign interest in the speakers—the manager of the Whatever 4 Cafe, the proprietor of a local bridal boutique, an architectural preservationist from some obscure foundation—but they bored him senseless. All anger, indignation. With not an original thought among them, each felt the need

to throw in his ten cents. The locksmith didn't dare retrieve a magazine from the end table; instead, he busied himself reading a wall
poster that diagrammed the components of braces. Bonded brackets.
Rubber bands. Archwires. A vocabulary of appliances as intriguing
as those in his own shop. He refocused only when the woman attorney mounted the makeshift proscenium.

"You win," said Jude Basso. "Like the Himalayas."

The top buttons hung open on the woman attorney's blouse.
From his angle, Onur could see the magenta frills on her brassiere.

"What we need most right now," she said, "are volunteers."

She spoke about recruitment techniques, door-to-door cam-
paigning. Onur left forty-five minutes later as co-coordinator of
fund-raising. He knew as much about fund-raising as he did about
dancing the rakkas—but at least he lived in the community. His fellow co-coordinator, Jude Basso, had to take the subway seven stops
home.

Onur discovered his gift for political oratory the following Saturday
at the loading dock behind Caravan Kabul. The Afghani restaurant
was owned by two Iranian brothers, identical twins named Malik
and Majid; each sported a full gray beard. Although Onur had as-
sisted them several times in the past—once following a burglary,
twice after automobile lockouts—he still couldn't tell them apart.
For fund-raising purposes, of course, this didn't matter. While
one of the brothers and a frozen produce wholesaler inventoried
sacks of vegetables as they came off the back of the dealer's truck,
the locksmith stood in the flurrying snow and spoke of property
rights. Nearby, a visibly uncomfortable Jude Basso chain-smoked
cigarettes.

*You ask: what does this have to do with me? I'm no politician. I'm no rabble-
rouser. I don't want any trouble. That's why you've come to this great coun-*

*try, America—so you can avoid politics and trouble. At least, that's what I my-
self believed at first. You're likely thinking what I was thinking: I'll take their
'fair market value' and expand. Upgrade. Maybe move out to the suburbs. But
what then? Please hear me out, my friend, small business owner to small business owner. What are you going to do when the government comes after your
new restaurant, your new store, your new home? My father picked us up from
Anatolia—gave up everything he had back in Turkey. And why? WHY? I ask
you. To move where his property would be protected. Not his right to speak.
Or even to pray. No, no, no. His right to make a decent living. A secure living.
The Declaration of Independence was originally supposed to say "life, liberty
and property"—that's what the pursuit of happiness really is. Without property,
there is no stability. Without stability—Revolution! That's why we need to stand
up for ourselves.*

Onur placed his hand on the Iranian's thick shoulder; his voice
dropped to a confidential lull: *They drove you out of Iran in '79. I know
how it was, my friend. I know. But don't let them do it to you a second time. Remember how you swore it would never happen again? Here's your chance.*

The Iranian spit into the snow. He signaled for Onur to follow
him into the meat pantry, a small freezer that doubled as an office,
where the locksmith waited between dangling rabbit carcasses while
his host rummaged through the desk for a checkbook. To Onur's
shock, the restauranteur—Malik—wrote out a draft for five hundred
dollars. "Here," said the Iranian. "Tell them from me: go fuck themselves."

Similar success greeted Onur at the Cambodian deli, at the television repair shop operated by the Pakistani with the Bell's Palsy, at
the storefront offices of the Hungarian foam rubber supplier. All he
had to do was alter the proper nouns: *They drove you out of Czechoslo-
vakia in '39. Out of Cuba in '59. Out of Uganda in '72. Or occasionally he'd add
a touch of his own personal history: I've been to college, to the state university at
Albany, but did I abandon the neighborhood? Of course I didn't. Would I leave
my family? Of course I wouldn't. I take pride in being a locksmith—the same way
I imagine you take pride in being a landscaper—a piano tuner—a beautician—*

a liquor dealer—a masseuse. I cared for my widowed mother until she died—I still support her unmarried sister—the same way I am certain you look after your own. So I am not asking for any more than anybody else gets, my friend. But I am not willing to take any less—and I am certain that you are not either.

Onur made a point of leaving his business card at every office and kiosk and apartment that he and Basso visited. Why not? Considering his efforts, the least he deserved was free advertising. He'd distributed more than eighteen hundred by the end of the month—and also raised nearly a quarter of a million dollars—when the woman attorney paid another visit to his shop.

Onur heard the door chime, but did not look up. He was teaching his sixteen year old cousin, Yusuf Gurkan, how to pick a wafer-tumbler with a tension wrench. "When raking the tumblers, the trick is focus," explained the locksmith. "You put pressure on the sidebar with the steel wire, my boy, and you concentrate." Then Onur caught sight of Claudia and nearly sliced off his thumb.

The woman attorney did not appear to notice the mishap. She was leaning over the countertop, examining his family photographs.

"Who's that man?" asked Claudia.

She pointed to a sepia portrait of a dapper young Zouave in puff-trousers, a short red jacket and a matching fez.

"That's my great-grandfather," answered Onur. "During the Russian War. He later served as chief-of-staff under Ataturk."

"Impressive," said Claudia.

Onur grinned—inadvertently exposing his bad teeth.

Claudia returned his smile. "Is there someplace we can speak?"

The locksmith left his cousin in charge of the shop. He led the woman attorney into the stockroom, pulling the bulb light on with a string.

"So this is your secret lair," she said.

The musty, cedar-lined closet embarrassed Onur. He dusted off space atop a worn steamer trunk for the woman attorney to sit down.

Claudia tucked her skirt beneath her. "It's amazing, what you've been doing."

Onur nodded stupidly. "Thank you."

"The truth is," said Claudia, "I came to apologize. For the Emma Goldmann remark the other night. And for misjudging you. I'm a straight-shooting kind of gal, Mr. Erdem, so I'll say it like it is."

The locksmith leaned forward on his splintered wooden stool.

"You weren't our first choice for the steering committee," said Claudia. "Even three weeks ago, I considered asking Mr. Kurji to take your place. But what you've done since then is, well, just unbelievable."

"Oh *that*," said Onur, disappointed. "Nothing beyond the call of duty."

"The call of duty," she echoed. "That's probably what your great-grandfather would have said. Maybe we'll have to start calling you The Ataturk of Jackson Avenue. Or, better yet, The Ataturk of the Outer Boroughs. It has a ring to it."

Onur said nothing.

"You'd make your great-grandfather proud," said Claudia. "Steve Gussoff's getting thirty, forty calls a day. People wanting to volunteer. People wanting to give more money."

"That's good news," said Onur.

He was sitting so close to Claudia, he could smell her shampoo. "We're going to win this," said Claudia. "*On The Spot News* is doing a story, maybe Channel 5. And our lawyers—thanks to you, we've got a dream team."

"I thought . . ."

"No, no," said Claudia. "I do family law. I advocate for abused women."

She stood up and extended her hand—still outstretched rigid like a metal bar.

"May I come bother you again, Mr. Erdem?" she asked.

"It's no bother," said the locksmith.

Call me Onur—he thought, the moment she'd left—*Why didn't I ask her? Call me Onur. Call me Onur. Call me Onur.*

The locksmith redoubled his fund-raising efforts. He no longer had time for chess, for monthly backgammon tournaments with his Staten Island relatives. He delegated increasing authority to his teenage cousins, Yusuf Gurkan and Yusuf Nesim, who practically ran the shop in his absence. His waking hours—often from the crack of dawn through the marrow of the overnight—he passed canvassing the neighborhoods beyond the six square blocks of the impact zone.

You ask: what does this have to do with me? They're building that hockey arena in Jackson Heights, not in Corona. Not on 103rd Street and Northern Boulevard. If anything, you think, all those fans will be good for business. But let me tell you—small business owner to small business owner—that you're fooling yourself. Today it's a hockey rink, my friend, but tomorrow it's a sports complex. Parking lots, luxury hotels. Like Disney World. Let me ask you this: does a wolf devour only one lamb? If today they take what is mine, surely tomorrow they will take what is yours. Onur left a business card at every encounter. Yet as his sermons grew more urgent, as he haphazardly quoted Patrick Henry and John Stuart Mill and Burke's *Reflections on the Revolution in France*—to Egyptian cabbies and Ecuadorian grocers who didn't know political philosophy from a hole in the floor, the young locksmith became his own most loyal convert. Absolute property, he decided, made sense. The only thing necessary for the triumph of evil, he warned Jude Basso, is for good men to do nothing. Onur's deepset black eyes acquired a distant, slightly prophetic gleam. He condemned Lenin and the Queens Borough President in one malignant breath. When Mama Fairuza observed that she didn't see what the fuss was about—*Is it so awful that I should die in the suburbs?*—Onur nearly put her out on the street.

Claudia's visits became a weekly, then daily affair. She updated Onur on their legal progress: evidentiary hearings, preliminary injunctions. Once she brought with her a television crew from a cable access channel; on another occasion, she arrived with two city council members from Brooklyn, both Republicans, who'd wanted the hockey arena for an abandoned switchyard between their districts. Onur quoted for them Irving Kristol and Barry Goldwater. He preferred it most, of course, when Claudia arrived alone. That gave him an excuse to invite her back to the stockroom. Later, they graduated to the parlor where his aunt served them tea. All perfectly innocent, of course. But the locksmith knew by memory every inch of fabric in the woman attorney's wardrobe, what days she visited the hair dresser, which earrings she matched with which shoes—a fashion extravaganza etched indelibly into his heart. His interest transcended the political, but it wasn't as though he viewed his canvassing as an arrow into Claudia's affections. Not at all. Rather, the two causes had grown so intertwined in his hysteria that true happiness depended upon both.

And then one March morning—the ides—the pretty woman attorney and her husband arrived together at his shop.

"It's over, Mr. Erdem," she said. "The whole goddam shebang."

Onur surveyed the husband. He wondered how she could prefer this dopey-looking clod who had eyebrows like black moss and hardly ever spoke.

"Judge Katz tore us to shreds. An air-tight, seven-hundred-page opinion. The old geezer even refused to stay the order pending appeal. He said, and I quote, it is utterly inconceivable that the plaintiff might ultimately prevail."

The husband shrugged his shoulders, dejected.

"Are you crazy?" demanded Onur. "We can't give up."

"We have no fucking choice, I'm afraid."

Onur snapped shut a bronze padlock. He twinged at the memory of the city marshal dragging his father's furniture to the sidewalk in the pouring rain, of the caustic metallic odor that greeted him after the electrical fire.

"How long do we have?" he asked.

Claudia scowled. "The evictions begin May One."

The locksmith nodded. "Plenty of time."

※

Onur passed the night of April 30th locking people to inanimate objects.

The final eviction notices had already been posted for weeks. They came in various unlikely hues—mauve, chartreuse, vermilion— each affixed with four jabs of a staple gun. They reminded Jude Basso of quarantine warnings in science fiction films. From the Viennese waiter at the Whatever 4 Cafe came a harsher verdict: "Anschluss in Technicolor." Earlier in the day, police—not from the local station, but from distant precincts—had barricaded the cross streets. Outbound traffic, only: an entire community of one-way boulevards. Later uniformed officials had spray-painted bright yellow directions on the sidewalks, letters, numbers, indecipherable shapes, a patois recognized only by bureaucrats and bulldozers. Several families did depart; they loaded their Penskes and U-Hauls in sheepish silence. Others dispatched wizened fathers-in-law and toddlers and nursing mothers to the homes of nearby kin. A few businesses, too, carted off their wares: not just the mega-drugstore and the chain supermarket, but also both Korean newsstands and the Dominican drycleaners. Miraculously, that was all. When dusk settled on the last day of the month, the impact zone still teemed with life. By prior arrangement, the locksmith and his cousins went to work.

The three men set about their task systematically: they started at Washington and Hickory, chaining the orthodontist to a postbox, then worked their way north to the corner of Jackson and St. James. Along the way, they fastened and bolted like madmen. They secured people to awnings, to drainpipes, to bicycle stands. King Gordius of Phrygia, boasted Onur, didn't tie his chariot half so well. They tried, of course, to make the captives as comfortable as possible. Most carried water and reading materials to their posts. Restauranteurs issued pots as makeshift bedpans. But the team's ultimate goal had to be security: this was no cause for plastic handcuffs and slipknots. Onur made certain to secure himself and Claudia on either side of his own front door. The husband—"for the sake of reconnaissance"—had been given a cellular phone and been bolted to the trash dumpsters behind the Greek used car lot. "You're our cavalry," explained Onur. "Our eyes and ears." The locksmith had hardly latched himself into place when the roosters from Wirkowski's Live Poultry greeted the dawn.

"I can't believe you pulled this off, Mr. Erdem," said Claudia. She was wearing her baby pink tank-top without a brassiere.

"Call me Onur," said the locksmith. "Please."

The woman attorney looked away from him. "I was afraid to ask," she said. "How funny. I'm not usually like that."

A solitary black crow landed on the brim of a nearby trashcan. "You know, Onur," said Claudia. "You're quite amazing."

"Nothing has happened yet," he said.

"But really," insisted the woman attorney. "I don't know if I'm supposed to say this or not—I don't know much about Turkish conventions—but I think you're one of the most amazing people I've ever met. Sincerely."

Onur waited for her to say more, but she didn't. He retrieved several stones from the nearby sidewalk and lobbed them at the crow. He missed each time. Eventually, no more pebbles remained within reach.

"I love the way you dress," said Onur. "You know that, don't you?"

The woman attorney eyed him for a moment. She smiled—but maybe there was less warmth in her smile; he could not be certain. "No, I had no idea."

The locksmith was eager to say more—he had a whole disquisi-
tion prepared, in fact, one that he'd repeated to himself for days—
but the arrival of police on motorcycles cut him short. State troopers appeared in their wake, then the Commissioner of Public Works
wielding a bullhorn. Even the mayor made an appearance: Hizzoner
personally entreated Onur to obey the law. But it was the media that
generated the frenzy, the scores of reporters and cameramen and
executive producers, the sound trucks and satellite feeds, the big
name network anchor who compared the locksmith to Gandhi and
Martin Luther King. *No, Ataturk,* Onur corrected him. *I think of myself
as the Ataturk of the Outer Boroughs.* The newsman nodded and asked:
"Who's that?" Claudia, meanwhile, granted interviews of her own.
Other than bathroom breaks, conducted behind the veil of a plastic
shower curtain, they had no privacy. Certainly no opportunity for an
intimate conversation.

At mid-morning, a phalanx of fire engines rolled in. The glistening red trucks gave the lock-in the carnivalesque atmosphere of
a tremendous block party. Shackled to the phone booth at the corner of Hickory and 83rd—and supplied with several dozen rolls of
quarters—Jude Basso told the locksmith that the vehicles reminded
him of the Italian civil defense drills from his childhood. *More like
floats in a private parade,* thought Onur. He relished the flags billowing
over the ladders that provided a patriotic, all-American backdrop
for his soliloquies on Madisonian democracy. Someone had the good
sense to run an extension cord into the corner deli and to set up a row
of televisions on the adjacent sidewalk. Onur watched himself on all
three networks simultaneously. He regulated the volume by remote
control. The sun rose above the Commerce Bank, trailed across Roo-
sevelt Park and descended behind a stand of little-leaf lindens. Nothing else happened.

Around midnight: a false alarm. Basso roused the locksmith out
of a half-stupor to report national guardsmen with bolt cutters. They

circled his phone booth—but at the first sight of the press, they retreated.

Onur steeled his vigilance. Claudia's eyes soon drifted shut. He let her sleep. Her body shivered in the damp, and Onur dispatched a reporter for a blanket.

✳

And then it was over.

Fast. Like a Houdini trick. All done.

A woman reporter told him the news. She was down on her knees, the microphone like a club in his face.

"The consortium pulled out," she said. "No arena."

The locksmith drew back. "Do you mean we won?"

"That's what the Associated Press is reporting. How does it feel?"

"Claudia," he shouted. "We won!"

He unlocked himself—a rather intricate process—and went to work on her bolts. When she was completely free, she hugged him. Tight. His chest against hers. He could feel his pulse in his temples.

The woman reporter persisted: "You must be very excited?"

"Of course, we are," said Claudia. "Now we can return to our lives."

"What a relief that must be," agreed the woman reporter. Other reporters, young and energetic, closed in on the locksmith. He watched on the television monitors as they surrounded him. A broad-shouldered black man in a dark blue parka—Onur recognized him as the host of an edgy cable newsmagazine—thrust his way between the locksmith and Claudia. "You must also be relieved, Mr. Erdem," continued the woman reporter. "You must be excited to return to your business."

The locksmith couldn't breathe. "Yes," he said, mechanically. "My business."

"Tell us a bit about it. About being a locksmith."

He tried to answer—to explain his previous existence—but he couldn't. He no longer remembered the life he'd lived then, not really, except that Claudia hadn't been part of it. His entire past seemed suddenly unsalvageable, like a key blank trimmed too close.

"Tell us about your former life," demanded the cable host.

Another reporter barked a question. And then a fourth. Their words didn't register. *My former life*—Onur stepped backwards, but there was no escape—*My former life. My former life.*

They thrust their ugly black microphones at Onur's mouth, pressing him further back against his storefront, but he said nothing. *For the first time in months, he had nothing to say.* Nothing newsworthy, at least. Did they really want to hear about his former life? About backgammon or test-match cricket? About chess? About Mama Fairuza's second-rate Harissa sauce? Of course they didn't. Who could possibly want to know about surveillance systems and fire-proof safes and locks, mortise locks and cross bolt locks and janus-faced locks, and all the locks that you could spend your entire life jimmying and picking—and still never be free?

EXPOSURE

WEDNESDAYS AND SATURDAYS are my days off at the pharmacy, but Saturdays my wife is off too, so I do my flashing on Wednesday afternoons. In the mornings, I have my weekly rap session with Dr. Quince-Martin. She rents space on a corridor down by the waterfront—opposite a urologist named Littlecock—and, after a bad storm, the entire office suite smells of rotting fish. Dr. Quince-Martin makes a point of revealing nothing about her private life, but I've taken the liberty of looking her up on the Internet: her husband is Dr. Martin-Quince, also a shrink, and she acted off-off-Broadway between college and medical school. Bit parts, mostly. Uncle Charley's receptionist in *Death of a Salesman*. A servant girl in *Hedda Gabler*. I'm holding this knowledge in reserve. The reality is that I just see Dr. Quince-Martin to keep Dawn off my back. My wife is all into head-shrinking and pill-popping and talk therapy, says it "rewired her neural circuitry" after the miscarriage, though she doesn't seem so different to me. Personally, I find Dr. Quince-Martin horrendously narrow. One time, when I tried to tell her about flashing, her back stiffened like a coffin lid and she advised me of the limits to physician-patient confidentiality in Connecticut. So now we chat about turning forty, and my step-father's chemotherapy, and Dawn's harebrained plan to build an outdoor deck onto the kitchen. I don't mention anything about showing Mrs. Sproul my genitals.

Mrs. Sproul must be in her early eighties by now. When we had her in fifth grade, she already colored her hair an unconvincing shade of chestnut. Two deep wedges grooved the space above her sharp nose, and her small, sagging breasts played second fiddle to her knobby, uneven collarbones. I distinctly remember someone asking her how old she was—and that same someone receiving a severe lecture on decorum. That someone may have been me. I think I may also have asked the other fifth-grade teacher, Miss Tillary, how old her colleague was, and I recall she may have answered "one hundred fifty." So while I knew Mrs. Sproul wasn't in her second century, I cannot express the relief I experienced a few weekends ago when I found the listing "L. & W. Sproul" in the New Haven County white pages. Twice, already, my targets have been dead. The first was Annie Jarmiczek, who'd repeatedly turned me down for a date at U. Conn. She'd fallen through ruptured ice while pond skating. And then my ex-boss from when I worked at Methodist Hospital bled out during routine gallbladder surgery. Which is why, after thirty years, there's a certain solace in knowing that Wilma Sproul is waiting for me like a plump goose on Christmas morning.

I took a swing past the Sprouls' place last week. A trial run. It's a second-story garden apartment facing away from the avenue, separated from the commuter rail tracks by a ribbon of parking lot and a towering privet hedge. The basketball court at one end stands rimless and overgrown with ailanthus trees. All of East Bondleigh has taken an economic drubbing during the last few years, and what was once comfortably middle class is now lilting toward downright sketchy. But I suppose Mrs. Sproul's choices are limited on a suburban teacher's pension. Or maybe she prefers the invigorating loneliness of New England winters to the stifling loneliness of Florida summers. Her husband, L. Sproul, is dead. His name remains in the telephone directory, but he's been replaced on the mailbox lid with a hand-printed: "Mrs. W. Sproul." While I nosed around the vestibule last week, pretending to read the free advertising circulars, a curvy young woman with purple hair and a razor-sharp nose appeared from the outside step and pushed the buzzer for 2K. She had grocery bags propped against her hips, so I helped her with the door. Clearly the granddaughter—you could cut pills in half with those Sproul family noses. But not bad-looking. She might come back today, I realize—some sort of weekly grocery run—so I know I'll have to work rapidly.

At mid-afternoon, the rear parking strip is nearly empty. I ease in beside a colossal trash dumpster. The remnants of someone's tag sale line the curbside: a warped sofa; a string-less ukulele; table lamps and chandeliers in various styles. All of this still sopping from the weekend squall. But there are also a pair of large marble lions—like giant, ferocious bookends—precisely the sort of kitschy garden ornament that Dawn can't ever get enough of. That's my wife for you: all day long preserving colonial farm houses and country churches and God-knows-what, then she comes home and wants to transform our swampy half acre into Versailles on the Old Mill Creek. Usually, I'd do right by her and drag the abandoned statuary into the back of the Plymouth. There's enough polished stone here to make her month. But today, I can actually see Mrs. Sproul through the wispy lavender drapes—relaxing in the sunlight beside the window, her hair now artificially curled, but still *faux*-chestnut—and I know there will be no time for hauling marble. Revenge is a dish that requires undivided attention to serve.

It's a hot, soupy day, so there's no one loitering on the cast-iron benches behind the Sprouls' building. Just a few grackles feeding in the thick grass. I walk quickly, my bathrobe and ski mask in a gym bag under one arm, my gaze firm and fixed forward. The first time I went on a flashing expedition, now nearly eight months ago, I used a trench coat that I'd lifted off a rack at the local barbecue joint. It had a zip-out fleece lining and a concealed breast pouch for carrying a wallet or a passport. But it made me feel a bit like Dick Tracy.

Or even something of a pervert. And I kept tripping over the belt. Eventually, I felt badly about taking the guy's coat—he'd also left his Parkinson's meds in one of the pockets—so I returned it to the restaurant with an apologetic note about carrying it off by mistake. I didn't actually walk into the restaurant with the stolen jacket, of course— I just draped it across the giant bull's-head doorknobs around five o'clock in the morning. Now, I use a royal purple bathrobe that I got on sale at Sears. It makes me look like one of those mobsters who fake madness by wearing their pajamas on the subway. Pretty stylish. Not that it matters. If all goes according to plan, the last thing Mrs. Sproul will care about is my wardrobe.

I wait several yards from the entryway, under a shedding dogwood, pretending to smoke a cigarette. Soon enough, a mother nearly half my age appears with a double stroller. Not twins—just two kids about a year apart. The woman's got a plaster cast on one forearm, so she's appreciative when I offer to hoist the carriage wheels over the steps. I'm glad to be helpful. Then I slip inside behind her. Recent parents are always the key to entering any residential building. They have far more on their minds than collective security. If our own baby had worked out, I suppose I'd be the same way. Or if we could have another one. But it didn't. And we can't. So now my greatest concern is getting onto my former fifth-grade teacher's fire escape without arousing suspicion. I loiter in the lobby until the young mother enters her apartment and then I climb to the second floor—with excessive determination, just in case I'm seen. The winding hallways are lined by ornate sconces, but only one bulb in each is functional. There's also a skylight on the second floor. A brass plaque beside the trash chute warns against tossing lit cigars into the compactor. From the flat opposite the utility closet comes the sound of afternoon sex. I breathe through my mouth to block out the pungent stench of grubby carpet and wet dog, trying several doors until I find the stair access to the roof.

Outside, the sun is a glowing patch of haze. Not much up here but a stack of folded aluminum chairs propped against a low parapet. Also empty Rolling Rock bottles, configured to form a giant question mark. Some have cigarette butts floating in them. I stand in the shadow of one of the tall brick chimneys and trade my street garb for the mask and robe. I'm able to alter my getup in fifty-five seconds. I've timed myself. But when I lower my body down the fire escape toward Mrs. Sproul's window, it feels as though I've been changing my clothes on the roof for an eternity.

Okay, timeout. You're probably wondering what an ordinary, straight-shooting, middle class guy is doing showing his pecker to post-menopausal women up and down the Connecticut coast. A legitimate question. But I'm not sure how well I can answer it. If you'd told me a year ago, when my family room was loaded high with Hefty bags of hand-me-down toddler clothes, that I'd be systematically flashing senior citizens, I'd have laughed my ass off. Or socked you one. My temper's not my strong suit. But post-baby, now that the Minnie-Mouse tutus and Winnie-the-Pooh sweater-sets have been shipped off to Dawn's lesbian cousin, who's expecting in a matter of weeks, it seems entirely natural to play my ongoing game of show the salami. Somehow, it gives my daily existence as sense of wholeness, of direction. And there's a certain reassurance in knowing that, by taking on a small amount of personal risk, I can begin to even out the cosmic score.

We were at an early Christmas party down in Bondleigh Cove when the inspiration first came to me. It's an annual shindig hosted by the volunteer historian at Dawn's preservation society. Dr. Tugman's quite well-off—he's a retired orthodontist and used to live in a three-story Victorian up on Prospector's Hill—but after his wife fell off a ladder two summers ago, he relocated to one of those refurbished upscale complexes opposite the public beach. I mention all of this because his holiday party was right after Dawn lost the baby, and she didn't want to go out at all, but she has a soft spot for the old widower, compounded by mutual loss, and eventually I talked her into making a brief appearance. Just say hello and shake a few hands, I promised. One drink, tops. But as I'd hoped, she started chatting with the courtly old fellow, and with another woman whose father had designed some celebrated covered bridges in Vermont, and pretty soon Dawn was deep into her second glass of champagne.

I interrupted the conclave only to ask after the lavatory. I'd already poked my head into several rooms unsuccessfully—a broom cabinet, a linen closet, a pantry. Tugman chuckled. "You have to go *through* the pantry. It used to be the servant's bedroom," he explained. "And be sure to pull shut the shower curtain. I'm still without drapes in the second bathroom, I'm afraid, and there's no need to give the neighbors a thrill." The old dentist laughed, his crimson face aglow under his shock of white hair. "Of course, if you do want to give them a thrill, I suppose nobody will stop you." He turned back toward his audience, dabbing his forehead with a silk handkerchief. "That's the tradeoff. A priceless view of the Sound out front, but in back it's all kitchens and toilets." This last remark sent the man reeling into another bout of mirth.

I crossed the parlor, where an overweight foursome crowded around the piano, crooning "It's a Long Way to Tipperary," off-key, then passed through the pantry into the second bathroom. It was a tidy little chamber, adorned in faded vermillion. Above the wainscoting, the wallpaper depicted the silhouettes of wildflowers—probably a popular design in its era, but today one seemingly more suited for toilet tissue. Tiny archers were carved along the frame of the mirror. The clothes hamper had been built into the wall. Maybe, when they'd refurbished these apartments, they also hadn't been able to find the servants' quarters. I took a closer look at the bath area. Tugman wasn't lying: from the window, you could indeed see the interior of the apartment across the courtyard. At fifteen feet, you could even make out the subscripts on the television newscast. And the individual polka dots on the viewer's dressing gown. I was about to draw shut the nylon bath curtain—when I recognized the woman watching TV in the opposite flat. Ms. O. Cotz-Cupper! The same screwy bitch who'd raised all hell when I wouldn't fill her sister's prescription for Vicodin. I'd told her: the name on the prescription has to match the name on the ID. No exceptions. In reality, if it had been amoxicillin or Lipitor, I'd have bent the rules, but hydrocodone is high-powered stuff. The kind of stuff the government tracks. So I wouldn't do it. Period. Then she called company headquarters, and got hold of the New England field supervisor, who backed me up, one hundred percent, but that's still a note in my permanent file. Customer complaint. What a goddam bitch! And somehow, while I was taking care of my business in the bathroom, I already knew my next step.

A few minutes later, I slipped out of the party with a black towel under my shirt. Then it was up to the roof, over a concrete dividing wall, down the opposite fire escape. Just enough time in between to strip and wrap the towel around my lower face. When O. Cotz-Cupper turned toward the window, I knew I'd succeeded. Her hands clutched to her blouse, as though she were covering her own nakedness, and her mouth opened like she wanted to scream, but she was afraid to. I could sense already that she wouldn't report me. That for years to come, she'd lock windows while sleeping and peek nervously behind closed drapes. She'd carry around a perpetual, latent terror—like an aneurysm waiting to rupture. A far greater punishment than the assault she expected. That seems like a fair trade-off for the permanent notation in my consumer relations file.

So I climbed back up the fire escape, changed back into my party clothes, and returned to Dr. Tugman's flat. By the time Dawn was ready to depart, an hour later, I was at the piano, belting out "Auld Lang Syne."

＊

And now I'm here on Mrs. Sproul's fire escape. She's gone over to the kitchen sink to wash some dishes, so she doesn't hear my tapping above the running water. I thump harder on the glass. Still no reaction. I have no choice but to stick my upper torso through the big open window, searching for something that will draw the old woman's notice. There's a stainless steel pot suspended from a nail in the molding. Perfect for banging against the iron radiator. That should do the trick—and it does. Now Mrs. Sproul turns to face me. I attempt to meet her gaze, but she's not looking at me. She's looking somewhere over my left shoulder. The old woman blinks normally, and the eyeballs shift back and forth, but the eyes themselves are unmistakably blank. Fucking brilliant! I'm flashing a goddam blind woman. It crosses my mind that I'll make her touch me—like the Braille version of flashing—but then something gives, and I lose my grip on the window sash, and suddenly I'm sprawled out across the linoleum.

"Who's that?" demands Mrs. Sproul.

I hold still and say nothing, as I might do if approaching a wild bird or rabbit.

"I know someone's there," she says. "Who are you and what do you want?"

Again, I keep silent. My head throbs. Blood is trickling down the side of my left ear, and it tickles. Immediately opposite me is a metal cabinet door with a calendar attached by magnets. The magnets read: "Have you taken your blood pressure medication today?" The calendar is turned to July, 1995. Beside the cupboard rests an olive-green wall telephone with a rotary dial. If the old woman goes for the phone, I know I'll be forced to restrain her. But she doesn't go for the phone. Instead, Mrs. Sproul pokes my flank with her open-toed slipper. Before I know it, she's leaning over my midsection and she's holding a carving knife in both hands. She's got it raised above her shoulder, like she's about to reenact the murder scene from a Roman tragedy. I can probably wrestle the weapon from her, but not without doing her physical damage. And that, of course, is across my moral line. "I may not see so well, but I'm not stupid," she says. "I can tell you're conscious by how you're breathing. Now account for yourself. Whoever you are. Speak up."

She doesn't sound frightened. Merely annoyed. As though confronting a wayward child. Of course, she can't see that my robe is hanging open. While I'm trying to decide my next move—whether I'll be able to crawl to the front door without getting stabbed—she's inching her bath slipper along my leg. Then—without warning—she drives her heel into my crotch. I groan, struggling for breath. When I try to sit up, I hit my head on the corner of the cupboard door.

"I warned you. Next time, it's the knife. Now, who are you?"

"Please, Mrs. Sproul," I say. "It's William Honegger. Billy. From the fifth grade."

She waves the knife aggressively, keeping it in constant motion—maybe to prevent me from lunging for it. "You don't sound like you're in fifth grade," she says.

"Not now," I say. "A long time ago. You taught me in the fifth grade."

"What was that name you said?"

"William Honegger. H-O-N-E-G-G-E-R."

The corners of her mouth tighten. She's thinking. "I remember William Honegger."

"You do?"

"Stupid boy," she says. "Dumb as a box of bricks."

I'm not sure how to respond to this. As absurd as it may sounds, her remark genuinely hurts me. Almost as badly as my testicles, which ache all the way into my shoulders.

"Funny that," adds Mrs. Sproul—more to herself than to me. "I always thought I'd remember the gifted ones. The future scientists, the scholars. The young ladies who'd turn heads entering a ballroom . . .

But all I recall are the most deplorable of the lot—the ones who lacked any hope." She's still poised to impale me, the knife trembling in her grip. "Life's a funny business. You can tell some of them are hopeless from the outset—even at the age of ten, eleven, twelve—and yet you've got to go on pretending otherwise. That's the only way."

I wipe the blood from my neck with my sleeve. "I wasn't sure you'd remember me," I say.

"Honegger, Honegger," says Mrs. Sproul. "Of course, I remember: dirty little runt. Had the makings of a pervert." She draws the knife back suddenly—as though to gain momentum. "You're not a pervert, are you?"

"I'm a pharmacist," I say.

"Hmmm. Could be." That's classic Wilma Sproul—never affirming anything. The same noncommittal "could be" she offered if you explained you hadn't done your homework because your grandmother had passed on. "Pharmacists aren't what they used to be, I suppose. In my day, pharmacy was a distinguished profession." Here, Mrs. Sproul begins coughing violently. Her temples pulse and the color drains from her long, downy jowls. She lowers the knife, straining for air.

I stand up. "Are you okay?"

"I'm fine. Stay back," she snaps. She removes a crumpled tissue from her blouse cuff, spits into it, then stuffs it back up her sleeve. "Now speak up. What are you doing here? I didn't phone for a pharmacist."

It's difficult to gauge her mental status. She sounds lucid, but there's something a bit hazy in her speech—though probably not enough to risk pretending that I've entered through the front door.

"I rang the bell," I say. "You didn't answer."

"I didn't?" she replies. "No, I suppose I didn't. That's what happens when you're nearing the end."

"You didn't answer the bell," I say. "So I thought I'd knock on the window."

This seems to appease her. "Very sensible." She shrugs. "William Honegger, a pharmacist. He was *such* a stupid boy."

I tear off a paper towel and run it under the cold water. The gash in my ear is far deeper than I anticipated. The cartilage protrudes through the skin.

"You have any antiseptic? I did a job on myself when I fell." "Whatever I have is above the sink," she answers. She has already lowered the carving knife to her side, and now she deposits it on the countertop behind her. Then she reaches for it again quickly—as though the peculiarity of my appearance has finally broken through her blood-brain barrier—but the weapon is already tucked into the pocket of my robe. I can see the first twinge of fear on her face as she searches, running her brittle fingers over the Formica like a spider's legs. "What do you want with me, young man?" she demands. "My niece will be here any moment now." So it's not a granddaughter. It crosses my mind that Mrs. Sproul may also be childless, like Dawn and me, and I feel sincerely sorry for her. For a moment or two. But there's a whole world of people who've got it rough—children battling cholera without tetracycline and that sort of thing—so you can't let it get to you.

"Doreen comes every week," says Mrs. Sproul. "She's fiercely devoted."

"Is she?" I ask. The cupboard above the sink contains a trove of germicides no longer recommended by the Food & Drug Administration. Hydrogen peroxide. Lugol's iodine. Mercurochrome. That leaves me with only two options: soap and water. "In that case," I say, "I'll just wash off my cut and get out of your way."

That's when the complexity of my predicament wallops me: I can't just walk out the door and put this behind me. She's bound to tell the niece that I've come crashing through her window—and one question will inevitably lead to another. When you've exposed yourself to fourteen women, you can't afford to be careless.

"I just wanted to say hello," I add. "I'm visiting *all* of my old teachers. On account of I'm turning forty next month."

"Forty and a pharmacist." The old lady coughs again—but not as roughly. "You haven't visited that nitwit Tillary, have you?"

"Not yet," I say. "You're my first."

This answer seems to please the old woman. "And why shouldn't I be?"

"You were my favorite." It costs me a lot to say this—but it's better than ten years in the slammer. That's the amazing thing about this country: you knife some guy in a bar, they give you a few months in jail. But you drop your pants in the wrong place, it's off to the federal pen and they throw away the key. "Not a day goes by when I don't think about a lesson I learned in the fifth grade."

"How very sweet," she says. "I'm pleased you didn't turn out as badly as we all thought. Surprised. Shocked. But pleased, nevertheless."

I don't have the ego to ask who "we all" are.

"That nitwit Tillary was the only one who thought you'd amount to anything other than a sex offender. But that was part of her idiocy. She thought *all of the children* were going to alter the course of western civilization for the better. Every one of you was an up-and-coming Michelangelo." Mrs. Sproul winced—at a thought as painful to her as angina. "It sounds all fine and dandy on paper. She's the angel. I'm the ogre. But if you believe all the children are up-and-coming Michelangelos, you can't teach them a darn thing. Do you see what I'm saying?"

"I guess so," I say.

"Don't guess," snaps Mrs. Sproul. "This isn't a game show."

While I'm dabbing my ear, Mrs. Sproul reaches her hand to my face and starts running her bony fingers over the features. At first, I fear she's going to poke my eyes out—her means of leveling the playing field. But she's just "looking" at me, in her way. Tapping the end of my nose. Measuring the width of my eyebrows. I feel like I'm being fitted for a balaclava under the care of a master tailor. Then she draws back. "Not a bad face," she says.

"Thank you."

"Not *handsome*, but it'll suffice."

"I hope so," I say, aware that the niece may stop by at any moment with the week's groceries—and I'm wearing only a robe. "I'm glad to see you're doing well, but I should probably be going now."

I start inching toward the foyer—just as Mrs. Sproul succumbs to another coughing fit. "My husband's smoking," she says, matter-of-fact. "Left me coughing and blind. Macular degeneration. Left Lawrence dead. At least, that's what they believe *this week*. So I am not, as you say, 'doing well.' But I'd be pleased if you would stay for a cup of tea. Keep me company until Doreen gets here."

I try to make excuses, but she ignores them and turns on the gas. "William Honegger," she says—again. As though repeating my name will somehow make it more palatable. "In spite of myself, I am pleased that you dropped in. It is very thoughtful. Not many of my little ladies and gentleman remember me anymore."

"They're probably just very busy," I say.

She sits down at the metal folding table. Reluctantly, I pull up a chair opposite her. The placemats depict capitals of Western Europe—London, Paris, Rome and Berlin. But in this frozen world, Berlin is still perpetually divided between East and West.

"Busy, my left foot. They probably just don't give a darn," says my hostess. "My fifth-grade teacher was Miss Llywarch. Adara. That's Welsh for 'catcher of birds.' She was a beautiful woman—a girl really, probably not even twenty-five. When the war started, she returned to Britain and was killed in an air raid."

"I'm sorry."

"That's the only reason I know what happened to her. Because she was killed by the Nazis. Otherwise, she'd just have evaporated into the ether." Mrs. Sproul looks as though she might weep, but she doesn't. The kettle whistles, a long mournful hum. When I try to help her pour the tea, she slaps away my hand. Hard enough to sting. I can only imagine what havoc she might have rendered with that carving knife. The old woman's hands shake fiercely while she fills our cups, but not a drop of the hot beverage lands outside the saucers. "Maybe I was too hard on Tillary," she says, apropos of nothing. "I suppose she meant well—in her way. When you do see her, please send my best." I pledge that I will. Then we sip hot tea in the stifling apartment while I struggle for something else to say. The old lady's eyes have acquired the filmy detachment of daydreams. I wonder if she is thinking about me, or her long lost students, or Adara Llywarch dying in the war.

"I should really be going," I announce. I'm ever conscious that the niece may be unloading groceries from her car as we speak.

Mrs. Sproul looks up from her cup. She appears surprised—as though she's forgotten about me. "Do you live around here?" she asks.

"Y—yes," I say, a bit hesitantly. But what harm can it do, right? She already knows my name. "I've got a place up in North Bondleigh. On Mill Creek."

"And you're a pharmacist?"

"That's what I said. At Metro Drugs."

"Could be," says Mrs. Sproul—in a way that makes me want to deck her. "Only drugstore around here used to be Rexall's. Back when pharmacists were legitimate professionals. Not foreigners who couldn't make it as doctors." Mrs. Sproul grins, as though this characterization brings her pleasure. She still has her own teeth, aligned in well-ordered rows. "Are you married, William Honegger?"

"Am I married?" I echo. Another straight-forward question—requiring only a one word response. But I don't give it. Instead, with a different word, I suddenly obliterate my fourteen years with Dawn. It's not unlike it was with Arnold/Sally. That's what we were going to call the baby. Arnold, after Dawn's late father, if it was a boy. Sally—just because we liked the sound of it—if it was a girl. But then we stopped calling it anything, and it stopped being anything. Just like that. So, for the moment, it's the same with my marriage. "No, I'm not married," I say. And I regret it instantly.

"Good," says Mrs. Sproul "Neither is my Doreen."

"I *really* should be going now," I say again. More forcefully. I'm about to add: I have plans to see my wife—but I realize this claim will no longer make any sense. "I need to get back to work," I lie.

"Stay a few more minutes. I would *so* like you to meet my niece," the blind woman says. "My Doreen is a bit feral. Like an alley cat. But she's a true dear. Quite frankly, a dullard pharmacist might do her some good."

"I wish I could, but—"

"—Oh, that reminds me. There is something else I want to show you," she says, ignoring my protests. "In the foyer."

Mrs. Sproul pushes her chair away from the table and disappears through the kitchen door. I feel obliged to follow. Or maybe powerless to resist, like one of the Pied Piper's children. And, although I know rationally that Mrs. Sproul survives quite fine on her own, there's something wrong to me about abandoning an elderly blind woman. So it's out of the sweltering kitchen, into the broiling foyer.

The foyer is a low railroad car of a room with matching armoires on either side of the entryway. One contains commemorative dishes of the Franklin Mint variety. *Gone With the Wind.* "Washington Crossing the Delaware." The other holds an assortment of cheap European souvenirs and African decorative arts—from which a research anthropologist might piece together the retirement itineraries of "L. & W. Sproul." My hostess shuffles to the second cabinet and points toward the top. She's indicating a silver plaque in the shape of a globe.

"Would you read that? Aloud, please."

I take down the plaque and dust off its surface; the metal could use a thorough polishing. "Forty years of devoted service," I read. "A life dedicated to her 'young ladies' and 'young gentlemen.' "

Mrs. Sproul nods approvingly. "That's right. Forty years. I *earned* that plaque."

"Forty years *is* a long time," I say.

"Forty years is a long time," she answers. "So they gave me a plaque. And now I can't even read it."

That's when the door buzzer sounds. Like a dagger through the stagnant air.

"May I visit the young gentlemen's room?" I interject—somehow, in my desperation, I've reclaimed the language of fifth-grade subservience. But then I bolt across the apartment without waiting for the old woman's permission. I don't seek out the bathroom, of course, but the master bedroom. Or, to be more precise, the walk-in cedar closet. It's dusty and stinks caustically of nail polish remover. Also a faint hint of mildew. Fortunately, Lawrence Sproul's business suits remain entombed on the hangers along the far wall. Lots of gabardine and tweed. Sports coats with suede elbow patches, the pockets smelling of stale pipe tobacco. All very collegiate. I'm somewhat shorter than the dead man was, but I manage to hike my belt up to my navel and conceal its odd location under a cashmere sweater. At least, Sproul's penny-loafers fit well. And the shoulders of his Oxford shirts are just the right width. I examine myself in the rectangular mirror above the bureau. I do appear marginally presentable, if thirty years behind the times. Yeah, right. Who the hell am I fooling? I look like I mugged the grandfather on a 1950s sitcom.

And then genius strikes. I un-tuck the Oxford and tear a gash in one of the jacket sleeves. I retrieve a bright yellow necktie, vintage seventies, from a chair-back and drape it loose around my neck. Noose-like. As though I'm impersonating a suicidal clown. From a wall peg, I retrieve a gray peddler's cap—and I set it atop my skull, jauntily askew. Now that's much better. I actually look trendy.

Or, at least *plausibly* trendy. Enough to snow Doreen. The niece is wearing an enormous denim skirt that looks more like a picnic umbrella. Or something Scarlett O'Hara might have worn during her

Woodstock phase. The skirt has bells along the seams, and they jingle while she walks. Her top is low-cut latex. Dressed like that, she's certainly got no grounds to criticize.

Doreen looks up from the groceries when I enter the kitchen. A polite smile, then she looks away. Indifferent? Shy? Something more? The girl obviously does not remember my helping her with last week's bags.

"Hi," I say, trying to sound nonchalant. "I'm Bill Honegger."

The defining feature of Mrs. Sproul's fifth-grade classroom was its spareness. What a contrast to fourth grade, where Miss Mandlebaum posted construction paper cutouts with each changing season: Valentine's hearts for February, Irish shamrocks for March, umbrellas and Easter bunnies for April. Or even Dr. Duggan, in sixth grade, who kept the same Monet water lily prints on the walls, decade after decade. But unlike the other classrooms at Orestes Bronson Elementary, which looked so forlorn during the summers, when you peered through the plate-glass at the boxed decorations stockpiled like military rations beneath the chalkboards, Mrs. Sproul's room looked more or less the same year round. As austere in October as in July. Only the chairs stacked atop the desks gave away the month. That, and that the floor-to-ceiling window shades stood open through the long summer holiday. During the school year, when Mrs. Sproul ordered the slats shut tightly, you had no way of watching the janitors lowering the flag before a storm, or of relishing the first dusting of snow on winter morning. Every school day, through the fluorescent dimness, Mrs. Sproul paced between the desks with her long wooden pointer. "Busy hands are happy hands," she warned us. "An idle mind is the devil's workshop." And we copied phrases like these, in D'Nealian script, until our little elbows ached.

My nemesis in fifth grade was a guy named Chuck Ziegler. He was one of Mrs. Sproul's "future scholars"—a fair-skinned kid with enormous blue eyes and an unequalled knowledge of reptiles and amphibians. At least among the ten-year-olds of coastal Connecticut. Chuck's father owned the local "Pet Paradise" and, at an age when access to snakes was more coveted than access to royalty, Chuck had parties where the popular boys could drape the boa constrictors over their shoulders. He was also the only student ever to earn a perfect mark on Mrs. Sproul's diagnostic spelling examination, after which he could commit no sin in her eyes. (In contrast, I scored something like seven out of one hundred.) But Chuck Ziegler, for reasons still beyond my understanding, devoted his towering fifth-grade intellect to one principal crusade: my ongoing and perpetual humiliation. I suppose I was an easy target: short, pudgy, in the lowest groups in math and reading. Not the kind of child to generate great sympathy among his classmates or teachers. So nobody but me minded when Chuck Ziegler sneaked under my desk and tied my shoelaces together. Or when he filled my lunch box with liquid paper. Or when he scrawled large black swastikas on my desk and told Miss Tillary that I'd drawn them. But the worst came one recess in the winter, on the box-ball court, when Chuck offered to shake my hand to seal a truce. With his other hand, he shoved a tree frog down my dungarees.

You don't know discomfort until you've had a live frog in your trousers. The damn animal must have panicked, because it started squirming around my groin. I also panicked and tried to retrieve it with my fingers. But getting a live frog out of your pants is far harder than getting one in. And I was terrified it might bite the end off my penis. We'd just learned about eunuchs in our lesson on Ancient Egypt, and I wasn't taking any chances. So I did the only thing I could do: I unzipped my fly and poked my pecker through, to protect it while I hunted for the frog. That's when Chuck Ziegler returned to the box-ball court with Mrs. Sproul in tow. "My dear young man," she said. "This will not be tolerated."

I still had one hand protecting my exposed pecker and the other deep in my jeans. "He did this," I shouted. "He stuck a live frog in my pants."

"Could be," said Mrs. Sproul wearily. "Charles, did you put a frog in William's trousers?"

"No, ma'am," said Chuck Ziegler.

"I thought not," said Mrs. Sproul.

"You've got to believe me," I pleaded. "There's a fucking frog in my pants. I'll take them off and show you."

Mrs. Sproul shook her head in dismay. "What language! You'll do no such thing," she said. She pointed at my exposed member. "Take care of that right this instant. Unless you want me to hit it with a yardstick."

I zipped up my fly. I could still feel the frog, struggling against my thigh.

"You'll come with me now," said Mrs. Sproul. "You'll keep your hands on top of your head and you'll come with me."

"But the frog—"

"On top of your head," she insisted. I complied. She paraded me past my classmates like a prisoner of war.

"You'll spend your recreation time with me," she announced. "Until you learn to use it responsibly. Now be seated. And place your hands on the desktop, palms up."

I attempted several times that morning to show her the frog—which soon suffocated under the weight of my leg—but she refused to listen. Her only goal was to keep my hands away from my privates. And then I was compelled to repeat this exercise every morning for the entire remainder of the school year. I sat beside Mrs. Sproul, indoors, while all of the other students enjoyed the spring sunshine. If my hands left the desktop, even to scratch my nose, she snapped her ruler across the artificial wood. But I dared not complain, certainly not to my parents, because then they would learn the alleged cause of my punishment. Even Chuck Ziegler wasn't prepared for this extreme a sentence. He began avoiding me. I'd become his badge of dishonor. But he never confessed to shoving the frog down my pants. Meanwhile, Mrs. Sproul's glare immobilized my hands as effectively as five sets of Mexican finger traps.

"You'll be grateful someday, William," she said. Every recess.

"The day will arrive when you'll thank me for molding you into a young gentleman."

※

"Thank you," I say. "But it's really not worth the trouble."

Doreen has offered to prepare a poultice for my ear. Some concoction involving bran flakes, aloe leaves and puréed tomatoes. "No trouble at all," she says, squeezing vegetables into the electric blender. "I'm the one who should be thanking you. Aunt Wilma doesn't get very many visitors." When the girl leans over the blender, driving the vegetables into the blades, her breasts nearly tumble out of her top.

"She was an excellent teacher," I say.

"Do you truly think that?" asks Mrs. Sproul. "Well, I think so too." Doreen squeezes her aunt's hand. The girl's other hand is pink with tomato paste.

"Of course, you were a wonderful teacher," she says—but in the manner that one speaks to elderly people about subjects that no longer matter. "Did you show Mr. Honegger your plaque?"

"—Bill," I say. "Please."

The girl smiles. She pours the contents of the blender onto a dishrag and drapes the cloth across my wound with a self-confidence that surprises me.

"Doreen is studying medicine," says Mrs. Sproul.

"Oh," I say.

"Holistic medicine," explains Doreen. "Herbal remedies."

"*Medicine*," Mrs. Sproul says again. More decisively. Then she adds: "Mr. Honegger's not married."

"Auntie!" The girl rolls her eyes—obviously for me, not for her aunt. "You're really in top form today, aren't you?"

"I'm just saying," says the blind woman.

"What are you saying, exactly?" asks the girl.

Her aunt sips from her second cup of tea. "Make hay while the sun shines," she says.

That's an expression I'll never forget. Probably copied it five thousand times. "Make hay while the sun shines." "Waste not, want not." "Can't never could do anything." An entire year of my life practicing penmanship on platitudes while Miss Tillary's class built the Great Pyramid out of papier-mâché. And after all that, my handwriting is still virtually illegible.

"Mr. Honegger is a pharmacist," says the blind lady. "*A pharmacist.*"

"That's right," I say. "I'm a pharmacist." But I wink at Doreen while I say this—trying to hint that my drug trade may be broader than her aunt suspects.

"If you want my opinion, dear, pharmacy is a very distinguished profession," says Mrs. Sproul. "He's practically a doctor."

"Practically," I say.

The niece has the poultice pressed to the side of my head. A cool lotion surrounded by her warm, gentle fingers. Impulsively, I raise my hand to my ear and place my own hand over hers.

"I'm sorry you fell," she says—as though our skin is not in contact. The girl lowers her voice to nearly a whisper. "It does her good to have people here. I hope you're not disappointed."

"Why should he be disappointed?" shouts Mrs. Sproul.

"He shouldn't be," says the niece.

"I'm not," I say.

We exchange a look of conspiracy.

"I was an excellent teacher," says Mrs. Sproul. "No matter what anybody says. I was a darn fine teacher. Darn fine." She breaks off to cough violently into her tissue. "I wouldn't do it any differently. Any of it."

Doreen's delicate hand is still pressed under mine. I'm afraid to move—afraid she'll pull away. How many years since I've done this—touched another human being with the outcome so uncertain? Not since meeting Dawn.

"Let them say what they will," says Mrs. Sproul. One large vein throbs behind her right eyebrow, but the rest of her face is suddenly lifeless. For the first time all afternoon, she looks as though the end really is near. Not just old, but too old. "We were teaching children—not competing for ribbons at a state fair. Or preening ourselves like debutantes at a ball. What did that sow Tillary know? Or any of them?! All that mumbo-jumbo about what the children wanted. *What the children wanted!* They were *children*, for heaven's sake. How could they possibly know what they wanted? I didn't even know what *I* wanted."

"It's all right," says Doreen.

"It is not all right," snaps her aunt. "It most certainly is not."

The girl's hand slides out from under mine. When the old woman starts sobbing, her niece is already at her side. "There, there," she soothes. "Would you like more tea?"

Mrs. Sproul shakes her head. She blows her nose with the force of a locomotive. "Forty years, and they wanted me to start over *their way*," she says. "With construction paper and papier-mâché! But I let them know what was what: if my methods were good enough for the likes of Adara Llywarch, then they were certainly good enough for me." Then the old woman turns to me and adds: "Miss Llywarch was my fifth-grade teacher. A brilliant woman. She was killed in an air raid during the war."

"I'm very sorry," I say.

"They don't make schoolteachers like that anymore," answers Mrs. Sproul. "Tillary wasn't fit to wash that woman's boots."

"It was their loss," says Doreen. "They didn't know what they had." Now her aunt says nothing. Not even: "Could be." She just sits impassively, her arms folded across her chest. I stand up. I know the time has come for my departure.

"I hope my visit hasn't upset you too much," I say.

The girl shakes her head. "Not at all. If you want to come back again, I'm sure Aunt Wilma would be happy to see you. Wouldn't you, Aunt Wilma?"

I try to read a deeper meaning into this question—a hint that the niece would also like me to return. It's hard to tell.

"Would you like Mr. Honegger to visit again?" asks the girl. Louder.

"Forty years," says the old blind woman. "My entire life."

"She would like it," says the niece. "Please do come."

"I'll certainly try," I say.

Of course, I know that I won't. And I can tell that Doreen knows this too. She accompanies me to the front door, and we exchange a quick handshake at the threshold. Then I climb back up to the roof and retrieve my clothing. My robe is still in Mrs. Sproul's bathroom, I realize. But that's fine. I doubt I'll be needing it anymore. Maybe the old widow will find some use for it. That seems like a fair trade, cosmically speaking, a stylish purple robe for the two marble lions that I now haul from the rear parking lot into the back of the Plymouth. I can already sense how much Dawn is going to like them. Once I've loaded them into the vehicle, side by side, I strap them into place with the seatbelts. Just as I might secure carpooling children. I enjoy looking at the marble lions through the rear-view mirror—forsaken animals on their way to a second life. A better life. Yes, a better life. We've just started on our journey home, and I can already feel their healing powers taking hold.

THE MAGIC LAUNDRY

*W*HEN HIS FATHER offered to stake him in any business venture of his choosing, Jeff Cutter decided to open a laundromat on the corner of Broadway and 117th Street in upper Manhattan. The old man was, of course, disappointed. He'd made his own fortune in a series of manufacturing enterprises as drab as they were lucrative—industrial adhesives, orthotic shoe insoles, articulating paper for dentists—and from his only son he had hoped for something a bit more glamorous. *Why not software design? Maybe robotics?* But after four years at Columbia University studying Demosthenes and Cicero, Jeff recognized his own limitations. He was an affable sort, neither inarticulate nor unhandsome, but too sincere to sell things and not shrewd enough to buy them. If among the classics undergrads at Columbia, he'd been considered rather a lightweight, he nonetheless preferred reading the Ancients (or a pick-up softball game, for that matter) to anything smacking of hard work and profit. A corner laundromat was about all he had in him. The elder Cutter asked: *How about a professional laundering service?* Or at least a dry cleaner's? But Jeff eventually won his father over with forecasts of a national chain of coin-operated laundromats that would do to full-service cleaners what Blockbuster had done to drive-in movies. The name proved the decisive selling point: The Magic

Laundry. Jeff's father thought it sounded Chinese—a killer advantage when it came to cleaning clothes.

Jeff spent his summer scouting out the neighborhood's three existing laundries. The largest, Kwick Wash Inc., catered primarily to the college crowd. While making use of fifty-one front-load washers and three dozen mega dryers, patrons could play arcade games and foosball in a dimly lit alcove or watch ESPN on a large-screen television. The owner, an overweight, chain-smoking Greek in his sixties, whose very presence seemed carcinogenic, turned a blind eye to paying customers who walked around with lit joints or gave blowjobs in the restrooms. Only two blocks away, serving a tamer crowd of predominantly black and Dominican women, a young Filipino couple named Segovia operated the Praise The Lord Laundry. Mrs. Segovia's sister-in-law was running for a city council nomination in the Democratic primary. The laundry doubled as her campaign headquarters. Two long fiberglass folding tables in back had been cleared of religious icons and plastic flowers to make room for a stack of placards reading "Santos for Harlem," and several mornings every week the Santos-Segovia faction of the local party held court around the detergent vending machine. One full afternoon in the Kwick Wash and another at Praise the Lord—drying the same load of clothing several dozen times in an effort to avoid appearing suspicious—convinced Jeff that neither establishment was the proper model for The Magic Laundry.

Madame Ursula's held more promise. A family of Polish immigrants ran the business, all women, all daughters and nieces of the proprietor. The eldest niece was a senior at Columbia whom Jeff had seen sporadically around campus; the youngest daughters, gangly twins, couldn't have been more than twelve. Madame Ursula was herself about fifty. She'd kept her figure and her long curveless hair remained the color of wild yellow irises. While none of her individual features displayed a singular beauty—her lips were a tad thin, her nose boasted a faint hook—they meshed into almost symphonic perfection. Rumor had it that she'd been a sex worker in Amsterdam after the Berlin Wall fell, also that she'd once counted Gomulka and General Jaruzelski among her lovers. Jeff had no way of knowing. But as an upperclassman, he had freely joined the speculation regarding Madame Ursula's background, itself a time-honored tradition among her clientele of graduate students and starter couples, for whom the owner's mysterious origins were as much of a draw as the laundry's cozy orange lamps and rosewood folding tables. Jeff had always admired Madame Ursula's élan. During his summer of spying, he also grew to appreciate her talents as a businesswoman. She doled out carefully chosen kindnesses: if a stranger off the street requested change for parking, she would offer to have one of her daughters feed his meter later in the afternoon. She made it her business to know as much about her customers' lives as they did not know of hers— but she was discreet, savvy, omniscient yet never intrusive. Jeff had washed the same bag of towels fifty times over three weeks before he uncovered her secret: Madame Ursula never touched the cleaning equipment.

The niece, he realized, ran the show. She emptied the coin canisters, programmed the water temperatures, changed the lint filters. While her aunt presided over the salon—cautious never to appear a mere laundress—the niece kept silent watch from her perch atop the antique safe that served as a makeshift counter. The girl's name was Katrin. When she wasn't clearing sheets of fabric softener from dryer drums or unclogging exhaust ducts, she sat with her long pale legs dangling from the safe and read inconspicuously. One morning, Jeff noticed that she was reading Thucydides. She must be knocking off her Western Civilization requirement over the summer, he thought. Yet three days later, while the girl stood on the sidewalk haggling with a child labor inspector sent by the state, Jeff passed by the safe and noticed that the volume was in the original Greek. He considered striking up a conversation: one classicist to another. But the bell above the door jangled unexpectedly and the girl was suddenly approaching—and Jeff realized that she thought he was spying *on her*, rather than on the laundry, because what other than romance would drive a sane person to wash the same red towels over again and again, morning after morning, until they'd faded to a pinkish gray? Katrin smiled at him. Jeff quickly plucked his towels from the dryer, nearly scalding his hands in the process. He didn't stop walking until he reached the bodega on the corner. Six weeks later—on the Tuesday after Labor Day—The Magic Laundry celebrated its grand opening. Three dozen triple-load washers. Forty-two 30-pound dryers. Walls plastered with movie posters from the thirties and forties. Jeff's father had suggested naming each machine after a Hollywood celebrity of the Golden Age, the way upscale delis often did with sandwiches, so little brass labels on the equipment paid tribute to the likes of Myrna Loy and Errol Flynn. The elder Cutter, fresh up from Florida and armed with the statistic that the majority of new laundromats fail within six months, also insisted upon an opening-day gimmick to crack the market. They offered free laundry from six am to midnight—served up with complementary daiquiris and piña coladas. *That* attracted a crowd: college freshmen, winos, a homeless woman who stripped to her underwear. Two plainclothes cops shut the party down around dusk and issued Jeff a summons for serving alcoholic beverages without a liquor license. After that, Jeff's business dwindled. He picked up a handful of regular customers, transfer students and families new to the neighborhood. He also acquired several unfortunates who had been banned from Praise the Lord and Madame Ursula's for repeated misdemeanors—stealing women's clothing, sexually harassing customers—or, as in the case of Mrs. Garcia, had willingly exiled themselves after verbal altercations with the management. But these patrons numbered in the teens, at most, and no quantity of glossy photographs from *The Grapes of Wrath* and *Double Indemnity* could compensate for Jeff's principal difficulty: would-be customers avoided an empty laundry the way diners avoided under-trafficked restaurants.

In desperation, Jeff considered hiring local high school kids to pretend that they were paying patrons in an attempt to break this self-defeating cycle. Then two miracles occurred on successive afternoons: on Friday, Madame Ursula invited him to dine with her. On Saturday, Mrs. Garcia announced that Mae West—a.k.a. washer number sixteen—had cured her chronic incontinence.

Madame Ursula's eldest daughter delivered the invitation: a note handwritten on monogrammed stationery. At first, Jeff feared it might be some sort of condolence card—that the omniscient laundress would know of a death in his family before he did himself. But the discovery of a summons to "a most informal supper" shocked him nearly as much. Jeff looked up from the letter to find the daughter, a lanky teenager with a hint of copper in her hair, waiting like a nineteenth-century valet. What did she want? A tip? He reached into his wallet and removed two crisp singles. The girl laughed and shook her head. "Are you coming?" she asked. He could hear her Dutch upbringing in her vowels. "Mama needs to know how many places to set." Jeff paused in confusion, then nodded. He had not considered the possibility, not even for a moment, that one might turn down an audience with Madame Ursula.

That evening Jeff rang the Luczaks' buzzer at precisely eight o'clock. The women lived on the top floor of a six-story walk-up several doors down from their business. On the way there, he noticed that the eldest daughter sat perched atop the safe. That meant the niece—the girl who suspected him of stalking—would be at dinner. But what of it? He'd done nothing wrong. Yet as he climbed the uneven wooden staircase that led to Madame Ursula's threshold, his ears burned red with shame.

His hostess greeted him at the door. She was wearing a white summer skirt with blue trim and a matching navy top. "So good of you," she said. "So very good."

Jeff offered her his bouquet. One of the twins carried it away and returned with the flowers arranged in a vase.

"I have never believed in making food to wait," said Madame Ursula. "Over dinner, we'll chat."

She led him through a cluttered parlor. The room contained far too much furniture: mahogany highboys and dropfront secretaries and savonarola chairs upholstered with purple velvet. In one corner, a plastic cover formed the outline of a harp; in another, an antique gramophone rested atop a baby grand piano. A swinging door led into an equally over-furnished dining room where the table had been set for ten. Eight of the places were already occupied by the Luczak girls. Madame Ursula seated herself at the head of the table. By default, Jeff sat between the twins at the foot. "My Rosa has already dined," said Madame Ursula. "I hope you do not find yourself too much in confinement. It is so truly a to-do to place the leaves in the table."

"It's okay," said Jeff. "I'm used to chow mein and pizza."

Madame Ursula motioned for one of the girls to begin the dinner service. "Well I fear I have no chow mein and pizza for you, Mr. Jeff Cutter. Tonight, we shall have escargot and Pemequid oysters. Oysters are to your liking, no?"

"Of course," lied Jeff. He'd never before tasted a Pemequid oyster. His primary goal was to avoid eye contact with the niece.

"I'm glad to see that you're an oyster connoisseur, Mr. Jeff Cutter," continued Madame Ursula. "Too few young men these days take such an interest. I am partial to Malpeques myself, but they have too much salt for Katrin's palate. Her tongue prefers a more fruitful oyster like the Pine Island, or an almond flavor like, I need not say, the Pemequid."

Jeff preferred not to think about Katrin's tongue. He waited nervously for his hostess to reveal the cause for his summons, but through dinner she spoke only of shellfish, of Turganev novels, of an article she'd read on the poaching of tigers. The word laundry never crossed her lips. Meanwhile, the younger girls whispered among themselves and giggled in periodic waves. Jeff felt as though he were caught in a summer-stock production of *Little Women*. He had read several stories in which unsuspecting young men like himself had been invited to such gatherings in the hope of arranging a marriage, and he began to worry about which of the underage girls his hostess had designated his. To his surprise, Madame Ursula concluded an anecdote about the cousin who supplied her with the free oysters, and she rose from the table. "Ladies," she said. The younger girls, as though trained, filed out of the room.

"It was a joy, Mr. Jeff Cutter," said Madame Ursula. "Now 'poof!' and I'm gone."

Suddenly, Jeff found himself alone with the niece. All that separated them was a graveyard of greasy dishes and balled-up napkins and empty oyster shells.

Katrin grinned. "You remind me of Elpenor."

"Of course," Jeff played along. "I do." He could think of no acquaintance with that name—if Elpenor were, in fact, a person.

"You don't have a clue," said Katrin. Her accent was thicker than her cousin's, but her voice flowed much more gently.

"Sure, Elpenor," ventured Jeff. "Hamlet's hometown."

"Elpenor," answered Katrin. "From the *Odyssey*, Book X. Odysseus' friend who drinks too much and falls off Circe's roof. You remind me of him."

"Okay," said Jeff. He refilled his water glass from the pitcher.

"We know nothing about him, of course," explained Katrin. "He was just some random guy who fell off a roof and was immortalized forever. But I imagine if we did know what he was like, he'd be something like you."

"Maybe," said Jeff. "I don't drink."

"We know," said Katrin. "If you did, we wouldn't hire you."

"What?"

The girl stood up and began to gather the dishes. "Don't look so surprised," she said. "My aunt wants to hire you to manage her business. I can't do it full time—not if I'm going to go to grad school next year."

Katrin rounded the table; she stood beside Jeff. The bare expanse of white flesh just below her collarbone breathed in and out only inches from his face. "I have a business myself, you know," said Jeff. When he realized that their conversation was to be professional in nature, he quickly grew disappointed and irritable.

"Get real, Jeff," said Katrin. "You won't last six months."

Jeff looked away from her chest. "I'm doing fine."

"You're not even making overhead," she answered. "The neighborhood can't support a fourth laundry. If you bail out now, your father can write off the machines." Katrin carried a stack of plates into the kitchen. "It's a good deal, Elpenor," she added when she returned. "Take it."

Jeff didn't answer.

"It's not magic, you know. I watch. I listen. I find out about people. I know your father fronted you the money in cash even though he wanted you to build rockets or something."

"Robots," said Jeff.

"Robots," agreed Katrin, speaking quickly. "And I know that you're single."

Katrin appeared surprised by her own audacity. She blushed, but didn't look away. They heard a car alarm raving at some distance.

"If we're done talking business," Katrin said softly, "you could invite me to dinner next weekend."

"You're serious," said Jeff. "You really mean it." His previous interactions with women had always been slow and uncertain. "Give me a minute. This doesn't happen very often."

Katrin smiled. "Elpenor only fell off the roof once."

They made arrangements to go out the following Saturday. Jeff felt grateful, also confused. She walked him to the door and he turned to face her at the threshold—even though he knew they would not kiss. "I have a question," he said. "What did your aunt do back in Poland?"

"You won't tell anyone?"

"Not a soul."

Katrin squeezed his arm. "We lived in Krakow," the girl said. "My aunt was the assistant supervisor of a public laundry."

The following day began with a bloodbath. A disturbed twelve-year-old boy from the General Grant housing projects had pilfered another child's puppy and tossed it unnoticed into one of the running washers. At the moment, Bonnie Williams had been changing her grandson's diaper in the restroom. She returned to find globs of knotted hair and a bloated cocker spaniel tangled in her brassieres and garters. Jeff offered her $1,000 in cash and free laundry for life to keep the matter quiet. What else could he do? Let her report it? Tell her to take the matter up with a prepubescent derelict? He paid another $500 in hush money to the mother of the puppy's owner. He even agreed to bury the drowned animal in a memorial garden for departed pets. Yet scouring the washer—a fifty pounder named Gregory Peck—Jeff felt only relief: thank God it hadn't been a child.

Saturday afternoon was usually a period of peak demand, but a bout of Indian Summer kept traffic light. Mrs. Garcia came in around four. With her were two other squat companions in their sixties, possibly sisters; they shared close-cropped gray hair and broad ski-slope noses that reminded Jeff of snow shovels. He paid the three women little heed, at first. Mrs. Garcia knew only two topics for conversation: her husband's hypochondria and her own legitimate illnesses. She had initially come to The Magic Laundry in the most unlikely manner. In September, her husband had experienced acute chest pains while dropping her off at the Praise the Lord. The Filipino couple had insisted upon summoning a doctor. A shouting match ensued. When the physician, an anesthesiologist who happened to be Segovia's half-brother, diagnosed the pains as acid reflux, Mrs. Garcia declared herself vindicated and shifted her loyalties to Jeff. He thought her a dour, embarrassing woman. Yet that afternoon—and the novelty caught his attention—she was smiling like the Buddha.

Jeff stopped scrubbing and listened.

"This one right here, Henny," said Mrs. Garcia. "I'm sure of it. I always use Mae West for mine and the Keystone Cops one for Al."

The sister named Henny laughed shrilly. "The Keystone Cops are some riot."

"Not to live with."

Mrs. Garcia wiggled her rump. "No more leaking. No more wicking for me. I feel like one of those Depend commercials." She beckoned Jeff with two fingers. "You got a regular goldmine here, you know that," she said.

Jeff approached nervously. He'd wrapped his sleeves around his elbows, but they'd managed to get soaked anyway. "Is everything okay, ma'am?"

"Better than okay. Hunky-dory. Mae West here fixed my bladder." "Your bladder?"

"I washed my overpants here last week and I've had complete control ever since. How common is this?"

"I'm not sure."

"Well you got to advertise better," said Mrs. Garcia. "Let people know what you're doing here."

Jeff took a step backwards. "I guess," he said.

"I tell you what," said Mrs. Garcia. "You done me a favor. I'll do you a favor. Half the people I know wet their beds. You'll have them taking numbers."

Jeff assured Mrs. Garcia that her assistance wasn't necessary— that he would prefer not to have it, in fact—but direct confrontation was not his strong suit. When he opened the laundry at six a.m. the following morning, two other women were standing in front of the iron guard gate carrying hampers. Every hour brought additional inquiries for the miracle-working machine—which was also rumored to treat herpes and lumbago. Potential customers called for reservations. Some walk-ins despaired of ever accessing Mae West—she was already booked five days in advance—and took their chances with less illustrious washers. Yet when the superintendent of a building on 126th Street announced that Gary Cooper, machine number eight, had substantially reduced his impotence, the entire establishment acquired a palliative halo. Later, a further discovery: washing the discarded clothes of friends or relatives—even if they did not wear them again—might have transformative effects. Jeff started a mail-order business. He raised rates to two dollars per load. On Wednesday, he grossed twice as much as he had done in all of September.

Nobody ever credited The Magic Laundry with any earth-shattering miracles of the cancer-curing, world peace variety. It appeared that Jeff's machines, like their owner, recognized their limits. Yet each morning brought word of hemorrhoids soothed and passions reignited and reconciliations with long-estranged siblings. Different washers gained reputations for aiding with specific problems. Humphrey Bogart, number three, helped smokers quit. Ronald Reagan, number twenty-eight, blocked out bad memories. Monetary difficulties were the province of number nine, Orson Welles. Bonnie Williams won $248 dollars on a scratch-and-match ticket and pinned a thank-you card on the iron guard gate. A Carmelite nun experienced a particularly vivid dream about the Virgin Mary; she promised to praise The Magic Laundry in her prayers. Jeff's meteoric rise soon drew media attention. A chirpy female reporter netted an exclusive interview with Mrs. Garcia and photographed her kissing Jeff's cheek in front of Mae West. The headline on Friday's *New York Post* read: Machine Dry. Jeff's father even flew up from Cormorant

Island to congratulate him on his "business acumen"; he insisted that they each smoke a Cuban cigar. "If you've got it, you've got it," the elder Cutter told the *Post*. "And my boy—make sure you quote me on this now—he's got it."

The reporter turned to Jeff. "Do you really think your machines perform miracles, Mr. Cutter? Increase fertility and improve test scores?"

"I'll answer that," interjected Jeff's father. "Our washers here at The Magic Laundry help those who are willing to help themselves."

"What exactly do you mean?" persisted the reporter.

The elder Cutter elaborated. "We do our part. The customers do theirs." Jeff's part, it turned out, was too much for one man. When business had been sluggish, he did not think twice about leaving the store unmanned. With thousands of dollars in the till at any given moment, he could no longer afford such a luxury. He hired four employees in two days: three college students to cover the overnight and a gay black man known as Doc Happy to back him up during the day. Doc Happy was seventy-two and played the harmonica professionally in the evenings. Jeff had hoped that the old man's presence would give him more time to read—at least to review the Homeric passage about Elpenor before his date—but training an employee was a job in itself. When Saturday evening rolled around, Jeff still hadn't cracked a book.

High on confidence—although worn to the bone—Jeff prepared for his dinner with Katrin. Deep down, he doubted the powers of the miracle washers. Still, he cleaned his slacks and sweater in a machine reputed to foster romance. Clark Gable, number one. If you've got it, he assured himself, I guess you've got it.

Jeff picked Katrin up at Madame Ursula's. It was his first New York City date. He'd had a serious girlfriend back in Florida through his junior year, but she'd fallen for a German scuba instructor while on vacation in Honduras. Jeff's mother sent him their wedding announcement from the *Cormorant Island Sentinel*. When the couple went diving in Indonesia on their honeymoon and the groom died of an asthmatic attack, Jeff's mother sent him the obituary as well. After that, Jeff kept a low romantic profile. All of the women he'd met in New York were a little too something—though exactly what, he couldn't say—and he feared they might interpret his advances as insults. He'd expected to find Katrin sitting atop the antique safe in jeans and a t-shirt. Her low-cut black dress and high-heel shoes caught him off guard. The girl was exchanging whispers with her copper-haired cousin when Jeff peered through the window. She glided out to meet him, waving at the cousin and flashing him a puckish smile. "Where to, Elpenor?"

"Oh, Jesus," said Jeff. "I don't know."

Katrin laughed. "Most girls would be really angry at you just about now. You know that, don't you?"

Jeff liked that she wasn't mad. "But you're not most girls," he said.

"We'll have Senegalese," she said. "Don't forget your wallet."

Katrin led him to a cozy, informal West African eatery on the ungentrified slope of Morningside Park. The tables were long, cafeteria-style. They sported checkered plastic coverings—some white and red, others white and green. The carcass of a mutilated payphone hung from one of the rear walls. Katrin embraced the maitre d'—a stylish dark-skinned woman in tight clothes—and she and Jeff took at seat beside the fish tanks. They were the only two white faces in the place.

"You should order the theibou djeb and aloko," suggested Katrin. "Snapper with plantains. And you should deep-six this miracle washer nonsense."

Jeff couldn't focus on Katrin and choosing his meal at the same time. He dropped the menu helplessly on the table. "Why on earth would I do that?"

"Because it's not you," she said. "Because it will consume every last waking minute of your time and you won't play softball again all fall."

"I hired four people today. Now *I* have a manager."

Katrin's cheeks flushed. "Bully for you, Elpenor," she said. "Has it crossed your mind that what you're doing is wrong? That you're taking advantage of those people?

"Of Mrs. Garcia? She's happy as a freshly-diapered baby."

The waitress came for their order. Jeff pointed to the theibou djeb and aloko. Yet when she asked if he preferred the aloko with peppers or with tamarind sauce, Katrin came to his rescue. She still had the upper hand after the waitress left.

"How about wrong to the Segovias or Timon Demopolis? How about wrong to my aunt?" Katrin's breath quickened. Her breasts rose and fell. "She can't afford many more weeks like this one. Do you know how hard my aunt works to keep her business going?"

Jeff pounced. "You mean how hard *you* work. I watch things, too."

"Yes, dammit, how hard *I* work," Katrin shot back. "I'm going to go to grad school next year and I'm going to teach classics and . . ." She stopped suddenly. "Look, I'm sorry."

"Tell me more about Elpenor," he said.

And she did. Their intimacy was instantaneous and almost brutal. They talked about the unspeakable—about her uncle's death in an electrical fire, how her father had killed her mother and then himself. They discussed under what circumstances it would be moral to assassinate the president. She admitted that she'd made out with a middle-aged woman in the ladies' room at the Kwick Wash. When the restaurant closed, they continued their conversation out onto the sidewalk and up to the steps of his building. It was nearly two-thirty. Several gypsy cabs slowed down to see if they wanted a lift; otherwise, the streets were deserted. Jeff didn't want to detain Katrin beyond reasonable first-date hours, but he didn't want the conversation to end.

"Usually the *guy* walks the *girl* home, Elpenor," said Katrin. Her face flashed red in the light from the twenty-four hour pharmacy.

Jeff didn't know what to say. "That's a beautiful dress," he said.

"You can keep it," answered Katrin. "I'll leave it here."

She took him by the hand and led him up the stairs to his own apartment. They stood face to face at the door. "I'll give you the dress now," she said. "You'll give me sweats and a t-shirt in the morning."

"Are you sure you want to do this?" he asked.

"I don't do anything I don't want to," Katrin answered. Then she leaned forward and added the words that would haunt him until the final time he saw her: "Just so you know, Elpenor, this has nothing to do with the laundry."

Katrin wasn't alone in objecting to the miracle washers. When Jeff returned from lunch the following afternoon, he found Timon Demopolis leaning against the change machine and chain-smoking volcanically. The owner of the Kwick Wash displayed a six-figure cashier's check. He reminded Jeff of the sweepstakes winners on television—only the Greek wasn't smiling. *We do equal partners*, said Demopolis. *Sixty me, forty you.* To Jeff's amazement, he even gave up smoking when asked—albeit, by tossing his lit cigarette onto the linoleum and letting it smolder until Jeff crushed it under his shoe. *Maybe your machines are contagious*, said the Greek. *We move a few to my place and mine do miracles as well.* His every other phrase ended with *my dear friend* or *my dear young man*. Only later, when Jeff rejected his "final" *fifty-five, forty-five* offer, did the Greek resort to such phrases as *You cock-sucking faggot* and *I'll grind your nuts to shavings and gouge them into your eyes.*

Demopolis merely threatened. The Filipino couple acted. They must have cashed in all of their chips at city hall because every day brought another official inspection. The Health Department cited Jeff for mold in his storage room. The Buildings Department gave him thirty days to rewire. His "No Smoking" signs proved too small; his aisles weren't wide enough for wheelchairs. Doc Happy accidentally overturned a bucket during a visit by the state's environmental authorities and they wrote Jeff up for improperly disposing laundry water. He even managed to run afoul of several left-wingers at the attorney general's office in Albany who were threatening him with prosecution for unjust enrichment and mail fraud. But what really got to him were the private law suits from unsatisfied customers: one from a prematurely bald rabbinical student whose hair hadn't grown back, another from a Dominican woman who lived above the store and claimed his machines were interfering with her psychic powers.

And then there was Katrin. So complex, so everything. They spent all of their time—except the hours supervising their respective laundries—together. They made excursions to the pier at Orchard Beach (where Katrin taught him to haggle for fresh fish) and to the Peekskill farmer's market (where she showed him how to select the ripest watermelons). She told him about Holland: the Sunday marriages at the Haarlem Kerk, the newlywed aristocrats releasing hundreds of white doves. He told stories of endless twilights on Cormorant Island, of flocks of spoonbills, pink and gentle, like birthday gifts for a hundred baby girls. Sometimes they discussed classics: Virgil, Ovid. But mostly just in passing. He often feared that she thought he knew more than he did. To tell the truth, he didn't quite understand what she saw in him. He asked her once and she answered: "Everybody has their burdens to bear, Elpenor,"—and then she squeezed his crotch through his jeans. If Jeff's washing machines hadn't reunited seventy-three-year-old Mrs. Goldwasser and her high school sweetheart, or helped Mrs. Gates to lose forty pounds, his life with Katrin would have been truly magical.

Jeff did not know what to do. Part of his difficulty was that he'd come to view The Magic Laundry as a public service. Whether through actual wizardry or some mass placebo effect, his machines had improved—were improving—the lives of hundreds of people. Strangers baked him pies, invited him to weddings. His father was finally off his case. What was more, now that Doc Happy had learned the ropes, Jeff had ample time to wade through Catullus and to visit the indoor batting cage. And hadn't he rinsed his clothes in a magic washer on the night of his first date with Katrin? Could this all be *so* wrong? But it *did* feel wrong, especially when Election Day rolled past and the Segovias pinned a sign on their gate reading: "Out of Business—God's Will."

Jeff walked past Madame Ursula's several times—on the opposite side of the street, striding quickly—and he was stunned to see the place desolate. Katrin sat atop the safe, reading. Her aunt moved nervously at the window, sitting down, then standing up, like a debutante being stood up for a ball. Katrin never spoke to Jeff about her business woes. Still, they clouded his every hour. During his junior year at Columbia, a male friend had confided in Jeff that the guy's girlfriend was pregnant and that, despite his pleading, she didn't want to have an abortion. The couple fought bitterly, every night. Still, they continued to date. They kept dating and arguing all the way through the first trimester. And then they stopped speaking about the fetus, ignored it as it grew ever larger on its journey to babyhood. This, thought Jeff, was like that.

One afternoon, while strolling on the plaza behind Grant's Tomb, he made the mistake of suggesting that he'd be willing to support Katrin—to support all the Luczaks—if she went to graduate school.

"Fuck you," she said.

Jeff stopped walking. "What's that supposed to mean?"

"Do you want it in Greek?"

Jeff was suddenly conscious of other pedestrians: an elderly man with brittle knees walking an arthritic terrier, two overweight teenage girls jogging. "Look," said Jeff. "I was just trying to be helpful."

"I told you," said Katrin, stiffly. "Nobody ever makes me do anything I don't want to do. *This*—you and me—had absolutely nothing to do with *that*."

Jeff looked away. Nearby, a muscular kid in a flannel shirt was displaying his skateboarding skills for his girlfriend. Jeff feared arguing. He said: "Of course, it does."

"Fine, it does," Katrin answered. "Have it your way."

Her words were ambiguous. "So you'll let me help you out?"

The wind picked up and sliced into Jeff's back. He wanted to hug Katrin for warmth—to squeeze away their fight—but she stood too far away. "You have to stop," she said. "It's fraud. It's taking advantage of people. It's total bullshit. If you want to run a laundry the way other honest people do—and God knows why the fuck you would—that's your prerogative. But I'm telling you, you are going to stop." Katrin tugged on the hood strings of her sweatshirt. "I love you, Elpenor. But I love me more."

"Okay," said Jeff. "I'll think about it."

"Okay," said Katrin. "You'd better."

That evening they had great sex and then Katrin told him about how she'd read that, as children, both Tom Brokaw and Dan Rather had ridden in electric dryers for fun. They laughed late into the night. Though they didn't talk about the laundry business per se, they didn't *not* talk about it as they'd been doing for nearly two months. Jeff's world seemed rich with enchantment. But he woke up, during the cavernous hours of the early morning, with renewed dread. He looked over at Katrin, sleeping: how helpless her face appeared nestled in the pillow, how unlike the strong-willed, intense scamp of the daylight. Jeff eased his body out of bed and retrieved her jeans and t-shirt from the carpet. It was worth a shot, he thought—and he would be doing it *for her.* If anyone deserved a miracle, he told himself, it was Katrin. What he was doing might be devious, even a bit presumptuous, but not actually wrong.

When Jeff returned from the laundromat, his bed was empty. He checked to see if Katrin had gone off in the dress she'd given him on their first date, or maybe in one of his own shirts, but his closet and bureaus appeared undisturbed. She must have left in her underwear, he thought. Walked three city blocks in her underwear! Jeff considered phoning the police, but didn't. Too much explaining. What he wanted to do was to call Katrin at home to beg forgiveness, at that very moment, but he knew to wait until morning. Instead he pondered her daring, half-naked escape: secretly, against his wishes, he found it breathtakingly sexy.

Jeff had no advance warning, no call from the police. He climbed down the front steps the following morning, like any other, the dawn just nipping over the elevated tracks. He passed his corner bodega and decided against buying a newspaper. At 119th Street, he noticed a blue police cordon and yellow crime tape. It couldn't be Katrin, he thought. It just couldn't. But at the corner of 118th and Broadway, he realized that it wasn't. It was the laundry. Charred, gutted—her front split open like the jaws of a rotting beast. Several passersby had congregated at a safe distance: Mrs. Garcia's two squat friends, a one-armed black man carrying a stack of books under the other. Jeff gazed helplessly into the rubble that had once housed Douglas Fairbanks and Rudolph Valentino until a female investigator from the arson squad insisted upon asking him questions about his property insurance. He vacantly mentioned Demopolis' threats; no arrests were ever made.

That afternoon Jeff received a polite hand-delivered note from Madame Ursula, sympathizing with his loss and offering him the post of general manager at her laundry. He never answered it. Instead, he joined his father in the dental equipment business. Eventually, his firm supplied articulating paper to nearly all of the dentists in Florida.

THE HOUSE CALL

FOR SEVERAL TOPSY-TURVY YEARS after my ex-husband abandoned me to middle age, I had cancer on Mondays and Thursdays. One spring it was a bladder tumor that made urinating frequent and painful; later, I suffered from something called an oat cell carcinoma, which sprouted in my lungs and then slithered its way into my brain and my femurs. Yet for most of my half-decade as a patient at the Havilland Center, my problem was a malignant mass inside my pancreas with a prognosis grimmer than being struck by lightning. I was only forty-eight years old, but I was going to die. You can't imagine what it felt like gorging myself on Fudgesicles and Mallomars at the hospital cafeteria, waiting for my checkup, all the while knowing that I'd never survive to see my daughters graduate from high school—that I'd never find out how Dynasty concluded or whether Bush or Dukakis would be elected President. But that's exactly what I was supposed to do: internalize Harriet Steinhoff's suffering so deeply that the medical students who interviewed me genuinely believed that I was a widowed Connecticut homemaker dying of an abdominal disease, rather than a divorced actress who needed the two hundred dollars per session to make the payments on her Yonkers condo. That was the part I was best at. Being Harriet. Sobbing over wallet photos of Amanda and Alyssa, my perpetually seventeen-year-old twins. I suppose personal tragedy has always been my strongest suit. The challenge for me was the grading. On any given day at the Havilland Center, there were eight simulated patients demanding various forms of assistance—a teenager in need of prenatal counseling, a blind diabetic at odds with her home health aide, a retired architect who had to be told he had Alzheimer's. Burl Vincent, who played the architect, had once toured regionally as "Professor" Harold Hill in *The Music Man*; he'd been losing his memory for the medical students twice each week since 1978. The ingénues portraying the pregnant girl never lasted more than a month; either they landed roles on a more conventional stage, or they quit the acting life entirely. We all worked along a corridor of adjacent mock-examination rooms on the ninth floor of Hudson Hospital, where Oscar Havilland, the pork-chop-baron-turned-healthcare-philanthropist, had once been treated for liver failure. The medical students came from Columbia and N.Y.U. and Mount Sinai, from as far away as Pittsburgh and Providence. The schools paid a fortune to have their skills assessed. My assignment was to evaluate these future physicians on a series of highly defined tasks: did they explain the causes of pancreatic tumors in clear, easily-understood language? Did they express appropriate compassion? Did they wash their hands before and after the encounter? I never did figure out what distinguished "OUTSTANDING" hand-washing from scrubbing that was merely "VERY GOOD"—nor did I particularly care—which is why I was constantly reprimanded for marking too generously.

It didn't help any that the students were Zachary's age. Or I suppose I should say the age that Zachary *would have been*, because my son remains frozen at fourteen forever. So how could I pass judgment upon anybody else's child? Year after year, my grades drifted higher. I awarded two OUSTANDINGS for each EXCELLENT, then twenty-one OUTSTANDINGS in a row. The director of the Havilland Center, Dr. Fishberg, pleaded with me to elevate my standards; later, she resorted to an official warning on letterhead. Eventually, the Board of

Directors hired a pair of statistical consultants from Johns Hopkins, and I was asked to clear out my locker. Not that I minded very much. By then, I was also subbing as a kindergarten teacher, and earning enough to pay my bills, so I let Burl Vincent take me out to a farewell lunch at Pastarnack's Delicatessen, and I put my cancer days behind me. That was the spring I turned fifty. Another decade would pass before my tumor emerged from remission.

My son is buried alongside his grandfather in a sprawling, soulless Jewish cemetery just north of Interstate 287. The second grave had once been destined for my mother, but Mom's second husband subsequently purchased plots in Broward County, Florida—walking distance to the beach, he liked to boast—which meant we had a spare for emergencies. When Robert and I were still together, we visited Zachary each year on his birthday, but after Bob left me, I made a point of visiting one week late so that I wouldn't risk crossing paths with him. The truth was that Zachary's death hadn't destroyed our marriage. It had nearly saved it. Overnight, we'd gone from running on fumes to running on grief—we stuck it out for another decade, mainly out of misplaced loyalty to Zach—and then I guess Robert finally exhausted his share of the heartbreak. I didn't even hate him for it. But there's not much you can say to a man you've slept next to for twenty-three years, and buried a son with, that won't leave you feeling hostile or lonely, so I pretended April 4th was a date like any other. A few days afterward, if the skies looked clear and I wasn't called in to teach, I'd ride the county bus out to White Plains, switch lines at Elmsford, and hike the last half mile from the Chatham depot to the gates of the King Solomon Cemetery. Zachary had always given me the hardest time for never learning how to drive—I was the only mother in his grade who couldn't carpool—but I hadn't found it much of a hardship, not even living in the suburbs, and on balmy spring afternoons, it sometimes felt like a blessing. The cemetery hardly changed in the twenty years after we lost Zachary, but the environs developed quickly. Subdivisions and a twelve-screen multiplex replaced acres of horse pasture and berry orchard. Caterpillar bulldozers razed hills and filled ponds to create adjoining golf courses, one municipal and one private. For many people, I realize, that's progress—but I'm too old for that sort of progress. To my thinking, action films and cocktails at the nineteenth hole are no substitute for the melody of songbirds. So I was genuinely delighted when I embarked upon my pilgrimage to the graveyard last spring, ten years to the month since I'd left the Havilland Center, and I discovered that a mom-&-pop plant nursery had opened cattycorner to the hulking movie house. Out front, sawhorse tables displayed tightly-packed azaleas and peonies, as well as a wonderland of empty terracotta pots. Two low-slung greenhouses, pregnant with the rich honeyed-air of the tropics, offered up rows of exotic succulents. A spruce-raftered warehouse stored phalanxes of leaf-blowers and lawnmowers. Behind these structures, and extending as far as the first stand of oversized ranch homes, a small farm nurtured bell peppers and pattypan squash and pole beans winding around trellises. Okay, it was more of a vegetable patch than a genuine farm, but it brought me joy to look at.

The unlikely farmers were a pair of Korean-born tax lawyers with heavy Brooklyn accents, Sammy and Shelly Go, who'd quit the corporate life in their forties. I learned all this from eavesdropping while I browsed bouquets for Zachary. But then I sensed that the young woman who'd been chatting with Mr. and Mrs. Go was looking at me—staring at me—and I feared that I'd been too conspicuous.

I picked up an African violet—for effect—and examined the price tag. Then I glanced casually at my watch. The woman continued to stare. She was a short, small-framed creature with a chest as flat as a twelve-year-old boy's, and *de rigeur* sunglasses propped in her highlighted burgundy hair, but she also had large, kind eyes and a soft smile. She couldn't have been much more than thirty, maybe thirty-five. And she was gazing at me as though she recognized me—as though *I* should recognize *her*, too. My first instinct was that she might have been a friend of Zach's from school, one of those scores of teens who'd sent nearly identical cards and had sobbed puddles at the funeral. I had no memory of having met her.

"Mrs. Steinhoff?" she asked. "Is that really you?"

She smiled at me innocently, but I felt like a spy whose cover had been blown by a chance run-in with an old acquaintance. Nobody had ever before—or since—called me by my simulated-patient name outside the hospital.

"I'm Jeannie Ballard," she said in a fast, almost breathless voice. The girl balanced a paper shopping bag on her tiny hip; her pocketbook dangled off her elbow. "You don't remember me, do you? I was one of the second-year medical students from Yale who met with you at that place . . ."

"The Havilland Center," I offered.

"That's right," she said. "The Havilland Center. God, that was a long time ago." Jeannie Ballard looked wistful, vulnerable. Somehow, she'd resisted that varnish of benevolent detachment that renders most doctors capable of infinite sympathy, but not empathy. I was pleased to see this—that she'd lived up to her "OUTSTANDING." She kept her eyes focused on me, examining, but gently, and if we hadn't been separated by vast trays of pansies and begonias, I suspect she would have placed her small hand on my elbow. Instead, she lowered her voice and asked, as a concerned friend might, "Have you been okay?" She paused nervously, and added, "I know that sounds silly, but I was never really sure . . ."

I nodded. "It's a pleasure to meet you, Jeannie," I said. "But my real name's not Harriet Steinhoff. It's Miriam Littman."

"Of course," she agreed. "Miriam."

But she looked surprised that I wasn't Harriet. I took this as a compliment.

"You were *so* convincing," she said. "I really believed you were dying."

"That's very kind of you to say," I said. "Harriet was my favorite role."

Jeannie lifted the paper bag from her hip and rested it on a corner of the sawhorse. "I always wondered how much of what you told us was true. I mean, I know you didn't have pancreatic cancer . . . How could you have? But did you really have daughters in high school and a ninety-eight-year-old grandmother who'd once worked with Madame Curie?" I'd forgotten all about my grandmother in the nursing home—an unauthorized flourish that I'd inserted into Harriet's back-story. It amazed me that Jeannie Ballard still recalled the details of our brief encounter so thoroughly, that she remembered how Grandma Steinhoff had helped to isolate radium. She'd probably seen thousands of patients since then. Maybe tens of thousands. I flattered myself that I was one of the most memorable—and not merely one of the first. I hated to disappoint her with the truth.

"Let's just say it wasn't *all* untrue," I answered. "My grandmother *was* French and she *was* a chemist, but she didn't work with the Curies. And I had a son, not daughters."

"Well, you had me totally convinced," she said.

"Thank you again." I realized that I had to ask about her life too, even though I was in no psychological state for chitchat. "And you, dear? How is the world of medicine?"

"Good enough. I'm buying Christmas tree lights," she said. "My older son's in fifth grade and he's building a diorama about Indian Tribes—his father's brilliant idea—so I've been running from store to store all afternoon looking for Christmas tree lights. You don't want to know what it's like trying to find Christmas tree lights in April."

"But you found them?"

"Only the clear ones. Not the colored ones. But he'll survive."

"I'm sure he will," I said.

He'll survive. How many times had I uttered the same words about Zachary? How many scraped knees and missing lacrosse sticks and bouts of puppy-love had I predicted he'd survive? Because most boys do. Nearly all of them do. That's what the therapist had assured us, after his first bout of moping. Yet once in a while there's a child too sensitive for his own good—what mathematics professors like my ex-husband term an outlier—and then surviving loses some of its inevitability. Robert and Zachary had also built a diorama for school once: The Battle of Lexington and Concord. Patriots in the foreground, Redcoats marching lockstep in the distance. The best damn diorama Mrs. Pelican's fourth grade had ever seen. I didn't mention any of this to Jeannie Ballard. Even I recognized that gloating about your dead son's fourth-grade history project rarely endears you to casual acquaintances.

I sensed the tears welling behind my eyes. "Well, it was nice running into you," I said.

"Absolutely," said Jeannie Ballard. She appeared as though she wanted to say something more—even to offer me a parting hug—but she didn't. "Good luck with everything."

I turned away quickly and scooped up the first marginally-suitable flower I could find, a solitary blood-red Oriental poppy. Mrs. Go gave me a 25% discount: "Because you're a returning customer— You just don't know it yet."

Outside the nursery, a conclave of grackles rummaged through the crabgrass at the curbside and, farther out of the public golf course, Canada geese preened their rigid necks. The breeze had picked up, rustling the hemlock hedge. Puffs of friendly clouds played peek-a-boo with the afternoon sun. I'd already put a good fifty yards between myself and the plant shop, thinking about Zachary, about what had become of that Lexington & Concord diorama, when Jeannie Ballard's minivan drew up alongside me. The power window descended slowly. Like a guillotine in reverse.

"Need a lift?" she asked.

I didn't. I wanted solitude. But I also didn't wish to be overtly rude. I dug deep into my actor's trick-bag for a plausible pretext to decline her offer, but came up empty-handed. "I'm not going very far," I pleaded anemically. "Just up the street."

"Nonsense," she insisted. "Hop in."

The inside of the minivan was cluttered with children's galoshes, and library books, and a tomb of crushed soda cans in the compartment behind the gearshift. An air-freshener hung from the rearview mirror, masking the scents of daily living under lemon-pine. Photos of Jeannie's sons, freckled kids with big ears, were taped to the glovebox door. On the passenger seat lay a physician's white coat and a stethoscope. Jeannie cleared them away so that I could sit down.

"Do you make house calls?" I asked.

"Those are Campbell's," she answered, rolling her eyes. "My younger one went dressed as a doctor for Halloween, and now he insists on wearing his costume everywhere. We have a deal that he can take it with him on the way to school, but he has to leave it in the car." Jeannie Ballard folded the small white coat and tucked it under the armrest. She eased the minivan back into traffic, and asked, "Now where are you headed?"

Not to the cemetery, I suddenly realized. Not see to Zach. I'd come back again the next day—on my own—once I'd had time to recalibrate myself. So that meant I was headed home to Yonkers. I braced the poppy blossom between my knees. "Could you drop me in front of the train station?" I asked. "I can catch my bus there."

"I'm not letting you take the bus anywhere," answered Jeannie. She grinned. "You are a ten-year pancreatic cancer survivor, after all. There aren't too many of those around."

"Well, I live in Yonkers, but—"

"Yonkers, here we come."

She made a U-turn at a service station and pulled onto the state highway. It was already approaching rush hour and the traffic was heavy. "The boys have karate on Tuesdays," she said. "They spend Tuesday nights with their father."

So we both belonged to the jilted spouse's club! But Jeannie Ballard had earned her membership early; she might yet have other opportunities ahead of her.

"Are you still acting?" she asked.

"Now and then," I answered. "I do some summer stock."

The truth was that I hadn't done summer stock in several years. Compared to portraying Harriet Steinhoff, where I'd always been the star of my own one-woman show, there wasn't much luster in playing a Scottish townswoman in Brigadoon or a pirate's wife in Peter Pan. But I sensed that I was shortchanging Jeannie Ballard's expectations once again—first as a patient and now as an actress—so something must have gone haywire with my moral compass, because I said, "To be honest, I haven't had much energy for theater since the chemotherapy."

"Chemotherapy?" asked Jeannie Ballard.

"Not pancreatic cancer," I explained. "Just a small oat cell tumor in my lung. And maybe a bit of it in my brain and femurs."

Jeannie glanced at me—devastated. It had slipped my mind that she was a physician, that she knew the prognosis of oat cell metastases. I feared that I'd gone too far.

"I'll be fine," I added quickly. "I'm in remission now. I'm very lucky."

"Oh, that's wonderful news," said Jeannie. "About the remission, I mean." She reached over and touched my elbow with her tiny fingers.

"I'm sorry you've had to go through all that."

"It hasn't been as bad as you might think," I said. "I suppose playing Harriet Steinhoff all those years prepared me for the worst of it."

Then I narrated the rollercoaster course of my illness—coughing up blood on my fifty-fifth birthday, radiation, chemo, more chemo, fighting insurers who refused to pay for bone scans—pausing only to offer driving directions. I don't know why I did it. I could have told Jeannie Ballard about how my teenage son went out one Saturday night and intentionally stepped in front of a commuter train—or stumbled in front of it accidentally, because nobody will ever know for certain—and how I spent the next six months, lying in bed, cataloguing every infinitesimal mistake I'd made over the course of fourteen years. That's a story far more horrific than any personal illness, even an aggressive lung carcinoma. Even sudden death. But after all those years playing Harriet Steinhoff, it was easier to tell her story than my own.

"You're a very brave woman," said Jeannie. "I can hear it in your voice."

"I just play my part," I answered. "I sometimes second-guess myself about all those years at the Havilland Center. Because I never made it to Broadway. *Or television.* I hardly even did much community theater. But running into a practicing physician like you who I helped to train—even in the smallest way—makes all that time seem worthwhile." That part was true. Seeing Jeannie did make me feel useful. I could tell she was listening to me—unlike my own doctor, a dour Jordanian man with the bedside manner of a cigar store Indian. "You must make a wonderful physician, Jeannie. Your patients must be extremely fortunate to have you."

I wished I hadn't lied about the tumor. I'd gladly have ditched the Jordanian for her any day, even if it meant an increased copayment.

"Thank you," answered Jeannie. "You should never think twice about your work at the Havilland Center. Mrs. Steinhoff was the best first patient anybody could ever have asked for."

We rode several minutes in silence. I gazed out the passenger window at the passing strip malls, the banners advertising "Spring-Cleaning Sales" and boosting the local girls' softball team. It struck me that if Zachary had lived, he might have married a woman a lot like Jeannie Ballard. *He might have married Jeannie Ballard.*

"Do you have a specialty?" I asked.

She looked up, startled—as though she'd also been lost in thought. I already regretted my question. I hoped to God that she wouldn't say oncology.

"Not exactly," she answered. "I never made it that far in my training."

"Well, I'm glad you're not a specialist," I said. "Too many specialists these days. Not enough old-fashioned internists anymore."

I had intended this to be supportive, but Jeannie's hands started to tremble. Before I knew what had happened, she was sobbing violently.

"I'm not a doctor," she said. "There, I said it. Okay? I'm not a doctor." I don't think her words could have been more unnerving, more downright shocking, if she'd announced them while standing over my operating table. I feared for a moment that she might hyperventilate—even that she might drive off the road—but she took several deep breaths and composed herself rapidly. "I'm not a physician," she said again—matter-of-fact. "I'm sorry I've I led you to believe otherwise."

"It's all right, honey," I assured her.

"No it's not all right," she said. "It's just how things turned out."

"Because of the children?" I asked.

Jeannie shook her head. "Long before that. I didn't even finish the second year of med school. Actually, it was that afternoon at the Havilland Center that did me in. I remember having to tell that nice old man that he had Alzheimer's, and then there was the college student who could never have children, and you with your pancreatic cancer—and I realized I didn't have it in me. I could handle the long hours and the endless studying . . . but the sadness was too much for me. I know that must sound ridiculous, but I just couldn't go through with it. Or maybe I could have, but I didn't know it at the time . . ."

"It's never too late," I suggested.

"It's too late. Trust me," answered Jeannie. "Do you know what I do for a living now? I babysit for dead people." She smiled—but it was a bitter smile. "Mortuaries hire me to go sit in wealthy dead people's homes while their families attend funerals, so that burglars can't take advantage of the tragic circumstances. It turns out that even burglars read the obituaries . . . I bet you didn't even know a job like mine existed."

I didn't. "But you have your boys," I said.

Jeannie smiled. "That's right. I have my boys. Without them . . . I don't know what . . ."

Of course she didn't. Who did? I ran my fingers over the petals of the poppy blossom, tracing the thin veins of life to their roots. I suddenly realized that I wouldn't return to the King Solomon Cemetery the next morning, or the morning after that. Or maybe ever. That I'd played my part already and I was ready for another role.

"Sometimes I meet people like you—with cancer I mean—or Alzheimer's, or Parkinson's, or even just pneumonia—and I wish so much I could help them." Jeannie sighed. She retrieved a tissue from a cup-holder and wiped the stained eye-liner from her cheeks. "I would honestly do anything to help you, Miriam. If I could."

That's how far we'd gotten when the minivan pulled up in front of my condo. Several young children played on the front steps under the watchful eyes of their nannies. Squirrels darted friskily around the KEEP OFF THE GRASS signs. Across the street, a team of men in white undershirts blasted Latin music while unloading crates of bananas from a box truck. An ordinary, truly unremarkable suburban afternoon. Jeannie Ballard didn't say anything else, she just reached over the gear shift and squeezed my hand. Her touch was reassuring, therapeutic. For a brief moment, I let myself believe that if she'd been a real doctor, and I'd actually had cancer, she'd have been able to heal me.

THE EMPRESS OF CHARCOAL

THE NOTE ARRIVED on Yale University letterhead, neatly typed, three years to the month after she'd lost her husband:

May 15, 20—

Dear Elsa,

I imagine you don't remember me. I was a student in Professor Stanley's figure drawing class at City College during the spring semester of 1962, when you served as a model. After the course ended, I asked the Visual Arts Department for your name, but I didn't have the courage to contact you. I suppose you will think me foolish—and no doubt I am— but that remains among the greatest regrets of my adult life. My wife of thirty-six years passed away last August and my son helped me find your address on the Internet. Would you be willing to have lunch one of these days?

Sincerely,

Morton D. Belldauer, Ph.D. Professor Emeritus

Department of the History of Mathematics

PS: If you are not the same Elsa Kalamaransky who modeled at City College in 1962, kindly disregard this message.

Elsa was not the same woman who had modeled for Professor Stanley's class. She'd already been teaching five years at Bonneville by 1962, initiating her girls into the marvels of Balzac and Flaubert. But ever since the balmy, cloudless morning when she'd discovered Bruce facedown in his beloved Jacuzzi, skin bloated and puckered like a bobbing apple, springtime tormented Elsa with its insincere promise. It was during one of her lonely spells that she replied to Belldauer in longhand:

> *Dear Morton,*
>
> *What a delightful surprise! I confess I do not remember you, but 1962 was an eternity ago, wasn't it? My life here in Rhode Island has been a good one. As Emily Dickinson wrote, "To live is so startling it leaves little time for anything else." I retired six years ago from teaching at The Bonneville School, shortly after it merged with an all-boys academy. At the end, I was teaching only French language, but I was initially hired as an instructor of Italian literature as well. Are you a fan of Leopardi? I do hope so.*
>
> *As of now, the summer is surprisingly open. My late husband (39 years together, 3 apart) was an avid gardener, and although I fear I lack his natural gifts, I'm doing my darnedest to keep my thumbs green. I believe I can claim some success, as this weekend the peonies are staging a wondrous show.*
>
> *Please do come see the daylilies while they are in bloom. Most warmly,*
>
> *Elsa Kalamaransky*

She reread the letter twice before sealing it inside the envelope, unsure if she'd included too much or too little. She'd been one of six sisters, and all of her life she'd worked among women, so what little she understood of men came from interacting with Bruce and his colleagues in the Providence Philharmonic—not, most likely, a representative sampling of the species. At the central post office in Creve Coeur, she tore open the envelope to verify that she'd printed the correct telephone number beneath her signature, and she had to purchase a replacement at the counter.

Elsa sent the letter on Saturday morning. Belldauer phoned in the early evening on Wednesday, and now it was Saturday again, and she was expecting him at noon. "At my age, I don't like to put any-thing off," he'd joked in a voice as deep and resonant as a kettle drum. "Besides, the way I see it, I'm already forty-five years overdue." Elsa had expected him to sound more patrician, less ethnic Brooklyn—like Cary Grant without the effeminate tinge. But the professor did come across as very much the gentleman. Bruce, rest his soul, had been a slow-spoken tenor with an accent to shame the Kennedys.

She'd started planning their meal the evening that Belldauer phoned and, in hindsight, she'd gone a bit overboard: after all, he was a stranger who'd been sweet on her nearly half a century ago. Not even *on her. On a woman who had shared her name!* But Elsa had endured so long without cause to indulge, that now she couldn't resist a drive to the gourmet supermarket in Providence for fresh bluefin tuna and hand-picked Nyons olives. She tossed the tuna in a homegrown spinach salad. Then she covered the wrought-iron table in the gar-den with her late mother-in-law's daisy-print cloth. As lunchtime approached and the skies remained clear, she set out a basket of as-sorted breads, a porcelain platter of camembert and brie, and the swan-shaped glass water pitcher that her wealthy grandaunt had be-stowed upon her and Bruce as a wedding gift. All night long, a driv-ing rain had pummeled the neighborhood, forcing Elsa to reassess her plans, but by Friday morning, the air had turned crisp with po-tential. On the slate patio, puddles shimmered under the high white sun.

Belldauer's car—a dignified jet-black Oldsmobile—pulled up at the curb ten minutes early, but the professor waited inside the vehi-cle until precisely twelve. Elsa watched through the bay windows in the living room as he advanced up the front path and paused under the crabapple tree to adjust the sleeves of his sports jacket. He was trim and long-limbed, with a grand forehead and a bushy, salt-and-pepper mustache. The mustache, reflected Elsa, might take some ad-justing to. Otherwise, Belldauer was as handsome as any man she'd laid eyes upon—at least, since that distant night when Rachel Kalamaransky, her colleague at Bonneville, had invited Elsa backstage at the symphony to meet her unmarried and "pleasantly eccentric" brother. The professor even carried himself rather like Bruce, his magnificent head cocked slightly skyward, as he stepped onto the front porch, holding his bouquet of lilacs. How fortunate that she'd had the nerve to write back! Then her chest fluttered with second thoughts: what if he realized she was the wrong Elsa? What if he didn't, but rejected her when she later confessed? What if the other Elsa Kalamaransky had been significantly less busty? Or black? Or an achondroplastic dwarf? When the doorbell chimed, she found herself paralyzed with anxiety. After a pause, the bell rang again. Elsa clenched her eyelids together, as though she were about to dive into a pool of icy water, and she crossed briskly through the foyer to welcome her guest.

The portico stood a step down from the entryway, so when Elsa opened the door, she and Belldauer faced each other at eye level. He said nothing, at first. For half a second, he just stared at her, his brow furrowed as though reconstructing a puzzle in his mind from memory. And then he flashed her a broad grin. "Goodness, Elsa Kalamaransky," he said. "It's really you, isn't it?"

"Please, come inside," answered Elsa. "I'm so glad you're here."

Soon they were standing in the parlor, surrounded by upholstery and knickknacks, and again he was examining her. She accepted the lilacs from his outstretched hand and her gaze followed his nervously around the room. Photos of her long life with Bruce cluttered the piano bench and the end tables, including several from their first honeymoon in the Canadian Rockies, and now Elsa regretted not having moved them upstairs.

"Did you have an easy drive?" asked Elsa.

"Oh, it was fine. I just can't believe it's actually you," said Belldauer. "The Empress of Charcoal, in the flesh."

"Excuse me?"

"That's what I used to call you. The Empress of Charcoal," he explained. "I suspect you'll laugh at me if I tell you why . . ."

"Try me," answered Elsa. She felt herself growing confident, even flirtatious. "But first, let's head onto the veranda. As far as I'm concerned, it's far too lovely an afternoon to squander another moment out of the sun."

She took hold of the professor's hand and led him through the sliding glass doors. Belldauer's skin felt warm to her touch. Outside, on the low-hanging branches of the Japanese maple, a pair of orioles serenaded each other; from beyond the forsythia hedge rose the cries of the neighbor's children, and the occasional blast of a firecracker. Elsa tucked Belldauer's lilacs into her plastic watering jug and centered the bouquet atop the gas grill. Bruce had enjoyed hosting barbecues for his fellow musicians, but ever since she'd lost him, Elsa used the device as a sideboard. "Now where were we?" asked Elsa, smiling coyly. "Oh, yes. I was about to laugh at your story."

"I wouldn't blame you," said the professor. "As I was saying, the office adjacent to Dr. Stanley's belonged to the chairman of the history department. Big, meaty fellow—I've forgotten his name. In any case, the two of them shared one of those long glass-enclosed bulletin boards, and Stanley used to post our charcoal sketches next to this pictorial genealogy chart of the royal houses of Europe. So one afternoon, I was standing in the corridor, looking over the various ways the class had portrayed you, and somehow 'The Empress of Charcoal' popped into my head. Foolish, no?"

"Not in the slightest," said Elsa. "May I offer you a drink?"

"It's only noon. I wouldn't want to give you the wrong impression."

"Nonsense," she retorted. "I still have a pitcher of frozen banana daiquiri left over from my niece's birthday picnic. How about I pour us each a glass and then I give you a walking tour of the garden?"

"I never say no to a lady," answered Belldauer. "Or to a chilled cocktail."

Elsa retrieved the crystal decanter from the mini-fridge and filled two cognac glasses. She'd prepared the contents the evening before, several weeks *after* her niece's birthday celebration, but it was a harmless lie. The truth was that she hardly drank at all—champagne on New Year's, Manischewitz at her sister-in-law's Passover dinner, an occasional Bloody Mary at a wedding or shower—but she didn't want Belldauer to think her puritanical. Secretly, she also hoped to limber up his judgment.

"Here's mud in your eye!" she declared. "To second chances!" They clinked glasses and she drank.

"It's amazing how you expect something to turn out one way, and it works out so differently, yet it's still just as good," said Belldauer.

"What do you mean?"

"It's hard to explain." He sipped from his glass. "I still remember how stunning you looked that first afternoon when you slid that Japanese dressing gown off your shoulders, and all you were wearing was that startling blue bracelet around your wrist . . . For some reason, I expected you to be reserved, aloof . . . and you're so friendly."

"I suppose I might have come across as aloof *back then*," said Elsa. "I can pretend to be less friendly, if you'd prefer." She sensed the heat of the daiquiri in her temples. "Or even downright mean."

"That won't be necessary," said Belldauer, beaming. "I have a strange confession to make. After I wrote to you, I still wasn't sure that I'd have it in me to meet you face-to-face. I'd be lying if I didn't admit that I miss Louise. Like hell, I miss Louise. Every day. I'll be reading a book or listening to the radio and my mind begins drifting to what she looked like during those final nights at the hospice. Of course, my son—he's a head-shrinker at Johns Hopkins—assures me it will get better . . ."

Bullshit, thought Elsa. It might be *different*, but never better. She still woke up every morning, three years later, shocked not to find Bruce, his paunch poking over his boxers, hogging the pillows onto his side of the bed.

Elsa squeezed Belldauer's wrist. "Poor dear," she said.

"Honestly, I wasn't thinking too clearly when I sent you that note," he continued. "I had no idea what I'd do next—whether I'd even follow up at all. But do you know what sealed the deal for me?"

"What?"

"That you'd kept your maiden name." The professor shrugged. "I know that sounds ridiculous, but I liked that you were still a Kalamaransky."

"Why couldn't Kalamaransky be my husband's name?"

"I did the math when I received your letter. If you've been married thirty-nine years and widowed three, you were still single when you posed for us . . . It makes a man wonder . . . Had I only written to you then . . ." Belldauer allowed this idea to drift unfinished into the azaleas. "I've always been vehemently opposed to women changing their names when they get married," he said. "It's a particularly retrograde practice, to be blunt, based on historical notions of wives as chattel. I'm proud to say that Louise was born a Kappelgruber and, rest her soul, she died a Kappelgruber."

Elsa wasn't sure she agreed with Belldauer about name-changing, but she found endearing the vehemence with which he voiced his opinion. "Are you ready for a stroll around the yard?" she asked. "Before the morning glories and the portulaca close up shop for the afternoon?"

Elsa topped off Belldauer's drink and passed it back to him.

"And on the subject of math, Mr. Professor Emeritus at Yale University, maybe you could tell me about the variety of mathematics you studied."

"*History* of mathematics," Belldauer corrected her.

Elsa polished off her second daiquiri. "*History* of mathematics," she echoed. "Twice as impressive."

She reached for his hand again, this time clasping it more decisively, and steered him between the neatly manicured beds of dahlias and gladiolas. Now that she'd spread store-bought bark chips around the perennials—as she'd already done for several years with the zinnias and pansies—the entire patch looked far more professional.

"Most of my work focused upon cuneiform tablets, on whether the Babylonians ever developed an authentic trigonometry," said Belldauer. "I also authored several papers on advanced functions in the Sumerian system—cubic equations, Pythagorean triples. I developed a particular expertise regarding a tablet called Plimpton 322. Truthfully, I can't imagine it would interest you in the slightest . . ."

"You might find yourself surprised," Elsa answered. But rather than inquire anything further about Mesopotamian numerology, she pointed out the various strains of daylilies. "This over here is Honest Abe's Beard," she said, cupping the petals of a tall blossom fringed in black. "Those two red ones behind the phlox are Emma Goldman and Alexander Berkman. What was it Goldman once said? 'I'd rather have roses on my table than diamonds on my neck.' Personally, I couldn't agree more."

"You've bred all of these yourself?"

"Heavens, no. Not *me*. Bruce." Elsa wondered if she was talking too much about her husband—but, after nearly four decades of marriage, what else was she supposed to talk about? "He played the oboe. You should have seen him: such a large man blowing into such a tiny instrument. But his real passion wasn't music. It was cross-breeding flowers . . . In Bruce's study, I still have an entire filing cabinet full of daylily pedigrees that I can't make heads nor tails of. I can't bring myself to discard them . . ."

"Louise was a dietician," said Belldauer—reflectively, almost as though he were thinking aloud. "She worked at the university hospital."

Elsa said nothing. One of her own sisters had also been a medical dietician, specially trained to counsel renal patients, before she'd suffered a breakdown and filed for permanent disability. So the Louise Kappelgruber whom Elsa now imagined, wandering the dialysis clinic, warning diabetic truck drivers against eating foods that appeared white, looked like her own dear, hopeless Gladys. Elsa didn't mention any of this, because she wanted Belldauer to think about his wife as infrequently as possible.

They circled around the far corner of the garden—past the firewood pile, the strawberry patch, the shaded hemlock arbor where Bruce had installed a polished cedar bench. The quarter acre beyond the hemlocks, up to the stockade fence, was overgrown with oak and hickory saplings. This was also where, in a small clearing, Bruce and his brother-in-law had been attempting to restore a twenty-one foot cutty cruiser that they'd salvaged from a rummage sale. The craft's lichen-coated prow still waited for them on cement blocks, oblivious to Bruce's aneurysm, unaware that Gary and Rachel had since retired to the dry heat of Phoenix. Belldauer tapped the side of the vessel with his fingers, generating a hollow thud. "One of my former students owns a boat like this," he observed. "He takes me out on the Sound two or three times every summer." This reminded Elsa of her girls from Bonneville, all of whom were now adults, many with fully-grown children of their own. One was even a grandmother—to twins! And another, Maria Coats, was the provost at Bryn Mawr College. Elsa had many regrets in life—not having children, not spending more time with Bruce—but choosing a teaching career was never among them. She reached for Belldauer's elbow and led him further into the lush greenery, keeping her feet on the flagstones to avoid the mud.

She paused in front of Bruce's favorite lily—his prized accomplishment. The blossom wasn't *officially* blue according to the American Hemerocallis Society's standards—technically, it was aquamarine—so Bruce hadn't won their challenge award. But it was certainly blue enough to fool the average observer. "These beauties here are the Ida Kalamaransky blooms," said Elsa. *Named after Bruce's mother*, she almost added. But she caught herself in time, and blurted out, "Bruce named them after my mother." She held her breath, waiting for Belldauer to call out her lie—but he didn't. He merely smiled warmly, so Elsa leaned forward and sniffed the blossoms, more to conceal her face than to inhale the mild aroma. "Aren't they glorious?" she asked. "They always remind me of those lines from the Wordsworth poem about daffodils:

> *"I gazed—and gazed—but little thought*
> *What wealth the show to me had brought . . ."*

Much to Elsa's amazement, Belldauer answered:

> *"For oft, when on my couch I lie*
> *In vacant or in pensive mood,*
> *They flash upon that inward eye*
> *Which is the bliss of solitude;*
> *And then my heart with pleasure fills,*
> *And dances with the daffodils."*

The professor held his lapels like a ringmaster while he declaimed, clearly proud of his performance. "You look surprised," he said.

"I *am* surprised."

"Why? I'm an historian of mathematics, so I can't be cultured?"

Elsa feared she might weep from joy. "Of course, it's not that . . ." she answered—but at some level, it was precisely that, and in any case, she had no opportunity to present an alternative explanation. Instead, a sharp, high-pitched whistle made her look up with a start—and then a staccato of explosions sent her diving into the hollyhocks with her arms over her head. Bright sparks, orange and pink, shot from the grass around the zucchini plot. Nearby, a portion of the chicken-wire trellis collapsed, toppling with it the nascent pumpkin vines. Then Elsa's entire world turned beige as Belldauer shielded her from the blasts with his sports jacket. He stood bowed over her, like a hawk protecting its brood, and her cheek pressed against his chest.

After what seemed like months—but must have been only seconds—a deathly hush descended upon the garden. Elsa could hear her own sharp breaths and the cadence of Belldauer's heart, the two sounds merging into one complex rhythm. Then, from above, a lone catbird began trilling its chipper reveille. Elsa drew her hands away from her face and climbed out of the flower beds. The elbows of her blouse were streaked with clay, and a run slashed across the knee of her left stocking.

"What on earth was that?" she asked.

"I'd guess three or four bottle rockets," answered Belldauer. "And half a dozen cherry bombs."

"We're being bombed?"

"Firecrackers," he explained, as he dusted splinters of bark from his trousers. "It appears as though your neighbors have turned their artillery on us."

The professor stepped into the vegetable patch and poked under the chicken-wire with a jagged stick. Elsa watched anxiously as he kicked a spent rectangular canister out from the undergrowth. She wanted to warn him to be careful, but feared he would think her a worrywart. "Don't go cleaning these up on your own," said Belldauer. "Your fingers are far too adorable to risk losing. I'm afraid you'll have to ask your neighbors to call in a professional—just in case any of these shells are still active."

"I don't understand," said Elsa. "We've never had any trouble before." It figured that, on her first date in forty-two years, she'd face an armed attack. If this actually were a date, this is—and not just one-time reunion. "They seemed like such decent boys," she added. "Their mother's a rabbi. Rabbi Bonomi. Italian Jews."

As though on cue, the Bonomi boys appeared at the break in the forsythia hedge. They were both pudgy kids with broad foreheads and impressive jaws, topped with matching shocks of auburn hair. The older youth, who could not have been much beyond ten, pushed the younger child toward Elsa and Belldauer. "My brother, Zachary," he said, "has something that he'd like to say to you."

Zachary stepped forward in increments, his eyes fixed on the damp grass.

"I'm sorry," he said—his voice soft and tentative. Elsa thought he might sob, and she felt an urge to hug him. "I did something dangerous and I'm very sorry I did it."

"Firecrackers *are* dangerous," answered Belldauer. "How old are you, Zachary?"

"Eight and seven months."

Belldauer winked at Elsa. "Do you know what I liked to do when I was eight and seven months? I liked to study the stars."

Zachary Bonomi kept his head down, his arms tucked to his chest. The older brother stepped forward and placed a reassuring hand on the boy's shoulder.

"A telescope," said Belldauer, "that's what a young *mensch* like you needs."

Elsa could sense that her date had once been an exceptional father. Speaking to these boys, he sounded as avuncular as the Wizard of Oz—only Jewish.

The professor reached into the breast pocket of his jacket. His hand emerged moments later, fingers wrapped around a short brass tube. The metal gleamed. Belldauer tugged on the cylinder and it expanded rapidly to become a foot-long telescope.

"Here you go, kid. But you shouldn't use it until the sun goes down."

The boy reached tentatively for the telescope. He peered into the broad lens, then turned the apparatus around and gazed down the narrow end.

"Can I keep it?"

"You can share it with your brother," answered Belldauer. "But on one condition. You promise not to set off any more firecrackers."

"Anywhere?" asked the boy.

"Yes," Belldauer said firmly. "*Anywhere.*"

Zachary looked to his brother for guidance. The older boy nodded. "Okay, it's a deal," said Zachary. "Thank you."

Then the boys turned and ran, a blur of dungarees and sunburnt flesh. "I'm not sure what to say," said Elsa. "Do you always carry around a telescope to give to wayward schoolboys?"

"I do, in fact," answered Belldauer. "But not for wayward schoolboys. I'm rather a devotee of the night sky—it's reassuring to think that I'm seeing the same constellations as Euclid and Archimedes." He stepped back onto the path, and this time it was he who took her hand. "You'll have to decide whether you want their parents to pay to have the firecracker shells removed," he said. "I can't say I envy you that decision."

They began walking back toward the house, arm-in-arm, like a Victorian couple on a promenade through Vauxhall Gardens.

"You are certainly a man of many surprises," said Elsa. "I'm afraid to find out what else you have hidden away in those pockets of yours."

"You should be," answered Belldauer. His voice contained a new seriousness, a sense of purpose. "Let's sit down and I'll show you."

He dried off a chair for her at the lunch table and drew up his own alongside it. Then he cleared off a small square of tablecloth between the bread basket and the platters of cheese. Elsa realized what he was going to show to her at the very moment he removed the drawing from inside his coat. The sketch had been folded over many times and bore deep, irregular crease marks. One corner of the paper canvas had been shorn away entirely. In several place, the charcoal itself had streaked. But there was no mistaking the subject of Belldauer's forty-five-year-old illustration. It was a young woman— a *nude* young woman—standing arms akimbo on a wooden stepladder. Fortunately, the portrait neither looked like Elsa nor unlike Elsa. Whatever his other attributes, the young Morton D. Belldauer had not been a particularly gifted sketch artist.

"I can't believe you've kept it all these years."

"I had a terrible crush on you for an entire semester," answered Belldauer. "Bear in mind, you were the first woman I'd ever seen without her clothes on."

Of course, thought Elsa. That wouldn't have been at all remarkable, back in 1962. What a different age that had been! Bruce, too, had been the first man she'd ever seen fully unclothed.

Elsa held the precious drawing as tenderly as she might hold a baby. Her hand trembled and she braced it against the tabletop. "You had talent," she observed.

"I didn't, but it's very kind of you to say so," answered Belldauer. "I've taken it up again, though. Drawing, that is. Ever since I retired from the department . . . I've got my art supplies in the trunk of my car."

He reached for the pitcher and poured them each a final daiquiri, shifting back and forth between glasses to ensure an equal distribution.

"I know this is going to sound crazy," said Belldauer, "but I was wondering if you'd let me draw you again . . ."

He sounded so innocent, so gentle. Like a fourteen-year-old schoolboy seeking permission to kiss her for the first time. The man's big dark eyes gazed into hers, brimming with tender hope, and his devotion made Elsa feel bashful. Her own eyes darted away from his quickly. Across the lawn, chipmunks scampered on the stone retaining wall opposite the cellar steps, and a dopey, overweight woodchuck sunned himself shamelessly beside the sprinkler head. She felt Belldauer's attention fixed upon her, waiting for his fate to be sealed.

"Are you serious?" Elsa asked. She had never modeled before, and she wasn't sure she'd even know how to do it. It was probably one of those feats that proved far harder than it first appeared, the sort of challenge her Bonneville girls had always relished—like drinking a gallon of whole milk in five minutes. Besides, she sensed that Bell-dauer had a specific sort of modeling in mind. "You don't mean . . .?"

"If you'd be willing. Just like in class."

"Oh, good heavens, Morton. I haven't done anything like that in years . . . I'm out of practice . . ."

"You'll do the best you can," he replied. "Let's make today the first day of your second modeling career."

"*Today?*"

"Today. Right here in the garden." Now Belldauer glanced away, his voice shifting to a softer, less fervent note. "I do hope I'm not offending you," he apologized. "I don't mean to put you on the spot."

"Not at all." Elsa downed what remained of her drink and rose deliberately from her chair. "Go get your supplies, Morton. I'll be back in a moment."

"Thank you," he answered.

She retreated into the house and quickly exchanged her blouse and skirt for Bruce's navy dressing gown. The silk charged her skin with desire. How unfathomable that she'd only met Morton Belldauer several hours earlier. She felt as though she'd already known him for an eternity, that the time before he'd entered her life was no longer readily accessible. Maybe this was what her Bonneville girls were feeling when they composed those essays defending Emma Bovary for having sex on a first date. Elsa assessed herself in the bedroom mirror: her rutted skin, her tired mouth, the flesh too thick between her chin and her neck. What a loon she must be, at the age of seventy-one, to compare herself to Emma Bovary. When she returned to the garden, clad only in the robe and a pair of sheepskin slippers, Belldauer had already set up his easel on the tier of flagstone across from the wishing fountain.

"You look ravishing," the professor said. "I'll never forget Dr. Stanley warning us that the models were employees hired solely to further our artistic development—that we shouldn't look upon them as women . . . I intended to do exactly that until the moment you walked into the studio." Elsa scanned the perimeter of the yard. Over the years, the rhododendrons and forsythia had grown high enough to block the neighbors' view. In any case, it was her own property, wasn't it? She had every right to engage in an artistic pastime on her own property! Who would dare say otherwise?

"Where would you like me?" she asked.

"How about in front of that fountain?" suggested Belldauer. "Maybe you could climb up onto the wall so I can capture those white flowers behind you."

"Honeysuckle," said Elsa. "During the nineteenth century," she added nervously, "teenaged girls were forbidden to sniff honeysuckle because the blossoms were believed to induce unseemly dreams."

"They're stunning flowers," he answered. "A perfect frame for a portrait of a stunning woman."

Elsa slid out of her slippers and inched along the stone wall as though advancing toward the end of a narrow branch. Belldauer stepped from behind the easel and watched as she allowed the robe to fall slowly from her shoulders.

How exposed she suddenly was! How vulnerable!

"I feel like a schoolgirl," said Elsa. "All jitters and nerves."

Belldauer stared at her body pensively, his fingertips pressed over his mouth. He looked as though he were discovering her for the first time. Elsa felt the shame building inside her. What a disappointment she must be! Here he was, clinging to a forty-five-year-old vision of youthful beauty, while all she had to offer were sagging breasts and cellulite. She wished she'd had the good sense to keep her clothes on.

Belldauer appeared troubled. More surprised than disappointed. "That blue bracelet of yours," he said. "What was it? Cobalt?"

"I don't know," stammered Elsa.

"Do you still have it?'

"Maybe," she replied. "I could check for you."

Why had she said that? For the sake of the charade? Or because she was mortified to pose naked on a stone wall in front of a complete stranger? Morton Belldauer was, after all, nothing more than a stranger who'd written her a letter by mistake. Elsa reached for her robe. "I'll be right back," she said, and she scurried through the sliding glass doors into the living room.

Inside the house, of course, there was nothing Elsa could do except to wait until a sufficient interval of time had elapsed. She obviously did not own the other Elsa Kalamaransky's cobalt bracelet—or anything she might substitute in its place. If Belldauer learned the truth, she wondered, would he still track down the correct Elsa? Or would he cut his losses with her? Bruce, in Belldauer's shoes, would have worked his hardest to laugh off the entire episode. He certainly wouldn't have held her little falsehood against her. Quite the opposite: Bruce was one to appreciate a stunt so audacious and madcap. He might even have attempted something truly nutty, once he'd forgiven her—like inviting the other Elsa K. to join them both for dinner. But Elsa sensed a sober streak in Morton Belldauer that might prevent the man from looking beyond her deception so easily.

She waited for the grandfather clock to strike three. On the third peal, she strode back onto the veranda. Belldauer was seated on the edge of the stone wall, posed thoughtfully on the very stones where she was to model.

"I couldn't find the bracelet," said Elsa.

Belldauer nodded. His fingers kneaded his magnificent forehead.

"I couldn't find the bracelet," she continued, feeling her tongue grew loose in her mouth, "because I don't have the bracelet."

"How foolish of me to expect it," he answered. "It has been forty years . . ."

He was still scrutinizing her—probably trying to reconcile her naked body with the image frozen in his memory. Elsa drew in her breath.

"I *never* had the bracelet," she said. "I have a confession to make—"

Belldauer held up his hand. "Don't," he warned sharply.

"But I have to," continued Elsa. "I wish so much that I'd been that woman in your drawing class, but I wasn't."

"Please, don't," Belldauer repeated. Louder. "I already know."

"You know?"

She could tell by the deep sadness in his face that he'd seen through her. "I believed you at first. Forty-five years *is* a very long time. But I knew the moment you removed your robe," said Belldauer. "You were so shy just now, so gloriously shy. How did you describe it? 'All nerves and jitters.' But the one thing I'll never forget about the woman who posed for us in Dr. Stanley's class was how confident she was, how comfortable in her own skin. I'd never seen such sophistication. That's not the sort of self-possession one ever forgets—not even after forty-five years." So there it was. Over. Done. What a fool she had been.

"I'll assume this means you don't want me to pose for you," said Elsa. Belldauer frowned at her, his face beset with gravity. This must have been the face he used when investigating mysteries in cuneiform. Elsa felt a dark, unforgiving ache pooling within her chest.

"Nothing survives forty-five years without evolving," he answered. "Not attraction, not love, not even memory. So maybe I'm imagining all that self-possession and sophistication." He stepped behind the easel decisively. "Of course, I still want you to pose," he said. "Just like you did in Dr. Stanley's class. Why should a lost cobalt bracelet make any difference?"

"What are you saying? That you want me to pretend I'm the right Elsa?"

"You are the right Elsa," he answered. "I'm sure of it."

So she climbed onto the fountain and let the robe slide once again from her shoulders. The breeze brushed gently against her bare skin, and she watched as Morton Belldauer copied her body, stroke by stroke, his hands moving with a powerful and coordinated intensity. Occasionally, their eyes met and she absorbed confidence from his certainty. She was already beginning to recall, with increasingly vivid detail, the much younger Morton Belldauer, surrounded by other intense young men, who had sketched her in Professor Stanley's figure drawing class so many years before.

ANIMAL CONTROL

SOME SMALL TOWNS in New England still elect their dog catchers, but down here animal control has always been a civil service post. You log forty hours of coursework in chemical immobilization and euthanasia, pass a multiple choice exam, write out a check for eighty-five dollars payable to the Virginia Department of Agriculture—and before you can say sweet Jesus on a flapjack, you've got a job you can't lose, short of sticking your pecker in a rabid groundhog. But that doesn't mean it's all country ham and gravy. Not hardly. You don't know stress until you've told the parents of a nine-year-old kid that you're going to put down his beloved Lassie or Old Yeller. Which is why, when the field supervisor pokes his head into the dayroom, I get a wallop of those cat-on-a-hot-roof jitters. There's just me and Josie today—Lisa May's out on her honeymoon in Las Vegas—so I know some unlucky critter somewhere has my number.

It's nearly noon and I'm reading a book about hoaxes. My sister-in-law's recommendation. Josie is cooking up catfish in a pan. The dayroom smells like frying.

"Ready to earn your bread, Mr. Dipple?" asks the field manager. He's not a bad egg, as bosses go, but he's third-generation veterinarian, so he thinks he's just a speck better than everybody else. He insists on calling us Mr. Dipple, and Miss Jackson, and Miss Bickmore—

though I guess Miss Bickmore's going to be Mrs. Butts from now on—and we're supposed to call him Dr. Molinary, at least to his face. As if we work in a grammar school or a post office. What takes the cake about Doc Molinary is he wears cream-colored suits, like Errol Flynn, even in winter. "I have police already on the scene," he says. "County patrol on their way."

"Let me guess. Another stolen monkey." We've got a big research hospital in Spotsylvania County now—and last year a gang of animal liberation folks attempted to spring free a chimpanzee. Damn monkey went bonkers. We spent nearly six hours trying to coax it down from the ferris wheel at the fairgrounds. "If I buy another thousand bananas at that Winn Dixie, the manager will have me committed."

"No monkey business, I'm afraid," says Molinary. "Try a tiger."

I look at my watch. April 1st is still two days away. "A tiger?"

"On the loose in Hollow Grove. Escaped from an outfit licensed in North Carolina. The Forepaugh Family Traveling Circus." He hands me the manila folder that contains the intake sheet. "You'd better hurry. It's seems our tiger has already made away with an eight-month-old baby."

Josie flips off the gas range. "So much for lunch," she says.

"Good luck, Mr. Dipple. Good luck, Miss Jackson," says the field manager, a bit too formal—like some Old West mayor sending John Wayne to fight bandits. "You go after the tiger. I'll handle the reporters. We'll see who comes back alive."

Doc Molinary smiles, pleased with his own joke. I smile back. I don't bother to tell him that his fly is unzipped.

※

It's a gorgeous day, probably over seventy. Makes you think those Global Warming people know what they're talking about. The birch trees along Princess Anne Street have started to leaf. Robins are feeding in front of the Washington Mutual. Young mothers crowd the walkways beside the Rappahannock. It's hard to remember that, a century before I was born, General Burnside lost twelve thousand men trying to take this ground from Lee's Virginians. Don't get me wrong: I'm not some wacko with a Confederate battle flag on his bumper. I've got nothing personal against people moving out here from Washington or Alexandria. Everybody has to live somewhere. I just think it's important a guy know what happened in a place before he showed up.

I adjust the rearview mirror and ease the van into traffic. It feels odd to be driving with the sirens. "There used to be these giant elm trees all along here," I say to Josie.

"I'm sure there were. Good, sturdy lynching trees," says Josie. She's only in her late twenties, but she's the first Black animal control officer in Virginia. Her fiancé teaches criminal justice at Mary Washington. "Say, you're the movie buff. Isn't there an old movie about a tiger on the loose? Something with Gregory Peck?"

It's true. I do watch a lot of movies. My marriage to Gwen is like that.

"*Bringing up Baby,*" I say. "Katherine Hepburn keeps it for a pet. But it's Cary Grant, not Gregory Peck. And it's a leopard, not a tiger."

"Well, pardon me for living," says Josie, grinning.

"On the subject of tigers, you got a location in Hollow Grove?"

Josie reads me an address from the folder. She must sense something in my reaction, because she asks, "You familiar with the place?"

I know the Minard place, all right. I grew up out in Hollow Grove—back when it was the only subdivision between D.C. and Richmond. All that land had once been Minard land. Years later, when I was at Virginia State, I took a class in Southern history, and the professor, who had this thing against suburbs, kept calling Hollow Grove "Levittown for crackers." That's total bullshit, of course. My papa taught accounting at a private high school and my mama did social work for the county. But there's no point explaining things to people who don't want to know them.

"I used to be familiar with the place. Before you were born," I tell Josie. "Screwy family lived out there, but I'm sure they're all gone now." I take the Hollow Grove exit off the turnpike and cross the railroad tracks onto Culpepper Avenue. "Fact is, I'm surprised the old place is still standing." Or maybe it's not still standing, I realize. The same address doesn't have to mean the same building. It could be a Chevy dealership these days. Or a porno theater. That's why I never drive out here. If I had kids, maybe I'd want to show off my old stomping grounds. Who knows? But I don't have kids.

It turns out the entire subdivision is gone. Ploughed over by the new Interstate to Charlottesville. There's a motel where my house stood. It's got a Dutch theme. Windmill over the office. Tulips and daffodils out front. That's one thing we never have a shortage of in this lifetime. Bad ideas. I don't tell Josie I used to live here.

Then we turn up Lady Randolph Street—and it's the same house. An old colonial with two chimneys. There's about six gazillion squad cars out front—state police, Spotsylvania County, Prince George County, Fredericksburg traffic enforcement—not to mention enough fire trucks for an Independence Day parade. The television crews have set up shop on the other side of a sawhorse cordon. I'm not even out of the van when the commander on scene, this huge bald guy with a walrus mustache, is practically up my nose. "You animal control?" he demands.

"That's what it says on the van," I say.

"It's about time," he says. "This one takes the cake. I got an escaped tiger snatching a baby off the back porch and carrying it up a beech tree."

"It is injured?"

"Hard to say. You can't see much with all those the evergreens. It was crying for a while, for what it's worth, but now it's stopped."

I shake my head. "Not the kid. The tiger."

"Oh, the tiger," says the commander. "How the hell should I know?"

"Well, let's go have a look," I say.

Josie hands me the tranquilizer gun and we start up the steep driveway. That's when I see her. She's much thinner today, you could even say too thin, but she still carries herself like a fat girl. Her hair is gray as steel wool. It matches her sweater. You can tell she's been crying, but now she's got this totally blank look and she's rocking back and forth like some sort of Bible-thumper. Her husband isn't half bad looking. A few years younger than she is, not too short—only his face is a bit blotchy. He's got his arm around Evangelina's shoulder.

I steel myself and walk directly up to her. "Good morning, Miss Minard," I say.

She looks puzzled. "Mrs. Stevens, now," she says. "Do I know you?" Not a hint of recognition. But I guess she has other things on her mind.

"Animal control," is what I answer. "Tell me what happened."

This might be a good point to mention that I wasn't a popular teenager. I didn't cut it as an athlete, I certainly was no rocket scientist in the classroom, and it didn't help any to be the son of Melvin Dipple, who taught bookkeeping with a pencil over his ear and chalkprints on the seat of his trousers. My brother compensated for his shortcomings with humor—and he won permanent social acceptance after he filled the deputy headmaster's Oldsmobile Tornado with six thousand nickel-plated ball bearings. I tried to follow in Albert's footsteps, but I just wasn't funny. By eleventh grade, I threw in the towel on cool. Instead, I took up birdwatching.

While Carter and Reagan bickered over leading the Free World, I went thrashing through the underbrush for woodpeckers and wrens. I wore a mesh pith helmet that my brother bought for a summer-stock production of *Lawrence of Arabia*. The hat came with a leather chin strap and a veil of mosquito netting. I also had a pair of Zeiss field glasses my Grandpa Cavanaugh brought back from North Africa. He was an artillery officer during the war. Probably the only Dipple or Cavanaugh ever to do anything important. For camouflage, I spread guacamole on my cheeks.

My goal was to spot all eight hundred species in the Peterson guide. Not that I cared so much about birds. What I wanted was accomplishment. Fossils or model horses would have done as well. But having picked birds, I hunted them with a vengeance.

Mostly, I kept to the subdivision. Sometimes I crossed the high meadow and ducked under the split-rail fence into the Minard's enormous backyard. The overgrown tea roses were great for hummingbirds, except when the hounds were outside. And the Minard's property was like a hidden amusement park. Some of the money from the farmland had gone into a private playground. A swingset. Monkey bars. A heart-shaped sandbox. They also had clay tennis courts, but they didn't maintain them. Being in the Minard yard never felt like trespassing, but I didn't dare ride on the swings. And then one evening—a long twilight in early spring—I was watching two large black birds perched atop the Minard's weathervane when Mr. Minard snuck up behind me.

Mr. Minard was tall and slender with a baby face, but in his forties he already walked with a stoop, and his skin was the color of cucumber pulp. I knew all about the man without ever having met him. If you lived in Hollow Grove, this was what you talked about. Darwin Minard had been raised by his mama—up north—then came back to the homestead with an overweight wife and the ugliest baby anybody could remember. The wife had sung opera once, but had a tumor on her voice box.

Mr. Minard dabbed his forehead with his handkerchief—as though encountering me was a cause of considerable exertion. "See anything interesting?" he asked.

"Ravens," I said defensively.

"Hmmm. Look like crows to me."

Mr. Minard broke off a sprig of forsythia and sniffed it approvingly. "How do you know they're not crows?" he asked.

They were crows, of course. We both knew that. But I also realized he thought I was a peeping Tom, which I wasn't.

"They're too large for crows," I said. "Their beaks are too thick."

He nodded. "Ravens. How do you like that?"

Mr. Minard snapped off several more sprays of forsythia and tucked them into a wet dish towel. He was assembling a bouquet.

"You think she's pretty, don't you?" he asked.

"Who's pretty?"

But just then I caught sight of Evangelina Minard standing at one of the dormer windows under the weathervane. She was the year behind me in school. Walleyed. Fat as a Turk. In the habit of fanning her neck with her hands. There was a limerick about Evangelina and a suckling pig graffitied in one of the boys' bathrooms.

Mr. Minard reached into his pants pocket and toyed with his keys. "What's your name?" he asked.

I considered a secret identity. All I could think of were Clark Kent and Peter Parker. "Jethro Dipple," I said.

"Well, Jethro Dipple," he said, "When I was your age, I used to hide in the *au pair's* closet. Fjola from Iceland. *Fj-o-la*. She was probably about twenty-five years old—and she would strip down in front of the mirror to look at herself. One day, I sneezed and she caught me— and I was positive she was going to tell my mother, but she didn't. For the rest of that summer, she let me sit on the bed while I watched."

"I should go home now," I said.

"No need for that," he said. "You're missing the whole point of my story."

"I wasn't doing anything," I said.

"I tell you what," said Mr. Minard. "Why don't you stay for supper? I'm sure Evangelina would be delighted."

I tried to object. Being un-cool was one thing. Being known as the guy who spied on Evangelina Minard was another. But what could I do? You don't have leverage when you're sixteen and covered in avocado dip. Either I followed Evangeline's father up to the big house, or I made a chancy dash through the brush. I searched for a break in the azalea hedge—but deep down I was a coward. Soon enough, I found myself standing in the Minard's big country kitchen.

The room's walls were large square timbers. All except around the hearth, which was exposed yellow brick. Assorted pots hung from the rafters. Silver candlesticks sat on the walnut dinner table. But there was also a modern oven, a dishwasher, and a double-doored Kelvinator refrigerator. The oven stood open, and a servant girl with an enormous rump was bent over it, rotating a turkey. Mrs. Minard hovered nearby, sipping a vermillion cocktail. She was big, but with shorts legs. Like a cartoon ox. Not un-pretty, just fat. Mr. Minard said I'd come to have dinner with Evangeline.

"Does he have a name?" asked Mrs. Minard, her voice like sandpaper. They both looked at me. "Jethro Dipple," I said.

"Dipple. I know Dipple," she said. "He's the one with the tiny little balls."

She meant the ball bearings. "That's my brother," I said.

"It seems like we're being inundated by Dipples," said Mrs. Minard—and she laughed fiercely. "No matter. I think it's about time Evangelina had a boyfriend."

As though on cue, the daughter walked into the kitchen. She was chewing gum.

"There you are, darling," said Mrs. Minard. "I was telling your friend here that you could use a boyfriend."

This was the only time—for a split second—that I felt bad for Evangelina Minard. Because we were not friends. We'd never exchanged two words in our lives. And we weren't going to be friends. Or I felt bad because the idea of her having a boyfriend—ever—seemed so totally impossible. The poor girl gasped when she saw me. She looked as though she'd just dropped a baby. "Oh my God," she said.

"Jethro here has been attempting to spy on you," said Mr. Minard.

I hid the field glasses behind my folded arms. Shame burned the tips of my ears.

"Gross," exclaimed Evangelina.

"You should be flattered," said Mr. Minard. "I told you it was only a matter of time before you turned into a swan."

This made Evangelina blush. "Daddy!"

"I have an idea," said Mrs. Minard. "Darling, we still have some time before supper is ready. Why don't you model for your friend here?" The woman turned to me and added: "Evangelina is going to be a great stage actress someday. She's very talented. All she needs to do is reduce a bit."

"Please, Mommy," said Evangelina. "I don't want to."

"It will be fun," said Mrs. Minard. "And good experience. Especially with company."

I looked to the servant for help, but the girl was painting butter on the turkey as though nothing were out of the ordinary. If Evangelina's father had turned me in for peeping, I could have lived with that. Somehow. But going from peeper to "company" was downright freaky. Evangelina must have thought so too. Her small dark eyes had taken on a watery, desperate look.

"Let's ask the boy," said her mother. "Jethro, wouldn't you like Evangelina to model for you?"

It crossed my mind that she might mean naked modeling. Or at least lingerie. In that house, anything was possible. "I guess so," I said. When I was sixteen, even Evangelina Minard was worth seeing in the nude.

My imagination quickly got the better of me. I was dreaming of bikinis, silk garters, kimonos from Japan. Evangelina Minard casually stepping out of peignoirs in front of floor-to-ceiling mirrors.

But my fantasies quickly came down crashing. The daughter disappeared through the kitchen door and returned an eternity later wearing a smock-like maroon evening gown a good forty years out of style. She had a string of black pearls around her neck and a hideous costume brooch pinned to her chest. The brooch was jade green and shaped like a moth. Evangeline posed with her plump hand on her equally plump hip. She had trouble balancing herself on her five-inch heels. Meanwhile, I tried to wipe off the guacamole with my sleeve. "My grand-aunt left us a whole steamer trunk of winter dresses," said Mrs. Minard. That explained the sudden, pungent odor of naphthalene.

"My grand-aunt was a Delacroix from Savannah."

"Isn't she stunning?" asked Mr. Minard. "Who do you think she looks more like—Marlene Dietrich or Greta Garbo?"

"You're showing your age, dearest," answered his wife. "I'm sure he's never heard of either of them. Try Farrah Fawcett or Raquel Welch."

It struck me that both of the adult Minards might be drunk. Mrs. Minard did indeed pour herself another cocktail. "Why don't you show us something décolleté, darling?" she urged her daughter "Maybe the lilac chiffon?" And Evangelina dutifully tottered out of the room.

"I tell you, Jethro Dipple, some young man out there is going to be very lucky one of these days," said Mr. Minard. "He's going to win the heart of a spectacular girl." I instantly thought of winning a piñata at the Mexican raffle. "And I don't mind saying, he's also going to find himself in an extremely advantageous position financially."

That's when I realized he knew the truth. They both knew. That their daughter was hideous as sin. Somehow, that made the fashion show even less bearable. I nearly bowled over the servant girl on my race toward the rear steps.

I can't imagine Evangelina's reaction when she showed up in her lilac chiffon evening gown—and her audience was gone. But she couldn't have been none too happy. By the following afternoon, the entire school knew I'd been spying on her.

❊

So here I am. Face to face with the girl who ruined me in high school. And also the lucky guy who finally won the piñata. In the same over-grown yard where I was once afraid to climb on the monkey bars. But everything's totally different now, of course. Because twenty-five years have gone by, and they've got a baby up a tree, and I'm pack-ing the only tranquilizer gun in miles. Fate can have a mean sense of humor.

I wait patiently while Evangelina tells me about the tiger. "I was inside hardly half a minute," she says. "Just taking Daddy's breakfast up to his room. I saw it through the upstairs window."

"You live with your father, Mrs. Stevens?" I ask.

Evangelina nods. She is sobbing again. Her husband adds: "She takes care of him. He's not right anymore, you understand."

So the old man's gone off the deep end. I can't help taking some pleasure in this.

"Do you think there's a chance. . . .?" Mr. Stevens lets his sen-tence trail away.

"We'll do our best," I say. "We always do." I'm not sure why I add this second part—maybe I don't want him to think we're cooking up anything special.

I turn away abruptly and follow the commander out to the tree. Josie is on her cell phone, discussing big cats with the Capital Zoo. We've also been joined by a ruddy, muscular guy in his seventies, a real Jacques LaLanne type, who keeps the animals for the Forepaugh family. His name is Ted Serspinski. His wardrobe staples are panama hat, alligator boots and bola tie. "The darnedest thing," he says, not too fazed. "But I suppose that's what we have insurance for." He has mentioned the welfare of the tiger, Duchess, half a dozen times. He hasn't said a word about the baby. We stop under the tree. It's in a thicket of cedars, so you can't see very far up. Occasionally, there's a flurry of branches.

"You're wrong," I tell the commander. "It's not a beech tree. It's a basswood."

"You fucking kidding?" asks the commander. "You a fucking botanist or something?"

I stay deadpan. "I wouldn't kid you. It's definitely a basswood."

The commander doesn't know what to make of this. He's resting one hand on the handle of his Billy club and the other on his service revolver. But I guess he thinks I'm a whackjob—and there's no sense arguing with a whackjob. "If it's a basswood, it's a basswood," he says. "You think you can shoot the damn thing from down here?"

I balance the tranquilizer gun on my shoulder and aim into the greenery. "Not a chance in hell," I say. "Maybe I can get a better angle from the roof of the house."

The circus guy doesn't like this idea. "You can't be serious," he objects. "She could fall out of the tree."

"Goddammit," says the commander. "If you get a shot, shoot."

"Are you sure about that?" I ask. "He might have a point. What if it knocks the kid out of the tree on the way down?"

The commander looks at me like I killed his dog. "Goddamit," he says again.

I turn to Josie. "Any ideas?"

"Actually, I do," she says. "According to Washington, we shouldn't do anything. If it hasn't harmed the kid yet, it's not going to. We should just sit on our hands until it decides it's ready to come down."

The commander spits into the dust. "So we're just supposed to wait for it to make the first move?"

"That looks like the plan," I say.

"They're going to send out their cat-keeper, but it may take a while," says Josie. "He's on jury duty and they've got to track him down."

That just takes the cake. Jury duty. Another lucky break for the Minards.

I send Josie back to the truck for my camping chair. Then I cozy up with my sister-in-law's book: *DUPED: The 100 Greatest Deceptions of All Time*. But it's hard to focus. I keep thinking about Evangelina, and about meeting her like this, and about how everything turned out. She's obviously not a great stage actress. And I'm not some expert on big cats who gets called in from D.C. I'm not even a vet or a cop. I'm just some civil service lackey with a dietician wife and no kids who knows a helluva lot about black-and-white movies. All in all, we're both rather damn ordinary. Which is pretty okay, I suppose, once you get used to it. But sometimes you can't help wondering how things might be different: if I'd been popular in high school. If I'd married Evangelina Minard. If Gwen hadn't had a hysterectomy. I fold the hoax book on my chest and lean back for a one-eyed nap.

At some point, a uniformed cop shows up with a bag of sandwiches. Somebody must have gotten his orders crossed, because another cop appears ten seconds later with two pizzas and a case of Dr. Pepper. It feels kind of strange to be chowing down while there's an escaped tiger in the tree above you—but that's what public service is like. You do what you can do. And sometimes you do what you can't do. In between, you stop for a pastrami on rye bread.

"You want to hear something amazing?" I ask the circus guy.

"What's that?"

"In England back in the '50s, they showed a television special on the spaghetti harvest in Italy. It was part of an April Fool's Day hoax. And people bought it—hook, line and sinker."

"Is that so?"

"They got letters from people asking where they could buy spaghetti trees."

I can tell the guy doesn't give two slaps about hoaxes. Probably has no idea he's standing half a mile from Stonewall Jackson's HQ. Or that in my twelfth grade, Duke Crenshaw passed around a petition to change the Virginia state bird to the "Peeping Dipple." Why should he want to know about me? All the circus guy cares about is his cats. And all Evangelina cares about is her baby. And all Doc Molinary cares about is keeping his first name out of the public record. We're a bunch of screw-ups, aren't we? People, I mean.

"You want another sandwich?" I ask circus guy. "We've got bologna, corned beef . . . and this one looks like bologna and turkey."

That's when the commotion erupts behind us. It's Evangelina's husband. The cops are trying to restrain him, but he won't back off.

"Let the guy through," I say.

The commander glares at me. "Let him through," he says.

Stevens comes directly to me. He must think I'm in charge. The guy must have come straight from the office—he's still wearing his tie and a tweed jacket with elbow pads. The tie has these tiny white anchors on it.

"What's up?" I ask.

"We've been waiting and waiting and waiting. This is killing us," he says, short of breath. "Can't you do something already."

The circus guy is standing next to me. "We've got to wait her down. It's the safest for both of them."

Stevens goes up like someone's lit a firecracker in his ass. "Both of them!" he shouts. "That's my goddamn son in that tree. If you don't do something—right goddamn now—I'm swear I'm going to do something myself."

The commander warns him to calm down. Like that does any good. Nothing to relax a panicked dad like a cop flexing muscle.

"You want us to do something," I say. "Okay, we'll do something."

"What about waiting?" demands circus guy.

"You heard the man. He wants action," I answer. "Anyone know how to get one of those machines they use on utility poles? You know what I mean . . . Apple pickers?"

"Cherry pickers," says Josie.

"That's right," I say. "Get me one of those. Fast."

❈

I've never ridden in one of these things before. For ordinary house pets, we go up in a ladder. Not glamorous, but it does the job. And it's cheap. Cherry pickers, on the other hand, are a once-in-a-lifetime opportunity, so I'm set on making the most of this.

At first, the guy down below does all of the steering. He pulls his levers and I'm up at the first branches, then higher than the Minard's roof. But it's me who has to direct the final few yards. "Left," I call out. "Up. Left. More left." The basket of the cherry picker snaps cedar branches as it moves. "Stop," I command. "Right there."

"Can you see it?" Josie shouts.

I can see it, all right. The tiger's just lying there, on a thick basswood limb. Minding its own damn business. And the baby's just lying there too. In a fork between branches. Eyes closed. Scratch marks on its bare chest—but tree scratches, not claw marks. The child is quiet as a gravestone, but he's still breathing. I raise the tranquilizer gun to my shoulder. At first, I take aim at the tiger. But then it strikes me that I could just as easily hit the baby. Get back at Evangelina for twelfth grade. Take a little bit of the random power in the world for myself. Mistakes do happen. Otherwise, I've got a clean record. Who'd ever know the difference?

I focus on the baby, then the cat, then the baby. Beyond them, though a break in the cedars, I can see all of Fredericksburg: the glistening Rappahannock coiling its way toward the horizon, the bell tower of Mary Washington's, the churches and tobacco warehouses and the strip malls spreading south toward Richmond. My wife's out there too, probably watching this on the TV in the nurse's station. Below me, Josie and the circus guy and Evangelina's husband are all shading their eyes against the sun. I guess this is what it means to have your life flash before your eyes.

"You all right up there?" calls Josie.

"I'm fine," I shout back. "Give me a second."

And then I fire. Straight into the cat's shank. The animal jolts upright—and then crumples, crashing through the thicket below.

I hear screaming at ground level. The circus guy cursing. The commander ordering people to back off. Evangelina wailing, "My baby! My baby!" I pull the cherry picker toward the branch and scoop up the kid in my arms.

I'm still not sure I made the right call. Truth is, I'm still not sure a baby's worth more alive than a tiger. But it's not my job to figure that out. No point in asking questions about what's fair and what's right. No point at all. Because the danger is you'll start answering them. And that's great if you're the President or something, but not so good if you're an ordinary guy. I know where I'll end up if I start asking questions like that, and answering them, and it's no place I ever want to be.

CAVITATION

O UR KID'S DENTIST had been kidnapped by pirates. His wife
too. Their adult daughters, who lived across the river in
Hager Heights, issued a tearful plea for the couple's re-
lease on the six o'clock news, and I genuinely felt bad for the women.
They shared their father's undershot jaw, so they resembled a pair of
middle-aged bulldogs. Not a look you'd want in a prom date, let me
tell you, but my sympathy went only so far, because their dad's reck-
lessness had left us in a pickle of our own. Who in hell's name takes a
pleasure cruise through the Gulf of Aden? My boy, Logan, is a particular child. Fastidious, if you will. So persuading him to brave a new
dentist proved about as much fun as taking the cat to be fixed. We
were already three months overdue for his biannual cleaning when
we resorted to outright bribery—his price tag a portable metal detector like the one he'd seen some geezer wielding at the beach. Vanessa
wanted to tell him that Dr. Bibbenheimer had gone on a long vacation, as we'd done three years earlier when his goldfish had died, but
I'd thought second grade was old enough for the truth.

"*Real* pirates? Like Captain Hook?" asked Logan.

We were en route to Dr. Jamison's office in Laurendale—my son
on the booster seat beside his mother in the back of the Mercedes—
and we'd covered this territory multiple times. The day itself was an
overcast Friday in November, blustery, the red cedars along the me-

dian shrugging with ennui. An afternoon without promise. I'd cancelled my OR schedule so Vanessa wouldn't have to take the boy to the stand-in saw-tooth on her own.

"Sure, like Captain Hook," I conceded—in no mood for another discussion of the differences between Neverland and the Arabian Sea. "Only Somali."

"I changed my mind," said Logan. "I don't want to go."

The kid folded his slender arms across his shrimpy chest.

"I thought we had a deal, buddy. You're on good behavior with Dr. Jamison and we buy you a metal detector on the way home."

"It's not fair to Dr. B.," he protested. "We should wait for him to come back."

The boy had a hard enough time yielding up baby teeth—even at the going rate of $20. He formed attachments that way. What the occasion called for was a "dentist fairy" to reimburse him above market value for the absent mouth butcher.

"Dr. B. may *never* come back," I snapped. "Dr. Jamison is a perfectly good dentist and it's time you started acting your age, young man."

I sounded like my own father—a military orthopedist who'd once extracted my cracked incisor with a cord coiled around a doorknob. Vanessa's eyes met mine in the rearview mirror: resentful, exasperated. Then the bawling commenced and she filled the kid's head with nonsense about Dr. Bibbenheimer cavorting across the decks of the *Jolly Roger* alongside Mr. Smee and Gentleman Starkey. By the time we arrived at the Laurendale Medical Plaza, the fortunate Bibbenheimer had been appointed ship's surgeon and shared the captain's table nightly with Hook's own family.

※

The captive dentist hadn't seemed any great shakes. Bibbenheimer must have been pushing seventy, and his office couldn't have been much younger: a musty walk-up above a shoe repair shop, its walls bandaged with glass-framed portraits of oral anatomist Pierre Fauchard and Apollonia, the patron saint of dentistry. We'd inherited him from Vanessa's sister, who'd used the codger for her twins. "He's lovely," promised my sister-in-law. "Very old school." *Behind the times* was more accurate, and his office stank of damp leather, but Logan took an instant shine to his so-called jokes—*Why did the king go to the dentist? To get a new crown!*—so we were stuck. One upside of the kidnapping was that I'd never again hear about "tooth trolls" or "cavity creeps" or any of the other cariogenic villains of Bibbenheimer's folklore.

Dr. Jamison came recommended by my medical school roommate, the newly-minted chief of pediatric neurology at Yale, where the gum prodder also held a faculty appointment; *Fairfield Magazine* had ranked him a "Silver Caduceus" provider five years running. His office—a shared suite on a corridor of orthodontists and podiatrists and chiropractors—was sterile as an operating room and displayed less personality than a chamber in a Scandinavian hotel. No toy-strewn carpet, no giant plush brushes or colossal papier-mâché packets of dental floss. No corny sign above the reception desk warning, "Ignore your teeth and they will go away." Only coloring books neatly stacked on a magazine rack, crayons available upon request. And the saw-tooth *looked* like a medical man: clean-cut, broad-shouldered, fit to row crew at Oxford or Princeton. After Logan had been given a maternal pep-talk and led into the treatment room by a busty hygienist, I mused to Vanessa, "I wonder if the pirates will make Bibbenheimer shave his whiskers." The old molar miner had sported a waxed handlebar mustache, white as alabaster—as though welcoming gate crashers to a geriatric Oz.

"*That's* what you're wondering about?"

"He'll be fine," I said. "Lots of kids are a tad nervous at his age."

Vanessa didn't appear reassured; she returned to grading exams. Although she'd given up fulltime accounting when Logan was born, she still taught a business finance course at the community college. She enjoyed it too—even if the students were dumb as Neanderthals with Down syndrome. Call my Nessie naïve, if you must, even foolhardy, but she's a paragon of patience. Always has been. Lord knows why.

I opened my briefcase and set to work on my son's campaign speech. His class at the Montessori school—officially the "Turtle Clan," rather than the second grade—would be electing a new "clan leader" before Thanksgiving, a replacement for a whiney, pigtailed blonde whose father had accepted an architecture gig in Atlanta. Logan did not want to run. Not at first. Candidly, his primary interests were hunting for hidden passageways and perusing coffee table books about buried treasures, interspersed with countless hours of woolgathering. But I promised him a trip to Hearst Castle—his vision of the Holy Grail—the following summer if he gave politics a shot, so he'd reluctantly challenged the twerp who'd planned to run unopposed.

"How's this, Nessie?"

My wife didn't bother to look up. I cleared my throat. At the front desk, a mousy receptionist typed behind headphones. Our only other company was some kid's butterball grandmother who dozed with her chin on her chest, trumpeting snores.

"*Dear Fellow Turtles and Tortoises,*" I declaimed. "*Let us rise out of our shells. Some may see us merely as soup, but do not mock us, for we are not mock turtles . . .* Not half bad, eh?"

"Honestly, Marty? You can't be serious."

"*Next time let us not merely outrun the hare,*" I continued, "*but serve him as rabbit stew . . .* You think it's too clever for seven-year-olds, don't you?"

"I think you should let Logan write his own speech."

That was some campaign strategy; we might as well have waited for Maria Montessori to rise from the dead and endorse him. And even if Logan ever got around to penning a speech on his own—

probably sometime after his classmates graduated college—it was likely to be heavy on treasure maps, light on empty but lavish promises. In short, a dud. I'd been class president at St. Paul's four consecutive years, so I knew a bit about electioneering. "Be reasonable, Nessie. Do you think John F. Kennedy wrote his own speeches? Ronald Reagan?"

"When they were seven? *Yes, I do*."

I didn't have a chance to pursue my argument. A wail—shrill, anguished, barely human—punctuated the antiseptic office, followed by the clatter of steel. The grandmother started from her slumber, overturning her handbag. Vanessa rose in alarm—without so much as a glance in my direction—and advanced toward the treatment room. The receptionist hardly had her headphones off, and was attempting to detain my wife, when the distinctive sound of Dr. Jamison's baritone swelled above the gush of running water.

"He bit me!" shouted the dentist. "Son-of-a-bitch motherfucking bit me!"

The incident cried out to high heaven for litigation. To my relief—and surprise—Dr. Jamison, once he'd had an opportunity to compose himself and to irrigate his wound, proved far more forgiving that I might have been under the circumstances. "It happens," he said, his aqua surgical mask dangling around his neck. "Water under the bridge. Right, pal?" Logan refused to make eye contact. "In any case, Dr. Rowe, Mrs. Rowe, the bottom line is he'll need at least three fillings for sure. There's also a suspicious area on the lower left I didn't get a good look at." Jamison offered me a firm handshake. Vanessa led our son out of the office while I booked the next session and waited for the receptionist to run my credit card.

We avoided the entire episode on the drive back to Marston Moor. Vanessa and I exchanged terse remarks about dinner plans, an overdue library book, whether I'd remembered to renew our membership at the racquet club. Gone was my enthusiasm for a Turtle Clan landslide, my puns about mossbacks at loggerheads. Only when we'd pulled into the driveway, beside the piles of dead wet leaves, did I say, "You can't go around biting people. You're not a dog."

Logan grimaced—more shell-shocked than defiant, as though Dr. Jamison had done all of the biting. "You're lying about Dr. B.," he said. "Pirates don't make friend with dentists. They hold them for ransom or force them to walk the plank."

"This isn't about Dr. Bibbenheimer, young man. This is about *your* behavior. You should be punished severely for what you did."

Not that punishing my son was an easy matter. You couldn't ground a boy without friends. Or you could, but then he'd just do what he always did—sit in his room and daydream. Once, after he'd caused a scene at his cousins' birthday party, which he'd attended under duress, because mini-golf was "pointless," I'd confiscated his treasure books. He shrugged off the penalty so quickly, immediately retreating into his own imagination, that I all but had to beg him to take them back the following week. The boy stood immune to everything except brute force—a prospect anathema to Quaker-reared Vanessa, who was all too glad to spare the rod and raise a wimp.

"How much do you think it will cost to ransom Dr. B.?" asked Logan, sparking with animation. "Maybe we could buy a metal detector and find the money."

I ignored this fantasy. "Next time you see Dr. Jamison," I said, "I expected you to apologize for today's conduct. Am I making myself clear?"

Logan didn't answer. He leered—sullen, resigned. I genuinely loved that boy—don't get me wrong—but sometimes I felt as though I were raising a changeling, that my baby had gone home with a Wolf Clan family by mistake. Alas, the boy's auburn locks and sharp, freckled nose branded the kid as mine; only the personality didn't mesh. If I'd stonewalled my own father, he'd have tanned the flesh off my ass. I killed the engine. Outside, the cloud-swept sky wavered toward dusk. "You answer me when I talk to you, young man. Got it?"

"We're not going back," interjected Vanessa. "Enough, Marty. If he doesn't like this dentist, we'll find a different one."

So that was that for Dr. Jamison. I believed, at a minimum, our son owed the saw-tooth a written apology, but my wife insisted a letter would be excessive. "He's suffering," said Vanessa. "Why can't you see that?" But what *I* saw was a promising young man having his future derailed by an overindulgent mother, a petulant attitude and a set of lousy teeth.

We did try other pediatric dentists. *Six* of them. Two afternoons each week for three consecutive weeks, I bailed out on my patients—postponing critical pneumonectomies, leaving neuroendocrine tumors to fight another day—so that my son could survey, and torment, the assorted fang hounds of southern Connecticut. Mercifully, we suffered no repeats of the biting incident, but that was largely because Logan couldn't be coaxed, duped or dragged into another dental office. The one time I attempted to deceive him overtly—telling him his mother had broken an ankle and we were to pick her up at the ER, while she'd actually gone to see a talk therapist—he caught on when we reached Dr. Adebayo's parking lot. I give Adebayo credit. The gum gopher was a Santa-bellied Nigerian fellow brimming with cheer, and he personally came out to the car to plead his case, but Logan nearly shut the power window on the guy's thumb, and when Vanessa learned about my ruse, I ended up exiled to the sofa. "We're going to develop a reputation, for Christ's sake," I griped. "The canine pluckers are going to think we're writing a guidebook on the sly. Or that we're engaged in some novel form of insurance fraud. Mark my words, Nessie. One day you're shopping around for mouth butchers, the next you're on trial for money laundering."

Vanessa shook her head. "Sometimes I think Mama was right about you."

"What's that supposed to mean?"

"Nothing," she said. "Just nothing."

I'd never seen eye to eye with Nessie's mother. She'd been one of those divorced homeopathy-and-natural-supplements biddies who always had something to protest: a power plant, a submarine base, a box retailer. I swear the woman's vision of heaven had been a pack of lesbian hippies in tie-dyes admiring cave paintings and making out with trees. But the sentiment was mutual: I'd once overheard her calling me a reactionary troglodyte with deviant priorities. That's an exact quote. The old hen had a thing for throwing around big words.

✳

Two days later was when the kid stopped eating. I remember the timing precisely, because it was the same evening Bibbenheimer's captors released their first video. In the grainy three minutes of footage, the dentist and his wife—and a Scottish naturalist kidnapped in a separate incident—paraded blindfolded across the deck of a mortar-mounted speedboat that bore no resemblance to the lateen-rigged galleys of yore. The trio appeared gaunt; the Scotsman walked with a pronounced limp. Bibbenheimer had grown a full beard to match his drooping mustache—a hirsute wraith of a man who recalled the last surviving Confederate veterans. In the foreground, a caucus of brigands mugged for the camera, laughing, occasionally displaying small arms or a machete. According to Lester Holt on NBC—breaking into regularly scheduled programming—the Somalis had demanded $20,000,00 per hostage. Our President had responded by threatening unlimited force. We'd been enjoying a relaxing Sunday brunch before our monthly visit to Vanessa's sister; I regretted not shutting off the TV.

"That's not *so* much money, is it?" asked Logan. "There's probably more than that lost under the sand at Cabot's Beach."

"Eat your eggs, honey," said Vanessa. "You're not feverish, are
you?" She assessed his forehead with the back of her hand. "He's
been picking at his food since yesterday."

"It's probably just nerves. Right, buddy?" I replied. "He's got a big
election coming up." I couldn't help feeling that his mother fussing
over the boy was part of the problem. "That reminds me. I have the
perfect slogan for the Turtle Clan. *'Snap to it!'* How's that for catchy?
Get it? Like *snapping* turtles . . ."

Vanessa stood abruptly and carried her plate to the sink. "Snapping turtles! Really?"

"Please don't fight," interjected Logan. "I'm not sick. But I don't
see why getting a metal detector is such a big deal? They're only like
fifty bucks."

I noticed his tongue fidgeting in the corner of his cheek. "Let me
take a look inside your mouth for a second, buddy," I said. "You don't
have a toothache, do you?"

"I'm fine," said the boy.

I rummaged through the odds-and-ends drawer beside the sink
for a flashlight. We had two, but the batteries were dead in both.
Then I retreated into my study and returned with a plastic penlight—
a souvenir from a Pfizer junket. "Open up," I ordered. "Now."

Logan let his jaw slack, yet with obvious reluctance, his upper
face a model of resentment. Sure enough, around the last baby molar on the bottom left—or, at least, what I thought was a baby molar, the gums appeared erythematous and swollen. Possibly an ab-
scess. Not that I knew the first thing about teeth—but it wasn't exactly
rocket science. Still, I didn't want to alarm Vanessa. So I shrugged
off the exam. "Looks like a bit of irritation. That's all," I said. But I
phoned in a prescription for amoxicillin the next morning and retrieved the pills on the drive home from the hospital. Just to be safe,
I assured myself. Besides, I'd determined to turn over a new leaf with

Vanessa—forty-three is too old to sleep on a living room sofa for long—and an antibiotic seemed as good a peace offering as any. On a whim, I also picked up a bouquet of carnations on sale at the checkout aisle. Cash & Carry: $14.95. I'll confess I often gave Vanessa a hard time for splurging on impulse items, but a small dose of hypocrisy never killed anyone—especially if nobody outside one's immediate family ever found out about it. When I arrived home, I felt genuinely chipper for the first time since Bibbenheimer had gotten himself shanghaied.

Vanessa greeted me at the threshold of the parlor. "Don't be upset," she said. "He had a really rough day at school. He gave that damn speech of yours . . . and well . . ."

I heard the device before I saw it—a bulb attached to a steel box by a slender metal neck like a Bauhaus vacuum cleaner. Logan steered the apparatus along the baseboards, prospecting the hardwood and the shag carpet. The machine's futuristic tonal staccato reminded me of the Geiger counter my nutso great uncle had installed in his fallout shelter. I swallowed my ire. "Sorry your speech didn't go so well, buddy," I said. "But it's not the end of the world. Bush Jr. was a turkey at the podium and he got himself elected twice."

Logan gazed up at me eagerly. "Can we go to the beach? *Please*?"

It was nearly Thanksgiving. Practically ice skating weather.

"I told him it was up to you," said Vanessa.

My son's eyes swelled with hope. I'd forgotten the bouquet in the car.

"*One* time," I said. "This weekend. But we're not going to make a habit of it, okay?"

The boy embraced my legs at the calves. "Thanks, Dad! I love you!"

Already I regretted my words. I could envision the boy at Bibbenheimer's age, shaggy and disheveled, gathering aluminum cans on the sand for pocket change.

✳

We drove out to the shore two days later. I had been enjoying summer weekends at Cabot Beach since my adolescence—when my father hung up his gold shoulder boards and settled into private practice in nearby Branford—but the coastal resort hamlet looked like a different country in the off-season. Billboards advertised boat storage, cheap flatbed transport. Plywood shielded Al's Bait & Tackle Stand and the adjacent Clam Shack. "VACANCY" flashed in neon across the marquee of the Pilgrim Arms hotel. At the marina, winterized bowriders huddled under canvas tarps; a metal barrier blocked access to the ferry dock. Logan insisted we listen to the radio news and Vanessa supported him. The previous evening, the President had launched an abortive attempt to rescue the hostages, and now the Somalis were threatening to kill them.

"My tax dollars at work," I grumbled.

"What's that?" demanded Vanessa.

"Nothing," I said.

Yet the notion of my hard-earned money squandered to free some bungling adventurer poked a stick in my craw. This wasn't a freak event or an unforeseeable accident, after all. The pirates hadn't raided Long Island Sound like marauding Vikings and carried off the dentist. Quite the opposite. He'd sailed straight into their jaws, practically inviting the buccaneers to slit his throat. Why should hard-working American families pick up the tab for his gross ineptitude? But I was turning over a new leaf, as I said, so I held my tongue and pulled Vanessa's Saab into the parking lot. The asphalt stood entirely empty, save a pick-up belonging to the state wildlife authority; the door to the vacant attendant's booth, unlatched, slapped in the wind. How strange, almost post-apocalyptic, the place appeared without bumper-to-bumper sedans, without fleshy couples unloading lawn chairs and bronzed teenagers lugging water coolers. I forgot to pull the Saab's safety brake; the vehicle beeped its frustrations. We'd left the Mercedes back in Marston Moor to protect its trim from sea air.

Logan led us toward the deserted beach. He carried the metal detector by the handle like an iron, his free hand below palm-up in a makeshift board. "Do you think Dr. B. misses me?" he asked.

It crossed my mind—fleetingly—that Vanessa might have been right about taking him to a shrink. At least, once. For an evaluation. This wasn't the only time the boy had become over-attached: when the postman's adult daughter drowned—a woman my son had never met, whom he didn't even know existed until the guy took two weeks off to mourn—Logan had proven inconsolable for weeks. As little as a shattered coffee mug or a misplaced umbrella could set him off. But who could say whether this was abnormal at seven? And even if the headshrinker voiced concerns, how did that help us any? We'd be shelling out a small fortune to be told what we already knew.

"I'm sure he misses *all* of his patients," said my wife.

She had a gift for consolation. Admirable, I guess.

We let the boy run ahead of us. Soon he'd mapped out a rudimentary grid of driftwood and was combing the sand with the voracity of an anteater. I'd underestimated the weather; the ocean wind gnawed through my parka. Vanessa and I ambled along the beach, keeping our distance from the child, but remaining close enough to rescue him should danger arise. We'd been out there off-season once before, I recalled, when there'd been an October whale sighting. But that had been years earlier—sixteen years, in fact—and the beach had crawled with amateur cetologists and marine biology students on field trips. How radiant Vanessa had looked—only twenty-three, willowy, sporting opera glasses instead of binoculars.

"He's a good kid," I said—apropos of nothing.

My wife smiled. "You really think so?"

"Why shouldn't he be?"

I reached for Vanessa's hand and—to my relief—she didn't resist.

"*I* know he's a good kid," she said. "Sometimes I think you're disappointed."

We strolled alongside the surf—indistinguishable from any other middle-aged suburban parents. A buoy jounced in the distance; gulls chorused overhead. I found myself suddenly rewinding sixteen years—before Marston Moor, before pediatric dentists, before fatherhood—to that lost October afternoon gazing at the perfect horizon. Or perfect, at least, in my mind's eye. Two days later, they'd discovered the dead whale marooned on the rocks.

"Sometimes I *am* disappointed," I conceded. "But that's because I want the best for him . . ."

Vanessa squeezed my hand. "Thank you," she said. "For saying so."

I wish I could report that had been a turning point in our marriage. Alas, it was not. Four hours later, equipped with $1.85 in assorted change, a pair of tungsten casting sinkers, a ball-bearing, and what might have been the clasp of a dog leash, or possibly a keychain, Logan reluctantly returned to the Saab. He did not look defeated, merely windswept. We'd hardly reached the Post Road when he asked, "Can we go back again next weekend? Please . . ."

I said, "Absolutely not," at the same moment Vanessa said, "We'll see."

We exchanged sharp glances. Nothing had changed. I asked Logan, "What makes you think you'll have any better luck next weekend?"

"I *know* we will," he said. Then he added—as though he'd been thinking of this for hours or days, "If you believe in pirates, Dad, you've got to believe in miracles . . ."

And I laughed. Not because I believed in miracles, or didn't, but because I'd recalled my father's favorite quotation. Shakespeare, I think. Probably the only line of Shakespeare that ever crossed the old man's lips. "*How sharper than a serpent's tooth,*" he'd say, usually as a veiled criticism leveled obliquely at my mother, "*to have a thank-*

less child." So now we had the tooth, but not even the goddam mouth butcher to uproot it.

※

We did end up at the beach again the following weekend. Not because I'd yielded to Vanessa's impulses, but because WCON-TV wanted to film the boy. He'd apparently shared the previous Sunday's antics with a classmate whose aunt reported human interest stories at the station, and soon an assistant producer was hounding me on the phone. How could I say no? Logan was also uncharacteristically excited. Not that the boy cared particularly about the media exposure for its own sake—but he believed that if he presented his case on television, other treasure hunters might join him in his quest. "And maybe Dr. B.'s family will see me," he added, "and they can tell Dr. B. that help is on its way." The first part of this wasn't so far-fetched. According to the assistant producer, one of the dentist's daughters had agreed to be interviewed briefly for the piece. To my surprise, Vanessa, of all people, was hesitant to consent to the filming.

"I don't know," she said. "It's so permanent. What if he regrets this later? Or if the kids at school see the story and start making fun of him?"

That was a joke. *Start* making fun of him? How could any kid his age *not* make fun of him when the boy hardly spoke about anything other than Montezuma's lost treasure and unexplored crawl spaces and a nitwit dentist half a planet away. I was surprised bullies from other schools weren't clamoring for transfers to join in the mockery.

"I thought you were into letting the boy make his own decisions," I replied. "Besides, it's not too soon to think about prep school applications."

Vanessa sighed. "I'm tired of arguing," she said.

So we drove out to the shore again. By then, Logan appeared to be in significant pain. Antibiotics had quelled the gingival infection, but done nothing to heal the underlying tooth, and even the mention of an alternative dentist threatened a tantrum. But what could I do? Sedate the boy? Bind him to a chair? Neither Dr. Spock nor the *Physicians' Desk Reference* had any wisdom to offer on captive mawcarvers. We did managed to keep the kid's calorie count up with a diet of soups and purées, but he'd still lost ten pounds. The architecture of his body welled beneath his flesh—ribs, trochanters, clavicle. Like an anatomy lesson. As part of our beach-going deal, my son agreed to consume two nutritionally-enhanced vanilla milk shakes, supplements I'd pinched from the pediatric cancer pantry at the hospital. What kind of kid, I wondered, had to be bribed to drink a milk shake? He'd also accepted a pair of baby aspirin. I refused to allow any radio news during the forty-minute excursion, so we enjoyed a medley of soft rock and oldies until The Beach Boys' "Sloop John B" gave way to Gordon Lightfoot's "The Wreck of the Edmund Fitzgerald," then drove the last fifteen miles in silence.

We found the television crew waiting for us at the head of the dunes. The aunt of Logan's classmate couldn't have been more than twenty-five; she spoke like her Yankee forebears—dropping her r's, running her a's broad in 'father' and 'start.' Not *un*-pretty, in a hyperprofessional way, but sporting too much makeup for my tastes. Her cameraman, a grizzled lug in a lumberjack coat, appeared to be chewing tobacco. I tried to make small talk with Vanessa, so we'd come across as a happy couple, but my wife hardly spoke.

"It must take a lot of energy to come out here in the cold, Logan," said the reporter, whose name was Jamie Cross, once the film was rolling. "What gave you the idea of using a metal detector to help search for ransom money?"

She'd seated my son at a wooden picnic table, facing the shore; behind him crashed a panorama of swells and breakers. At first, I feared she might be ridiculing the child—and, by association, his parents—but her expression was dead earnest.

"I wanted to help Dr. B.," answered Logan, matter-of-fact. "He's the best dentist ever."

"That's so noble of you. Your mom and dad must be very proud."

Logan shrugged. "They want me to go to a different dentist."

The boy's tone made this proposal sound unreasonable, even abusive, as though we'd asked him to have root canal performed by a barber's apprentice.

"We *are* very proud of him," I interjected. "And not just for his fundraising. Logan is running for leader of the Turtle Clan—that's what they call the class president at Montessori schools. You should hear his campaign speech. Vintage Jack Kennedy."

Cross nodded—clearly indifferent. I flashed a similar plastic smile when patients asked me irrelevant questions in the recovery room.

"I won't go to another dentist. *Ever*," said Logan. "No matter how bad my teeth hurt."

That drew the reporter's interest. "Is that so? Do your teeth hurt now?"

My son grimaced. "Not *too* bad. Usually, only at night. Or if I'm eating. But when Dr. B comes back, I'm sure he'll fix them."

The reporter's expression tightened from indifference to genuine concern—the sort of concern that led busybodies to meddle, that provoked calls to Child Protective Services. I ran my tongue nervously over my own molars, as though scratching an itch.

"It's all being taken care of," I said. "Trust me. I'm a physician."

We returned home that evening with a copper spigot, corroded cooking grills from a Coleman stove, and a bicentennial quarter. Quite a jackpot.

※

That night I phoned Julia Feig at home. She was the older of Bibbenheimer's two daughters—the one with a number listed in the white pages. I recognize my timing wasn't exactly ideal: earlier that evening, the networks reported that the kidnappers had beheaded one, and possibly more, of their captives. But I'd learned to follow the surgeon's creed: *sometimes right, always certain.* I realized lay folks often said that as a joke, and I could see the humor, yet in my experience, there was wisdom in it too. So I called—without informing Vanessa, who was watching CNN in the den with our son. For a woman in shock, and possibly orphaned, Mrs. Feig displayed impressive composure.

"My name is Dr. Martin Rowe," I explained. "I believe you're familiar with my son, Logan. The kid with the metal detector . . ."

"Do I know you?" asked Feig.

"Marty Rowe," I repeated. "My son is *Logan* Rowe."

"I apologize, Dr. Rowe. You've caught me at a bad moment." She paused to shout '*I'm on the phone*' to an unheard interloper. "Let me take your number—"

"Please, Mrs. Feig," I said. "My son is in pain. And starving. On account of *your* father . . ."

"Excuse me?"

So I shared our family saga as concisely as possible—embellishing the connection between my son and her dad, even praising the codger's dentistry. "All I'm asking for is five minutes of your time. Less. Just please tell him your old man would want him to see a different dentist—and I swear I'll never bother you again."

An icy silence followed.

"Mrs. Feig?"

"Very well," she said. "I'll talk to him."

So I carried the phone into the den. Logan sat ensconced beside Vanessa on the loveseat, feet tucked under the cushions. He held the remote control in one hand like a magic wand and petted the cat absent-mindedly with the other. "Phone call for Logan," I announced.

"For *me*?"

"It's Dr. B.'s daughter. Julia."

Logan grabbed the receiver. "Hi," he said.

And then he listened. The conversation must have lasted closer to ten minutes than to five, although Mrs. Feig did all of the talking. I could picture her simian jaw sliding in and out—like the dispenser on an antique candy machine. Vanessa shot me a fierce glare, shaking her head. The boy, for his part, looked as though he might sob.

"I don't know," he finally said. "I think we just have to have faith."

That drew an unheard response from Feig, another soliloquy of several minutes.

"I'm sure he will," insisted Logan—as though challenged. "I'm *100%* sure."

Bibbenheimer's daughter had launched into a third rebuttal when the news broke—first a chyron and then, almost immediately, a special report: the Scottish naturalist had been beheaded by his captors. Hours later, special forces rescued the dentist and his wife.

Three weeks elapsed before we took Logan to see Dr. Bibbenheimer. The mouth butcher had gone into semi-retirement—turning over his practice to his nephew—but he'd agreed to treat our son for the foreseeable future. "Either my hands will give out," the codger promised, once he'd watched the WCON-TV report, "or his teeth will give out." We'd gone to the parade in downtown Hager Heights the previous weekend as special guests of the Bibbenheimer family. I was amused to note that our local hero had shaved his facial hair. He looked older without the shield of his mustache—more vulnerable. From the lectern atop the steps of city hall, he asked: *Did you hear what the pirate said to the dentist? Say 'Arrr!'* The mayor grinned. Logan laughed so hard that Gatorade leaked from his nostrils.

Vanessa and I had already agreed upon a trial separation, but we'd held off telling the boy. Maybe because we feared the result. Or maybe because we remained hesitant, divided between our present selves and the whale-watching lovers we'd once been. By then, the school election already stood two days behind us, and the "turtle tally" had not gone in Logan's favor. I'd argued for a recount. I'd even taken the liberty of phoning Mrs. Rigott, his nitwit teacher, but she refused to divulge the margin of victory. "We have an secret ballot here, Dr. Rowe," she'd said. "So nobody's feelings gets hurt. But I'm telling you it's a *substantial* difference. *Not close.*" On the way to the dentist, the defeat still tasted bitter in my throat.

"All I'm saying," I said, "is that it's a flawed process. Maybe he *didn't* win, okay. But how can we know if there's no way to confirm the results?"

"I'm *glad* I didn't win," said Logan. "Because then Robbie would have lost."

"You worry too much about losers," I snapped.

I'd almost added: *Just like your mother.*

"Can I ask you something?" asked Logan. "Dr. B. will always be my dentist, won't he?"

I decided to let his mother answer. It was obvious that we'd gotten nowhere in two months, that my son was destined to stay the kid he was—no matter how hard I tried.

"For as long as he possibly can," said Vanessa. "Always is a very long time."

"And you'll always be my mother and father, right?"

Vanessa's eyes met mine in the rearview mirror; for an instant, she appeared uncertain. Our son's question hung in the air, so innocent and hopeful, reaching for eternity. In the ether lurked pirates, and dentists, and miracles, and turtles, and a universe of the infinite contingencies best left unspoken. A cosmos of silence. And then we both answered at once.

IN SICKNESS AND IN HEALTH

M easles, your kid's brain soft and swollen like a saturated sponge. Pertussis, asphyxiating on his own breath. Diphtheria. Rubella. POLIO! Lady, have you ever seen a child crippled by polio?

Usually, they shut the door on him. But the pale girl stood in the entryway and offered up a patient, almost forgiving smile. She held the child—no taller than a fire hydrant—by one hand.

Mumps, said Gadney, *I forgot about the mumps.*

The girl's smile broadened. *What a funny name*, she said. *Mumps.*

Gadney ran his index finger between his neck and his collar. It was beyond all reason for a public health officer to wear a jacket and tie—especially during the Cormorant Island summer. It was—as he'd told his boss—total bullshit. But here he was anyway, dressed like a fucking Mormon missionary, still making no progress.

Mumps are no joking matter. You're talking meningitis, orchitis, nasty swelling . . .

Rhymes with wumps, said the girl. *That made me laugh so hard as a kid.*

The child wrested his arm from his mother. *Mumps, mumps, wumps*, he said. *I want them now.*

Gadney sensed his professional authority slipping. He looked down at his clipboard for inspiration. *You know what I think*—said Gadney, deviating from his script—*I think you're all goddam nuts. Christian*

Science, my ass. If you didn't have some giant church to back you up, they'd throw all of you in jail.

To Gadney's surprise, the pale girl's expression remained friendly. *Maybe,* she said. *But tell me something,* she continued. *You're the third guy they've sent down from Gulf Coast City, you know. Why does it make you so angry?*

These diseases can be fatal, pleaded Gadney. *And there's measles this year. Bad measles, and it's bound to get here . . . already killed nine Old Order Amish in Missouri.*

Okay, let's say you're right about these vaccinations, said the pale girl. *That's not what I'm asking. I'm asking why you care. He's my boy, not yours.*

The child was swinging on a tire suspended from the porch rafters. As though on cue, the boy suddenly asked: *What are wumps, Mama?*

Gadney had a complicated answer for the pale girl—"herd" immunity, the potential for mutations, dreams of complete eradication—but, unfortunately, the occasion called for a simple one. He considered saying that he had a child of his own at home, but that wasn't true. Instead, he stood on the sun-mottled porch—as helpless as laundry on a line—and said absolutely nothing.

I'm sorry, said the pale girl. *You're just doing your job, aren't you?* She fingered a necklace of small colored crystals, raising it nervously to her lips. Gadney liked the way her blond curls somersaulted out one side of her kerchief; it struck him that she wasn't much more than twenty. *You're looking ill yourself,* she said. *Am I allowed to invite you in for a glass of freshly squeezed carambola punch? It's 100% organic.*

Gadney—still speechless, fearing the onset of heatstroke—followed her across the threshold and into the over-air-conditioned dimness. Three weeks later, he rented a U-Haul and brought over his furniture.

※

The great benefit of a fresh romance, Gadney realized, was the opportunity to reinvent oneself. It allowed taking to your own history with a scalpel. Excised forever were his ex-wife, the mutual recriminations, the restraining orders, what she said he'd done to that godawful Jack Russell terrier of hers. He had no need to explain his employment record—his six humiliating months as a singing telegram in Denver—his arrest for passing a bad check in Pennsylvania. He was no longer Gadney Hill who'd been suspended from nursing school for cheating, Gadney Hill who'd lost his last P.A. job for pushing a Jehovah's Witness down a hospital stairwell. He was Gadney Hill who'd put a lot of bad shit behind him and had earned a new start. It wasn't that he lied, either. All he did was retell the stories in such a way that he never strayed too far from the moral high ground—which was no more than anyone would have done in his shoes.

The girl, Tracey Rose, also carried baggage. Her husband, it turned out, had been the volunteer firefighter killed in the sagebrush conflagration on the Panhandle. He'd also been her introduction to Christian Science. Before that, she'd dabbled in homeopathy, in straight chiropractic, even in Ayurvedic medicine. Her parents had been perfectly respectable Roman Catholics from Boston— her father, in fact, had been a rather celebrated hepatologist—but they'd both succumbed to cancer before her sixteenth birthday. His and hers tumors of the brain and pancreas. Radiation, chemotherapy, surgery—they went through the works, for nothing. So when her grandaunt moved her to Florida, Tracey Rose explored the alternatives. Multitudes of them. That made disputing medicine with her all the more difficult.

They had their first argument on the evening Gadney moved in— their housewarming spat, he later called it. In lieu of champagne. Not that they hadn't come close, earlier, when the boy, JJ, vomited blood. In Gadney's world, this called for a beeline to the nearest emergency room: do not pass go, do not collect $200. His mental glossary proposed esophageal varices, Ménétrier's disease, possibly Ebola, but he kept his own counsel. Tracey Rose spoke with her practitioner on the telephone for nearly three hours—Gadney suspected they were praying—and the episode prove transient. Probably just irritation of the digestive lining. So it wasn't until the following week, kindergarten only days away, that Gadney challenged the reigning orthodoxy. Tracey Rose was sitting at the kitchen table, sowing flower seeds in a germinating tin. *I'm trying alyssum for the front beds, pansies and calendula for the back*, she said. *What do you think?*

Gadney stepped behind her and massaged her bare shoulders. He loved the knead of her flesh, the power of muscle on muscle. *What I think is*, he said, *I think you should take your kid to the clinic.*

She shrugged off his hands. *Different people do things differently. You wouldn't make religious Jews eat lobster, would you?*

There's a difference between not eating it and denying it tastes good.

Tracey Rose continued to trail tiny seeds into a moist troth of soil and vermiculite. *Meaning?* she asked.

Meaning, this isn't a question of faith, said Gadney. *This is a question of reality. You're not telling me you won't get the kid inoculated because his soul is going to burn in the afterlife or something. You're telling me—against all reason, against two hundred years of scientific evidence—that vaccination plain doesn't work.*

Tracey Rose sighed. Earlier she'd rubbed her eyes with her gardening gloves, and now streaks of loamy soil scarred her cheeks like war paint. *I'm saying*, she said—her voice whetted—*that different people do things differently.*

Tell me, demanded Gadney. *Do vaccines work?*

Tracey Rose didn't answer, at first. Her sleeves were rolled up above her gloves and she glared at him like a retired boxer contemplating the ring. Overhead, the ceiling fan slapped through silence. *The measles vaccine causes autism*, she said. *There's a Congressman from Indiana who had public hearings. He turned up tons of empirical evidence.*

Of course, this autism shit was counterculture, not Christian Science—but Gadney knew that was a dead-end argument. *You're missing the point*, he said. *Even if one particular vaccine does cause autism in rare cases—and I'm not saying that it does—will you admit that, on the average, vaccination saves lives?*

According to Norma Shoemaker, answered Tracey Rose, *the life expectancy for men was longer in colonial Massachusetts than it is today.* Shoemaker was the practitioner whose two daughters played with JJ. *But please, let's stop fighting.* Tracey Rose squeezed his wrist tenderly. *Let me go tuck in JJ and then we'll celebrate our first night under the same roof, okay?*

That was an offer Gadney had a hard time arguing with. He wasn't so much concerned with the safety of the boy, after all, as he was about this obstacle between him and Tracey Rose. When he'd attended nursing school in Philadelphia, he'd briefly dated a Norwegian masseuse who spoke thoroughly fluent English, but whom a faint language barrier prevented from appreciating the nuance of his jokes. This was like that. How could Tracey Rose ever understand who he was—what was inside of him—if she held such wacko ideas about doctors? Her intransigence frustrated him—even angered him—although rationally he understood that his displeasure was foolish. In all matters non-medical, after all, they enjoyed each other swimmingly.

Gadney knew he was lucky. He'd lived with six different women in the first thirty-one years of his life—when you're good looking, you can do that—but he'd never experienced anything like Tracey Rose's generosity. She volunteered mornings in the children's room of the public library, afternoons as a guide at the nature preserve—always with JJ in tow—yet still set a multi-course vegan supper on the table every evening. She culled pot roast from grilled eggplant, baked cheesecake from soy milk and arrowroot. All of the vegetables she raised at home. Yet what amazed Gadney to no end was that, after supper, she was always game for whatever sexual adventures he had in mind. He'd never come across a woman as willing, as compliant. She didn't say much in bed, but otherwise he had no complaints. Off and on, Gadney picked up hints that her marriage to the volunteer firefighter had not been a happy one—that his predecessor had displayed something of a wayward eye, possibly a wayward prick—and that Tracey Rose was relieved to have something that wouldn't roll out of bed in the night. She wanted a father for the boy, too. *That* she told him often.

As for the boy, well—what was there to say? Gadney got on with him just fine, considering. He took the kid to watch alligator wrestling at Wild Wally's Everglades Safari, and swamp buggy races on Big Seminole Key, and spring training baseball in Gulf Coast City. He bought him a set of miniature bongo drums, a glow-in-the-dark yo-yo, Incredible Hulk sneakers. Gadney wanted the boy to like him. He also wanted Tracey Rose to see that the boy liked him. And JJ, who was a happy-go-lucky, easy-to-please youngster—Gadney conceded the boy had a winning disposition, as much as any five-year-old possesses a distinct personality of its own—genuinely did like him. Not once did the boy direct resentment at his mother's lover. Far from an interloper who'd replaced his martyred father, the child seemed to view Gadney as compensation for what had gone away.

The three of them sipped paradise in that vine-smothered house on Conch Street, paid off with insurance money, nestled on a forested ridge above the public beach. And yet the anti-medical quackery tore at Gadney—not like a thorn in his sock, but like the threatening memory of a thorn in his sock. One afternoon, he logged onto the Internet and, much to his consternation, discovered that men in twenty-first-century Florida lived no longer than their forebears in seventeenth-century Massachusetts.

※

As Gadney's home situation improved, so did his professional life. He relished the trappings of serving as a public health officer: the authority, the badge, the permit that let him park in fire zones and handicapped spots throughout the county. It was like being part physician, part cop—without having to earn the credentials of either. Rumor held that the legislature was even considering a bill to let health officers carry guns. Gadney's father, who'd been a real cop, the chief of police in a Cleveland suburb, would have been damn proud. The work itself wasn't that bad either. Short hours, long lunches. During the summer, as the school year approached, he tracked down the nearly four hundred county parents who'd sought religious or philosophical exemptions from the compulsory inoculation laws. Not just Christian Scientists, but fundamentalists and hyper-Catholics concerned that the vaccines were derived from fetal tissue, and arch-libertarians resistant to government encroachment. On Lower Manatee Island—actually a peninsula strewn with ramshackle cottages—a stocky woman in her sixties, a self-proclaimed Seminole chieftain, threatened Gadney with a jagged fence post.

Although Tracey Rose subscribed to the medical tenets of The Mother Church, her other involvement with the Scientists was surprisingly limited. She didn't attend services and never visited their lavish reading room in Ft. Coleman. Except for Norma Shoemaker—the practitioner who phoned occasionally, more often about carpooling than spiritual affairs—she had virtually no contact with other congregants. As a result, Gadney came to know the local Christian Science community better than she did. He encountered them first on his vaccination visits, but later in his various capacities as sanitation inspector, veterinary quarantine warden, and occupational safety administrator. On one of these missions—investigating a charge of permitting dancing without a cabaret license—Gadney first came face to face with his nemesis.

The bakery-café that Norma Shoemaker owned occupied several storefronts on the second floor of an open-air shopping center in Cormorant Cove. Wooden benches graced the boardwalks outside, shaded by the branches of an ancient strangler fig, and off-season tourists savored virgin daiquiris and pastries beneath the epiphytes and Spanish moss. The interior featured long tables suited for refectory-style dining. An unlikely night club, thought Gadney. Looks more like a monastery. But there was nothing monastic about the seductive cases of key-lime pies and meringues that extended across the rear wall to the height of his shoulders. Behind one of these, orchestrating the ministrations of a dozen college-age servers like a master puppeteer, towered the woman who had to be Norma.

Norma was larger than Gadney in all dimensions—taller, broader, heftier. Yet she was surprisingly attractive, maybe thirty-five, unmarred by wrinkles or laugh-lines, like an Olympian goddess on temporary sojourn in South Florida. Somehow Gadney had imagined her mousy, shrewish—a middle-aged creature still ticked that she hadn't had a prom date. He waited beside the complimentary magazine stand, unnerved, feeling more like a stalker by the minute. Unexpectedly, Norma herself solicited his order.

I'll have a decaf coffee, answered Gadney—in spite of himself. *Black.*

Mighty hot day for coffee, she answered pleasantly. She scanned him up and down as though assessing him for signs of illness. Then she retreated toward the end of the counter and returned moments later with a steaming cup. *You're Tracey Rose's friend*, she said. *Aren't you?*

Boyfriend, said Gadney.

I knew that voice from somewhere, said Norma. *My girls just love that JJ. They're only six and four and already they're fighting over who gets to marry him. We should all get together and do something one of these days.* She lobbed him a broad, open-mouthed smile like a golden retriever's.

Gadney clenched his fists. *Nobody's going to marry him if he dies of measles.*

Norma's jaw went slack, so that her mouth remained open and yet all the pleasure drained from her features. *Enjoy your coffee*, she said in an even tone. *And my best to Tracey Rose.*

You need to get your kids vaccinated, said Gadney. *You're going to kill them. There's a measles epidemic, for Christ's sake.*

Norma Shoemaker stepped around the display counter without warning. She stood arms akimbo, her chest only inches from his chin, her sharp eyes honed into his forehead. Her white baker's fatigues gave her the look of a deranged surgeon or a medieval inquisitor. *I love my girls just as much as the next person*, said Norma Shoemaker. Her voice was neither loud nor angry, just solid. *More than the next person. Nobody says otherwise, okay? You think just because I believe in the healing power of the Lord, I'm some uneducated nitwit. Well, uneducated nitwits don't graduate first in their classes at the Harvard Business School and aren't chosen Florida Small Businesswoman of the Year two years running.* She scratched her head through her hairnet, as though deciding whether to brandish her resume further. *Now please enjoy your coffee—on the house*, she said, *and send all my love to Tracey Rose.*

Crazy as fucking loons, answered Gadney. His own voice was loud and shaky. *Child killers, every last one of you.*

A number of patrons turned their attention his way.

Fucking batty, he shouted. *A goddam cult.*

Gadney slammed his coffee cup down on a nearby table. He stormed to the front exit—aware that he was creating a scene—and allowed the door to slam shut behind him. *A goddam fucking cult*, he added—addressing nobody in particular.

Later, at the supper table, he repeated the same phrase. *A goddam fucking cult*, he said. *And she's a goddam Amazon. I was afraid she was going to come at me.*

Your language, please, begged Tracey Rose, glancing meaningfully at JJ.

I was just doing my job, added Gadney. *Dancing without a cabaret license is a serious violation.*

I'm sure it was all a misunderstanding, said Tracey Rose. *What did she say about the dancing?*

Gadney still singed from the contempt in Shoemaker's eyes when she'd said Harvard Business School. *Fucking instigator*, he muttered.

What's a fuhginstigator? asked JJ. *Mama, tell me.*

Please, said Tracey Rose to Gadney. *I'm begging.*

I'll take him to bed, offered Gadney.

He hefted JJ into his arms and carried the boy to his bedroom like a potted plant. The room stood dark, the windows half open. A street lamp bathed the boy's bed in a square of angelic light. Gadney seat himself at the child's feet. *Can you keep a secret?* asked Gadney.

Dunno, said JJ. *Depends what.*

If I took you to the doctor on the way home from school tomorrow, would you tell your mother?

I think so.

Gadney panned the gray room: the giant stuffed giraffe, the abandoned yo-yo glowing ominously on the bureau. *I think so too*, said Gadney.

On the drive home from school the following afternoon, Gadney detoured into Gulf Coast City and bought the kid a deluxe burger at Fast Food Heaven. Bacon. Garlic mayonnaise. Melted cheese. Don't tell your mother, he warned—and the boy didn't. But Gadney thought often about the spare efficiency apartment where he'd lived alone before he'd met Tracey Rose, of the cracked ceiling in the bathroom and the endless evenings of nothing, and when October rolled around, he'd still done absolutely nothing to vaccinate the kid.

The first pock mark appeared like a solitary tear on the cheek of Norma Shoemaker's eldest daughter, Jasmine. All of them were on what Tracey Rose called a "reconciliation outing"—a stilted afternoon of miniature golf. Gadney had promised her—after she'd cried herself to sleep for nearly a week—that he'd be on company manners with the Shoemakers, that he'd keep an open mind, and nobody could say he hadn't tried his darnedest. Hadn't he listened politely while Ed Shoemaker, a swimming pool manufacturer who both looked and thought like an ox, expounded on the impending revolution in synthetic terracotta? Hadn't he held his tongue when Norma invited Tracey Rose to wrap copies of *Science and Health* for distribution to servicemen overseas? Hadn't he even shaken the damn woman's tremendous paw and "agreed to disagree" with the utmost of civility? But the pock—! *Sure as shit*, insisted Gadney, *That's varicella.*

It's just a scratch, said Norma. *Isn't it, darling?*

Jasmine Shoemaker stood dopily in front of a giant concrete flamingo. She held the head of her golf club in one hand and scratched at her shirt with the other.

Nearby, JJ and Laurel Shoemaker took turns jumping off a short concrete retaining wall onto the putting green.

Mommy, said Jasmine, *my tummy itches.*

Gadney jerked up the kid's yellow shirt; blisters pitted her chest and abdomen.

Let go of my girl, said Norma Shoemaker.

There you go, answered Gadney. *Chicken pox.*

Please, said Tracey Rose. *Don't start anything.*

Gadney crossed the putting green—through the sand trap, around the red windmill—and took hold of the other Shoemaker daughter. The child screamed and flailed; Gadney pulled her overalls down to her waist. *Here's more for you.*

And what's good for the fucking goose, said Gadney, grabbing hold of JJ, *goes for the gander too. Chicken pox*, he announced, exposing the boy's rash. *I hit the fucking trifecta.*

Gadney released the boy, and the child ran into his mother's embrace. She scooped him to her bosom, kissing his head haphazardly. Gadney catapulted his purple golf ball into the blades of the red windmill. *It could have been measles*, he shouted. *What more will it take for you to inoculate them?*

Disease is caused by sin, answered Norma. *You cannot inoculate against sin.*

Tracey Rose looked at Gadney over JJ's shoulder; her eyes were wet and pink. Laurel Shoemaker cowered behind a miniature waterfall. Jasmine Shoemaker clung to one of her father's hairy legs, scratching at her neck. *How can you possibly explain three young children getting sick at the same time,* asked Gadney, choosing each word carefully, *by any means other than contagion?*

If they play together, Norma snapped, *they probably sin together.*

Norma Shoemaker spent the next two weeks shuttling between Conch Street and her own home in Cormorant Cove. She commanded the sickroom like a fleet admiral, issuing periodic orders for fresh bedding or damp towels for JJ's forehead. But most of her time was spent kneeling on the hard cedar floor, a weathered Bible spread before her like a pharmacopeia of magic recipes, her big, smooth features rapt in prayer. *God's healing balm,* she said. *An ointment of scripture.* Tracey Rose knelt at the practitioner's side. The two woman often joined hands. When Gadney passed the open door and saw his Tracey Rose's delicate fingers locked in Shoemaker's oversized talons, he seethed with jealousy. He'd been engaged in a three month tug-of-war for Tracey Rose's spirit—and now this deranged woman had yanked the rope free from his hands.

Overnight, Gadney became a refugee in his own home. His vegetarian feasts instantly gave way to carry-out dinners from Burger Emporium and The Fisherman's Fry. Evening after evening, he'd sit on the sofa in the living room, gnawing beef patties, swigging Michelob, fighting back tears. Sometimes he took a walk around the neighborhood and came back sobbing. Since Norma's arrival, he'd been exiled from the master bedroom—she'd commandeered the entire second story of the house—and deep down he feared that his banishment might not end with JJ's illness. The deranged woman was transforming Tracey Rose. Gadney didn't know how—but he knew.

During their few private moments together, Gadney sensed a confidence kindling beneath her anxiety. The wrong sort of confidence. The sort of confidence his ex-wife had picked up in the months before she put him on the street. As Norma Shoemaker solidified her grip over his girlfriend, Gadney increasingly avoided the house.

And then a child died. Not JJ. Not Jasmine or Laurel Shoemaker. But a child, nonetheless. She was a three-year-old Guatemalan girl from Waccasassa Springs in the central part of the state, but her death—and two dozen other measles cases reported in that community—pitched a fever through the Department of Public Health. Gadney returned from work that day with fire under his collar. He was caffeine-ridden, under-slept, ruffled. After eleven nights sleeping on the sofa, his entire body felt done-over with a meat tenderizer. *I can't take any more of this shit*, he shouted, disrupting the solemnity of the sickroom. *Enough is enough. I'm calling a doctor.*

He's feeling much better, said Tracey Rose. *His fever's way down.*

It doesn't matter, said Gadney. *I love you and I'm not going to let you do this anymore.*

Norma Shoemaker folded shut her Bible. She rose, with some effort, from her knees. *What will a physician do?* she asked—her voice still firm as a boulder. *Do you know what pediatricians prescribe for chicken pox, Mr. Hill? They tell you to let the illness run its course. Thanks to the wonders of Christian healing, my girls are already back in school.*

I'm not going to argue with you, lady, answered Gadney. *You twist my words in circles. I'm going to call a doctor and he'll decide what to do.* He picked up the yo-yo off the bureau and aimlessly twisted the cord in knots. *Am I making myself clear?*

Please be open-minded, begged Tracey Rose. She crossed the room to Gadney and held her body to his shoulder. *Come pray with us.*

Gadney wrapped one arm tenderly around Tracey Rose's thin waist while his gaze met that of the sick child. JJ was sitting up in bed. The heavy covers had been drawn above his chest, and the boy clasped the cusp of the blanket in his hands like a marsupial peeking over a pouch. He stared wide-eyed, saying nothing. *I can't do this,* said Gadney. *There's fucking measles in Pelican County. Maybe this fanatic has a right to kill her own children, but she has no right to kill mine.*

Tracey Rose broke free of Gadney's grasp. She looked him sharp in the face and said, *He's not your child.*

Gadney skipped work the following morning to pack. This time around he had no need for a U-Haul—he wanted to escape from Conch Street as rapidly his possible. Fuck the furniture, he thought. Let her have it. He would have chopped it all to pieces with an axe—chopped the entire house down, in fact—if he'd had the energy. As it was, he carried his belongings in milk crates, one by one, the length of the steep driveway to his van. Tracey Rose sat on the tire suspended from the porch rafters. Her hands were folded in her lap, her legs dangling through empty air. Neither of them spoke. A pair of moorhens bantered in the stagnant drainage ditch, and a catbird warbled unseen from the pine thicket, but all the rest was stillness and silence. Gadney hoped she would say something, anything that might assuage his anger.

His cell phone rang. Gadney spoke briefly with the elementary school nurse from Cormorant Cove, a broad-face woman with heavy eyelids whom he'd met the previous month at a free contagion workshop. Overhead, the midday sun scarred the sky like an angry yellow blister.

Guess what, Gadney said to Tracey Rose. *That cuckoo friend of yours. Her kids have got the measles. And what's more, she wouldn't even take the damn girls to a hospital—she insisted on home quarantine.*

Tracey Rose stood up and held her hand to her mouth. *But they were just sick.*

Chicken pox doesn't give you measles immunity, said Gadney. He kicked dust across the slate walkway with his boot.

Tracey Rose bit her crystal necklace. *You don't think—?*

Probably not. But the only way to be sure is if he get his shots. C'mon, honey. Let's take him to the clinic and put this all behind us. Gadney raised one foot onto the bottom step of the porch. *Please, honey. Measles isn't chicken pox. It could kill him.*

Tracey Rose said nothing, at first. Her mouth opened. Shut. Opened. She stepped forward as though she might let Gadney take her in his arms—and then she pushed her way suddenly past him in a flurry. *I love you, but I can't,* she said. *I just can't. Please don't be here when I get back.* She disappeared over the ridge and down the path that led through the barrens to the public beach.

Fucking CAN'T, cursed Gadney. *WON'T.*

Anger surged through him like heat through an iron pipe. He mounted the stairs and retrieved the child from his room.

Get up, ordered JJ, choking back emotion. *We're going out.*

No, answered the boy. *Mama said you might try to take me to the doctor, but that I should say no.*

Gadney patted the boy's arm. *No doctors, I promise.*

The child eyed him suspiciously.

I swear to God, said Gadney, holding up his hand.

Where are we going?

We're going for a play date, answered Gadney. *At the Shoemaker's.*

And Gadney stayed true to his word. He drove the boy to Coconut Cove and kept the child up beside the sickbeds well into the marrow of the evening.

FLOTSAM CONUNDRUM

S HE KNEW DOGS and I knew boats, so we were an ideal team. On paper, at any rate. In reality, we started arguing while still loading the empty cages into the runabout.

"You'd kill two living creatures to save one human being?" the girl demanded—as though I'd suggested fricasseeing babies. "I can't believe you really buy into that sort of speciesist bigotry."

"Well, I do," I answered. "That's me in a nutshell. A speciesist bigot."

The question she'd posed was: If we were on an overloaded vessel with two people and two dogs, who should be jettisoned first? It's a pointless debate. When a boat risks sinking, nobody has time to quibble about ethics. But she was gorgeous, and I was trying to be a good sport, so I'd replied honestly.

"If you didn't want to hear my answer," I added, "Why'd you ask?"

The girl grimaced. "The moral dilemma is whether one of the dogs has to go overboard first, because she weighs less—or whether the dogs and humans should draw straws. But what you're saying is that even if we're certain we'll have to cast off exactly a human's worth of bodyweight, we should still sacrifice both dogs. Two lives instead of one. I can't believe anyone thinks that way in the twenty-first century."

I hoisted the last empty cage into the bow. The summer sun was peeking over the mangroves, promising a scorcher.

"I consider myself rather enlightened," I observed. "In some places, might I remind you, dogs are a delicacy." I unhooked the mooring line from the bollard and wrapped it around the cleats on the gunwale. "Now may I ask a question of my own?"

The girl looked up at me with distrust, her face a white sail beneath her bright orange mane. "What?"

"How exactly does a dog draw straws?" I asked.

She rolled her eyes. "Fuck off," she said.

We'd been paired together by the sheriff's office. When the National Guard helicopters plucked folks off rooftops—the numbskulls who'd ignored days of mandatory evacuation orders—they didn't have space for large house pets. Nothing bigger than a bicycle basket. Instead, the Guard officers marked the roofs over abandoned animals with a splash of pink chalk. Dumb idea, if you ask me: one downpour could have washed away the markings. Of course, nobody did ask me—and fortunately, we'd had two dry days behind the hurricane. But the dam was going to be out above Pelican City indefinitely, which meant Sucram's Grove was going to remain underwater indefinitely, so they'd called in the harbor service to begin retrieving dogs.

Hager County—I'm proud to say—has the only all-volunteer harbor services in Florida. Fifteen of us, total. I've been patrolling the coastal inlets nine years, and I'm still more or less a newcomer. Scallop Sally has been on the job since the Kennedy Administration. She even remembers when they built the causeway out to Cormorant Key. We each work a handful of shifts a week. In my other life, I teach marine biology and field ecology at the community college.

Anyway, as I was saying, the sheriff's office paired each of us with a rescuer from the ASPCA. I'd hit the jackpot where my partner was concerned, at least in the looks department. Stacy Lorimer was a first-year veterinary student at FSU, but she had the taut body of a professional athlete. It didn't hurt that redheads have always been my Achilles' heel—my ex-wife is People's Exhibit A in that department—and curls didn't come any redder or fuller than Stacy's.

The entire bay between Glade Estates and Sucram's Grove is technically a no wake zone—part of a laudable effort to conserve manatees—but the rule smacked me as ludicrous with the entire coast inundated to a depth of twenty feet, so I opened the throttle on the runabout. We cruised through the murky water, intermittently swerving to avoid flotsam. Shellfish traps. Dislodged buoys. Lots of plywood. In movies, floodwaters always team with toaster ovens and tea sets, but most remnants of civilization actually sink rather quickly.

As we sliced across what had until recently been Cormorant Bay, but was now a swath of sea indistinguishable from its surroundings, we passed an enormous, tattered white blanket. Closer up, I realized the blanket was a carpet of golf balls. Literally thousands of them. The country club to which they'd once belonged had gone the way of Atlantis. In the distance, the towers of Cormorant Key's causeway rose from the depths like the joists of a ramshackle pier. Overhead, herring gulls circled. The birds bawled raucously. They appeared disoriented.

My companion relaxed in the bow, her back against the parapet of plastic cages that formed our makeshift kennel. She ignored me. To add to my torment, she started lathering sun lotion along her pale, muscular calves.

Once we'd been on the water about twenty minutes, I unlocked the cooler and offered her a Diet Coke.

"Can we agree to disagree?" I hazarded. "I don't plan on jettisoning any dogs—or people—in the near future."

The girl yielded a grudging smile. "I give you credit," she said. "At least you're not afraid to argue with me. Lots of guys are afraid of me."

"Who says I'm not afraid of you?" I retrieved a second Diet Coke for myself. "I'm quaking in my boots."

"Bullshit," said Stacy. She braced the can of pop between her knees and stretched her arms above her head. "By the way, where exactly are we?"

"The Gulf of Mexico." If she didn't want me to be intimidated, I wouldn't let on that I was intimidated. "Say, you have a boyfriend?"

Don't get the wrong impression: I'm usually not so forward. In fact, I'm shy with women. But I guess something in the girl's attitude provoked me to false courage. Or maybe it was that we were trapped on the runabout, that she couldn't simply flee.

Stacy ignored my question. "Where in the Gulf of Mexico are we?"

"Was that a yes or a no?" I persisted.

"That was a 'whether I have a boyfriend or not is irrelevant to this conversation and to our assignment,' " she answered, but she was grinning. "So are you going to tell me where we are . . . or am I being kidnapped?"

I checked the GPS and the depth chart.

"Believe it or not," I replied, shocked myself at our coordinates, "You're crossing the runway of the Cormorant Key airstrip."

The entire island, it appeared, had submerged.

I shifted the rudder eastward and slowed the engine, afraid a hidden treetop might disembowel the runabout. Soon enough, the mansions of Sucram's Grove approached us—their upper stories levitating above the current. A sturgeon leaped from the surf only yards off the portside prow, then vanished beneath the sea. I plugged our first destination into the GPS and followed its guidance. We wove between the tufts of coconut palms toward the second floor of a colonial-style dwelling. Sure enough, a scar of pink chalk stained the corrugated roof. The storm had peeled away a jagged portion of the metal rooftop—exposing one corner of the structure to the elements.

I moored us to the frame of a dormer window.

"Bandit," Stacey read off a clipboard. "Siberian husky. Age five."

I radioed our location to the sheriff's command center. Then I hacked a path through the window and window frame with the poll of my axe.

"I've done my part, Miss Lorimer," I declared. "Now you do yours."

✳

Stacy recovered Bandit in a matter of minutes, but the majority of the animals proved far more elusive. Of our first seven targets, only two others—a brindled St. Bernard and a mahogany Rottweiler mutt—made it onto the runabout. Three dogs couldn't be located. I accompanied my partner through upper story windows in search for the missing creatures, but to no avail. Either the beasts had escaped or they had drowned. The last animal, an elderly retriever named Max, lay dead on his master's bed. But steadily, as the sun glowered toward its zenith, we filled our cages. Stacy displayed considerable finesse with the tranquilizer gun—far more precision than I could possibly have mustered with the .44 Magnum that I carried on my belt.

"I've got to hand it to you," I said after she'd taken down a pair canines in rapid succession across a stuffy, poorly lit parlor. "You're good at this."

"I know," she shot back. "You sound surprised."

"Jesus. I was paying you a compliment."

She eyed me warily. "In that case," she said, "I ought to say thank you."

"You're welcome," I answered. "Just don't let it go to your head."

We'd drawn abreast of one of the high-rise condominiums the hug the Sucram's Grove waterfront. The Blue Flamingo. Eight stories. When my ex-wife left me two years ago, she relocated to a nearly identical complex in Belleau Gardens—moved in with a fifty-four-year-old abdominal surgeon. The bastard had taken out my mother-in-law's gallbladder, for Christ's sake. But even without this personal baggage, I'd never been a fan of these outsized developments.

I counted windows: Only five of the floors remained above the waterline. Fortunately, the entire front façade of the structure had been fashioned from tinted glass, so it was easy enough to clear an entryway.

"I've got a dachshund in 2A and another Doberman in 6G," said Stacy.

I replaced the batteries in the flashlight and passed it back to her. "I'd recommend against visiting 2A."

"6G," my partner announced. "Here I come."

She clambered from the runabout into the third floor corridor and disappeared through the door to a nearby stairwell. I updated the sheriff's office regarding our status and hunkered down with a fishing magazine.

Several of the canines had shaken off their tranquilizers and barked furiously. A trio of military helicopters hovered in the distance; later, a speedboat darted past and the pilot honked a greeting on his air horn. He had no business in the area, which had been quarantined to prevent looting, but that wasn't my problem. Not today. After forty-five minutes—more to escape the yapping of the dogs than from genuine concern—I gave up on waiting and followed Stacy into the apartment complex.

None of our earlier endeavors had prepared me for the intense, toxic odor of the unventilated high rise—a brew of swamp and raw sewage. Only two days had elapsed since the storm, but the walls of the stairwell already sprouted mold. My flashlight provided a poor antidote to the darkness. I focused on breathing through my mouth; this didn't help much. On the sixth story, I gripped an earthenware pot containing a dieffenbachia and I vomited copiously. Then I wiped my mouth with a leaf.

Almost all of the doors on the sixth floor had been propped ajar, just as the occupants had been instructed to leave them. At least the numbskulls got that right. You shut doors for fires, open them for floods—to prevent surges in hydraulic pressure. Apartment 6G stood at the far end of the passageway, opposite the chute to the trash compacter. I entered cautiously. The windows in the living room caught the late morning sun and rendered my flashlight superfluous.

I did not find my partner in that main room, or in the kitchen, or in what appeared to be a painting studio, a chamber furnished with only one three-legged stool and an easel. I heard no barking. The calm struck me as disquieting, so I didn't call out Stacy's name. On guard, I advanced toward the sleeping quarters.

The waist-to-ceiling glass in the master bedroom afforded an expansive view of the coast as far north as Port Isabel. Sunlight streamed between gauze curtains, bathing the room in a pale pink glow. And there stood Stacy before the rosewood bureau, examining herself in the mirror. My partner held a pair of dazzling silver-and-gemstone earrings to her earlobes.

"Don't let me interrupt," I said.

The girl's shoulder's jerked. "You scared the shit out of me."

She thrust the earrings into a jewelry box on the dresser.

"I couldn't find the Doberman," she stammered. "I got distracted . . ."

"I'm sure you did," I replied. "Don't stop playing dress up on my account."

The girl's expression tightened. "I wasn't . . ."

"It's okay. They look good on you."

Stacy slammed shut the jewelry box. "Whatever," she snapped. "Let's get away from here before I pass out."

She retreated as far as the cusp of the passageway, where a pantry opened onto the foyer, then stopped abruptly and inched her way back into the room. At the far end of the corridor stood a colossal raccoon. Sunlight glinted off his onyx eyes. Foam spumed between his perilous jaws. The creature staggered forward—two steps—as though drunk. I'd never seen a mad animal before, but I instantly sensed this beast suffered far more than dehydration.

"Shoot it," ordered Stacy—her soft voice as authoritative as a scream.

"Are you sure?"

"Shoot it, dammit," she commanded again. "Now!"

I drew my weapon and glanced toward her for reassurance. Every muscle in her tense face urged me to immediate action. And suddenly, as my shoulder jolted from the recoil, a series of angry pops ricocheted through the apartment—like bottles of warm champagne uncorking—and the raccoon collapsed onto its side. For several seconds, we both stared at the dead animal in mute shock. My entire body was shaking.

"Nice job," Stacy finally said. "You're good at this."

That broke the tension. "I'll take that as a compliment," I said.

"You should."

The girl approached the raccoon's corpse, prodded it with her boot. "Keep alert for bats," she cautioned. "Rabies doesn't come from nowhere."

"I didn't think you believed in killing animals," I ventured.

The girl shook her head. "I'm opposed to speciesism," she said—with no hint of irony. "That doesn't mean I'm a martyr."

"I see," I said. Frankly, I didn't.

My partner stepped around the raccoon's remains and I trailed her out of the apartment. In the corridor, we switched places, and I led the way with the flashlight.

"So now will you tell me if you have a boyfriend?" I asked.

"Maybe."

"Maybe you have a boyfriend?"

"Maybe I'll tell you," she said, laughing. "Maybe not."

※

Our encounter with the mad raccoon left me on edge, but Stacy actually seemed more at ease after the shooting. She told me about her ongoing conflict with her parents, how she'd transferred from medical school to veterinary school over their objections. "I've got nothing against people," she elaborated. "Okay, that's not exactly true. I have lots of problems with human beings, but that's not why I quit med school. It's just that I love working with animals in the clinic . . . and I never felt that way in the hospital." Since her parents were refusing to pay to educate a vet, she'd had to work fulltime as a cocktail waitress in Tallahassee—on top of her school schedule—to pay for tuition. While the girl spoke, she served beef kibble to our boisterous menagerie. She'd perspired straight through her cotton top.

I discovered that Stacy's family, like mine, had settled in Hager County long before the influx of snowbirds. Her great-grandfather had been the official state naturalist in the 1920s. Her father practiced dentistry in Fort Francis. Except for my time at Yale, and a brief summer gig in Alaska, I'd lived in jogging distance of Port Isabel my entire life. I also learned that her mother's baby sister had been murdered by the Red Ribbon Stranger in the 1960s, that this tragedy had colored every aspect of Stacy's childhood. I still didn't know for sure that she was single.

We tied up for lunch outside a residence on Nautilus Avenue where the owners had abandoned three mastiff puppies. They'd also freed their bright-green military macaw, but the creature remained perched atop a window gable. Stacy made an admirable attempt to retrieve the bird. She even considered a tranquilizer dart, before deciding it wasn't worth the risk.

Our next stop was a bungalow inside a gated retirement community, yet when we arrived, we found another harbor patrol officer and his ASPCA partner already on the scene. Some idiot had included the same address on both our lists. But the encounter proved educational: I found out how lucky I was that I'd been paired with Stacy Lorimer, and not Chet Picardo's assistant, a grizzled fifty-something battleaxe as burly as an ox who criticized his every blink. We traded Chet a pair of cheese sandwiches for a bag of pretzels, then left him to his misery.

"That was easy enough," declared my partner. "Only nine addresses to go."

I was starting to feel more confident about my prospects with Stacy. I even dropped my ex-wife's name into the conversation—letting the girl know that I was only thirty-three, and unattached. My mind had already advanced to the practical aspects of romance, such as where I might take her for dinner, when Stacy climbed onto the runabout with her bare arms full of fur. Ten flawlessly round eyes gazed up at me.

"What on earth are those?"

"Opossums," Stacy replied, matter-of-fact. "Cubs. Aren't they adorable?"

To me, they looked like obese guinea pigs. I watched in alarm as she set them down on the aluminum floor of the runabout. It dawned on me that my partner actually planned to keep these creatures.

"I do hope you realize we can't bring those back with us."

She appeared genuinely surprised. "Why not?"

"Because I don't want to get fired," I answered. "What if those things carry disease and someone's dog gets infected? Or if they turn out to be an endangered subspecies that we've plucked from its habitat? No way. I have strict orders from the sheriff's department: Domesticated animals only."

"You can't mean that," cried Stacy. "They'll die."

I felt like a jerk. Truly, I did. But two years ago, Alan Steinhoff helped a pair of fisherman bring in a wounded dolphin for first aid—and he got suspended six months on charges of "interfering with protected wilderness." So I'm not taking risks. Certainly not for glorified hamsters. "I do mean that," I said. "I'm sorry. But there's a good chance they'll send a television crew to cover our return, and the last thing I need is some angry pet owner asking why we couldn't find his schnauzer, but we managed to pick up a sack full of rodents."

"They're not rodents," retorted Stacy. "They're marsupials."

She had pushed the wrong button. "I'm well aware of that," I said in my driest tone. "The Virginia opossum. Didelphis virginiana. Order: Didelphimorphia. Family: Didelphidae. I know an awful lot about opossums, since you ask. Including one more thing than you do. Do you want to know what that is?"

"What?"

"That they're not welcome on our boat."

Her nostrils flared. "Says who?"

"Says me. Your captain. I hate to pull rank, but I am in charge here, and as much as I genuinely like you, I like working for the harbor patrol more."

The words sounded more domineering than I'd intended. Stacey sat with her arms folded across her heaving chest and glared at me. The sun-black beneath her eyes menaced like war paint. "Why can't we hide them? Nobody will ever know."

"And get caught smuggling? Because they would catch us," I said. "Look, I have no choice in the matter. Please don't make me out to be the bad guy here. I'm all for breaking rules, when you can away with it, but trust me on this one: My boss will go through the ceiling if we bring those things back." I sensed my explanation wasn't gaining traction, so I added, "Maybe they'll do okay on their own."

"They're going to die out here. Of starvation. Or dehydration. Or some predator will carve them up before that—if they're lucky. I wish I had more nerve, so I could drown them right now to save them from the torment."

"We could leave them some food and water," I offered.

"Fuck that. We could leave you some food and water."

Stacy stood up abruptly. "They're not things, by the way. They're very much alive." She scooped up the first cub and pushed it back through the broken window, into the dark interior of the decaying house. "And you're a total asshole."

※

Any camaraderie between us was lost after that. We navigated from house to house, rescuing animals—and Stacy uttered not one syllable more that was absolutely essential to complete our mission. At one point, I even suggested cutting short the workday, that I'd return on my own the next morning to pick up the final few dogs. She didn't acknowledge my offer. Never—not even in the bitterest days of my divorce saga—had I ever been the object of such hostility. I started second-guessing myself: Was my refusal so unforgivable? Had I gone too far with all that bullshit about pulling rank? I regretted the way I'd handled things, although not the underlying decision to abandon the opossums. What I regretted most of all was that Stacy had found the damn creatures in the first place. How many relationships—how many potentially happy marriages—got slaughtered at birth by a dash of bad luck?

By the time we'd crossed the final missing pet off the list, a Bernese mountain dog with a broken paw encased in a soiled fiberglass cast, the sun was already dipping toward the mangroves. Even our live cargo had been silenced by that relentless combination of heat and exhaustion. In the cloudless sky, a lone turkey buzzard glided in ominous circles.

"All done," I announced—recording the final animal's capture in the log. "Fourteen out of twenty-seven. Not bad for a day's work."

Stacy wore a stark frown. "We can still go back for the possum cubs," she suggested. "It's not too late. If we're lucky."

"We're returning to port," I answered.

She turned away. "I don't know how you live with yourself."

I drew the rudder starboard and the runabout circled toward land. I recognized that one more unpleasant task still lay ahead of me before the journey was done—but I despised myself for having to do it. For the first time in years, since I'd quit in my twenties, I found myself craving a cigarette.

"I have to ask you to do one more thing," I said. "I'm sorry about this too."

Her gaze locked on mine, but she didn't speak.

"Please empty your pockets."

The poor girl looked as though I'd stabbed her. "What the fuck?"

"It's nothing personal," I said. "Just do it."

Now her expression grew as ferocious as the rabid raccoon's, but I also detected a hint of fear in her eyes. "Not in ten million years."

I stood up and crossed the deck.

"You touch me," she threatened, "I'll have your ass in jail for rape."

The smart choice would have been to wait until we reached port— to have a female officer search her in the presence of witnesses. But I genuinely liked the girl—enough to venture a senseless risk. Besides, I felt awful about the opossums.

The entire maneuver took under a second: I wrapped one hand around her waist and thrust the other into her shorts, turning the pocket inside out and grasping its contents all in one violent motion. The girl screamed. A smattering of rings and chains clattered to the floor of the runabout. Also a billfold of hundred dollar bills.

I showed her what remained in my palm: ruby earrings, pearls, a gold watch attached to a chain. She flashed me a look of sheer hatred. I deposited the booty on the lid of the cooler and waited for her to speak.

"Okay, now what?" she asked. "Are you going to turn me in?"

"Don't be stupid. But I am going to make us take those back. I do hope you know what came from where," I explained. "Don't you think people would notice when they came home and their valuables were missing? And that the only people with missing valuables were the ones who'd left behind dogs?" I sat down opposite the girl on a wooden storage crate, our bodies only inches apart. I let the runabout drift aimlessly on the tide. "You're just lucky the sheriff's dispatcher is an old buddy of mine. I'll tell him I accidentally left behind my lucky rabbit's foot. He'll know that I'm up to something—but he's not going to ask any questions."

"I guess I'm supposed to thank you now." Stacy didn't look the slightest bit appreciative. "For keeping me out of jail."

"No need," I answered. "But what you can do is come by my apartment tomorrow morning at three am . . ."

"Like hell I will."

"Three o'clock, sharp," I continued. "That's what time I'm going to have to leave to pick up those damn rodents of yours. If I get out and back before dawn, I might just not get noticed."

She looked puzzled at first, then doubtful. "For real?"

"For real," I answered. "I like my job with the harbor patrol . . . but I honestly think I might like you more. Good enough?"

"Maybe," she said.

Her face was close to mine now—her lips chapped yet perfect.

"That's all I get. Maybe?"

"It's better than maybe not, isn't it?" she asked.

I admitted that it was. A lot better.

"Three o'clock, sharp," she agreed. "Good enough."

Then she leaned forward and we sealed the bargain.

THE PRICE OF STORKS

HE TROUBLE BEGAN when the Flightless Nun decided we weren't storks.

Steinhoff had dubbed her the Flightless Nun because she was the first Federal Aviation Administrator without a pilot's license, but it didn't hurt that the chinless old wench looked like an extra from Lilies of the Field. Do I sound hostile? Well, we'd been assured by both the Safe Passage folks and by the Fish & Wildlife people that approval for the stork run, officially called a "coaxed migration," needed only rubberstamping—that this was no different from last October's expedition, when we led the whooping cranes from Wisconsin to Florida. Then the new administration took office, and the Flightless Nun branded us a commercial enterprise, because Steinhoff and I were getting reimbursed to guide the storks north to Manitoba. Suddenly, we found ourselves subject to volumes of regulations—regs we couldn't possibly obey if we ever hoped to convince eight juvenile carmine-crested storks that our ultra-light aircrafts were their parents. So that, in a bird's egg, is how we ended up stranded at a motel outside of Bontea, Mexico—thirty miles southwest of Matamoros—when Steinhoff burst an aneurysm and required evacuation to Brownsville.

I figured that with my partner out of commission, they'd postpone this year's run and let the storks summer south of the border. Reintroduction is a long term project, after all—a matter of generations, not seasons. To my amazement, the Washington office of Safe Passage phoned within hours of Steinhoff's departure, promising they'd have a replacement pilot on the ground by the end of the week. I'll admit I was none too thrilled. Carl Steinhoff and I had been conducting wildlife flights together for nearly a decade—first nature photography, then conservation work—and adjusting to another flyer's style takes both time and trust. Besides, we'd been studying the damn birds all winter: mastering their technique, memorizing their idiosyncrasies. I didn't see how a newcomer could just swoop in and expect to fill Steinhoff's shoes. Yet my job was to mimic storks, not to make personnel decisions, so I kept up with daily maneuvers at the wildlife preserve, alternating between Steinhoff's plane and my own, escorting our avian offspring to and fro across the salt flats. I'd just returned from one of these workouts, dust clad and sunblind, when a jeep pulled into the hangar. The driver, a redheaded girl in her twenties, sported reflective sunglasses. Her jaw was too square to be pretty.

"Can I help you?" I asked. "This is a private airstrip."

"Glad to meet you too," she replied. "You're Jack Leppa, aren't you?"

I didn't relish a stranger knowing my name, especially in Mexico, and I reached into my pocket for my jackknife. "Do you want something?"

The girl stepped from the vehicle and offered me her gloved hand. "Stacy Sulcram," she introduced herself. "I'm your new partner."

I hadn't anticipated a woman. It's not that I have anything against female pilots, it's just that a woman creates a different dynamic—a temptation—and, at thirty-nine, I've come to recognize that temptation is a synonym for trouble. Besides, I was already paying alimony to one ginger-haired aviatrix. Yet, like I said, I'd been hired to imitate storks, not manage human resources, so I showed the girl our planes—two retrofitted Messerschmitt phantoms—and then drove her out to a limestone bluff overlooking the bird sanctuary. The air stank of brine and rotting vegetation. A warm wind rippled the bulrushes. In the distance, eight crimson tufts glistened atop a sandbar.

"So what do you know about storks?" I asked.

I figured she'd claim more expertise than she actually had—and honestly, I was looking for an opportunity to put the girl in her place.

"Less than nothing," she replied.

"That's not very much."

"I don't know very much and I don't care very much," she said. "What I do know is that I need money for school, and playing 'mama duck' for a few weeks is a lot safer than doing stunts for air shows." Stacy stepped toward the edge of the bluff, so near I feared that she might fall. "I come from a family of stunt pilots. My father and both my brothers performed on the air show circuit for years. That's what got them killed."

"I'm sorry," I said.

The name Sucram suddenly registered. I recalled reading a newspaper story about a fatal mid-air collision while we were up in Wisconsin.

"Not as sorry as I am."

Stacy turned on her heels and hiked back to my pickup. I followed. She didn't speak again until we were en route to the motel.

"You're wondering how Safe Passage found me, aren't you?" she asked. "The short answer is there are lots of people who can pilot a light plane, and there are lots of people who can drop their lives on a moment's notice and fly off to Mexico, but there aren't very many people who meet both of those qualifications." She laughed—but hers was laughter utterly devoid of joy. "Except me," she added. "So here I am."

"Well, I'm glad you're here."

"I highly doubt that," she said. "But thanks for pretending."

❋

In the morning, we took to the skies. Any doubts that I harbored about the girl's piloting abilities burned off with the Mexican sun: Stacy had the birds trailing her across the salt flats within minutes, and when we switched places, so that I led the flock and she rearguarded, she rounded up stray storks faster than a herding dog could corral sheep. Skills that had taken Steinhoff months of painstaking effort to acquire, his replacement mastered before lunchtime. Unfortunately, nothing on God's green earth is more attractive than a gifted aviatrix, so when we called it quits for the day, and ducked into the dimly-lit roadhouse opposite the motel, I hardly even noticed Stacy's square jaw anymore. We settled into a corner table and I ordered us a round of Pacíficos. On the juke box, a female singer covered Elvis's "All Shook Up" in Spanish.

"That was some rather impressive maneuvering," I said. "You're good."

"You sound surprised."

"I am surprised."

A waitress too old for her tight-fitting outfit served us the beers. We raised our bottles in a toast and I savored the cold brew. Stacy flashed me a smile.

"You and your partner were close, weren't you?" she asked.

"You could say that," I replied. "He's married to my sister."

"I didn't know." She sipped her beer. "Is he going to be okay?"

"Okay is a relative term. He's going to live." I'd been holding the phone away from my ear when my sister described the extent of Carl's brain damage. "Let's talk about something else. Something cheerful."

"Sorry," said Stacy. "Cheerful isn't my strong suit."

Nor mine, I thought to myself. Nor mine. I said nothing. We sat in silence, enjoying each other's presence, paying joint homage to the sad state of the world. The Spanish version of "Dock of the Bay" pulsed in the background.

Our waitress approached, but instead of clearing our bottles, as I'd expected, the woman pulled a stool up alongside our table and seated herself. She had obviously been beautiful once—her high cheekbones and delicate chin still visible under her weathered skin. "You're the man flying the bird plane?" she asked.

"Maybe," I said. "You have birds that need flying?"

The waitress surveyed the busy saloon. "Not birds," she said in a hushed voice. "But my friend has other things that need flying. You take his cargo with you when you fly across the border and he'll pay you cash. You understand?"

"Not interested," I replied. "We fly birds. Nothing else."

"Fifty thousand dollars," whispered the waitress. "American dollars."

We'd been in Mexico only four months, but already six different dealers had offered me ready money to ferry cocaine over the border. Compared to the other proposals, fifty thousand greenbacks was chicken change.

"We're not interested," I said again—louder.

The waitress shrugged and stood up.

"If you change your mind," she said, "you ask for Erendira."

"We won't be changing our minds."

Stacy had watched the entire encounter with a look of detached amusement. When we were alone again, she said, "Fifty grand is a lot of fucking money."

"Blood money," I snapped. I leaned forward with my elbows on the wooden tabletop. "I've got nothing against drugs," I explained. "I'm not even averse to taking risks. If it were just me, who the hell knows what I'd do. But I've got those birds to think of. It would be the birds' lives I'd be gambling with, and I can't do that."

"You're serious?"

"Dead serious," I answered. "Because I do care about storks. And do you know how many carmine-crested storks there are in the world?"

"Not many?"

"Fifteen. So that means more than half of all the carmine-crested storks on the entire planet are my personal responsibility. Our personal responsibility. How can you not find that awe-inspiring?"

Stacy grinned. "You are one weird dude, Jack Leppa," she said—and she wrapped her small warm hands around mine.

I hadn't always cared about birds. For the first twenty-five years of my life, I didn't care much about anything. My story is none too unusual: army brat, ROTC, four years flying refueling tankers for the Air Force. Then some pen pusher noses around in my personnel file and discovers that I minored in photography at Dartmouth, and since the USAF is short on photographers, I'm swiftly dispatched to catalogue the flora and fauna of an obscure atoll in the Indian Ocean—before the military blows the place to smithereens. So there I was, landing my puddle-jumper on turquoise lagoons, snapping pictures of flamingos and ibises that would soon serve as artillery fodder, and one of the gears in my brain hit a snag. Six months and countless nights of soul-searching later, I resigned my commission and joined Steinhoff's charter outfit, offering aerial tours of the Everglades and Dry Tortugas. We made a go of it for seven years, then went belly-up in the recession and signed on with the Safe Harbor folks.

Nobody's going to get rich flying coaxed migrations, of course. But it was steady money, season after season, until the Flightless Nun got her wimple in a twist. I shared my frustrations with Stacy one torrid afternoon—two weeks after her arrival, nine days after we started sleeping together—while we were performing some routine maintenance on the Messerschmitts. Or rather, Stacy was performing the maintenance, and I was handing her tools.

"It's a goddam mess inside here," she said—looking up from under the engine box. "You've literally got gauges hanging from paperclips. How you haven't fallen out of the sky yet is completely beyond me."

"We don't always do it pretty, miss know-it-all, but we get the job done," I answered. "We haven't fallen out of the sky yet."

"Dumb luck," she said.

"Just remember that if you ever do think you're going to fall out of the sky," I added, "make sure you fall far away from the storks."

Stacy rolled her eyes.

She climbed down the ladder and wiped her gloves on her overalls. We were laboring at the western fringe of the airstrip, where the local gentry housed their Cessnas and Learjets, taking advantage of the breeze off the hills. She hoisted herself onto the hood of her jeep and lit a cigarette. "What are you looking forward to?" she asked.

"Getting out of here," I said. "What else?"

"I mean in the grand scheme of things," she said. "What's your long term plan?"

"I don't have a clue," I replied—which was the truth. "What's that sense of making long term plans when you might burst an aneurysm at forty-two?"

Stacy lit a match and watched it burn toward her fingertips. "I figured you'd say that," she said. "Do you know what I'm looking forward to?"

"What?"

"Not flying airplanes."

"You're serious?"

"Couldn't be more serious," she said. "Just because I'm good at something doesn't mean I have to like doing it. I heard a story on the radio about this famous Portuguese folk musician—she plays the fiddle or the ukulele or something like that—and she's great at it—the best in all of Portugal—but she doesn't like doing it anymore. What she really wants to do is become a puppeteer, but she feels she has a moral duty to keep playing her instrument." Stacy tossed the match to the dust. "A moral duty! I think that's crazy. I want to make sure I don't end up like her."

"So what do you want to do?"

"Go back to college. Maybe become a kindergarten teacher or an elementary school librarian—something safe and fun and involving children." Stacy's features hardened. "You're disappointed in me, aren't you?"

"Not at all."

"Yes, you are. I can tell."

An Ikarus C42 passed overhead, its propellers roaring through the midday heat.

"It's just that you're such a gifted pilot," I said.

"And you wouldn't want me to waste my talents," continued Stacy, finishing my thought for me—although in harsher words that I might have chosen. "Can I ask you something personal?"

"Anything."

"How far would do go to protect those storks?"

I sensed a trap. "Pretty far."

"Would you kill another human being?" asked Stacy. She took a deep drag on her cigarette, then stubbed the butt out on her boot heel. "I guess what I'm asking is: If you had to choose between a human life—the life of a total stranger—and an entire species of birds, which would you choose?"

"I suppose that is the sixty-four trillion dollar question," I said.

She refused to back down. "And what's the sixty-four trillion dollar answer?"

I dabbed my forehead with my bandanna. On the horizon, low dusty clouds melted into the low dusty hills of Nuevo León. My sanity sustained itself, I had come to recognize, because I no longer entertained those sorts of all-encompassing questions. It's much easier to maintain a happy, functional existence patching up flight instruments with paperclips and pipe cleaners.

"I don't know. Honestly, I'd probably save the birds," I said—selecting each word with care. "I don't like strangers."

"You are predictable," said Stacy. "I'll give you that."

"If I'm so predictable, why did you bother to ask?"

"To be certain," the girl replied. A strangely tender, yielding expression played across her strong features. "I'm trying to decide how serious I am about you, Jack Leppa, so I want to know exactly what I'm dealing with."

We packed it in early that afternoon, and after a dinner of microwaved pizza and boxed Chianti, we made love until the couple in the adjoining motel room banged on the walls for us to keep down the noise. But in the morning, Stacy insisted on returning to her own room to shower and dress. As I washed out our plastic wine glasses, I found myself hoping the Flightless Nun wouldn't hurry to rule on our appeal.

The call from Washington came three days later. It turned out that the Flightless Nun had been enjoying an extramarital affair with a senior Boeing executive, a conflict of interest she had neglected to mention during her confirmation hearings. Her temporary replacement, a career bureaucrat, belonged to the same Audubon Society chapter as the executive director of Safe Passage—which meant our Messerschmitts were once again below the agency's radar screen. To celebrate our impending emancipation, I took Stacy out to El Conejo Ciego, Bontea's only restaurant. The proprietors, an elderly Lebanese couple, served up simple Mexican fare in a sheltered adobe courtyard whose walls displayed black-and-white photographs of pre-Civil War Beirut.

At first, Stacy and I discussed logistical matters—refueling parameters, altitude markers, the quirks of the various landing strips on our flight path. Inevitably, after the owners lit the courtyard's candelabras, our conversation turned personal.

"So what does this mean?" asked Stacy. "For us?"

I nursed my sherry. "Does it have to mean something?"

"I don't like uncertainty," she replied. Her pale skin glowed in the flickering candlelight. "We're going to be in Manitoba in three weeks. What then?"

"I don't know," I said.

"Well, you have to know."

A mustached waiter began to serenade the young couple at the adjacent table on his accordion. I reached over our dessert plates and caressed Stacy's cheek. She held my palm to her skin for a moment, then lowered my hand to the tablecloth.

"Up until a month ago," said Stacy, "when I thought of storks, I thought of babies. That's what storks mean to 99% of the people in the world. But now I can't help feeling as though those damn storks are what's standing in the way of us having a normal life together, of us having a family someday." A note of anger whetted her voice. "Do you remember how you said you might sacrifice a stranger's life to save those birds? Well, what if I asked you to sacrifice the birds for my sake?"

Her salvo had caught me entirely off guard. Up until that evening, I'd given no consideration to having children with Stacy—or with anybody else—anytime soon.

"Are you asking if I'd let the birds die to save your life?" I asked. "You shouldn't even have to ask that. Of course, I would."

"That's not what I'm asking, Jack," she answered. "I'm not asking if you'd sacrifice the storks to save my life. I'm asking if you'd sacrifice the storks because I wanted you to—because it was important to me."

"Why would it be important to you?"

"That's so not the point," Stacy snapped. "Even if it wasn't important to me. Maybe on a whim—just because I asked you to. Would you sacrifice the storks because the woman you're in love with is tired of them?"

"I couldn't do that," I said. "You know I couldn't."

In the silence that followed, the mustached waiter approached our table with his instrument, and I shooed him away with a two hundred peso note. Overhead, a pair of barn swallows darted between the rafters. Suddenly, we found ourselves with surprisingly little to say.

I paid the tab in traveler's checks and escorted Stacy out to the pickup. The low cloud cover of the afternoon had given way to a star-soaked desert night. Moonlight bathed the gravel parking lot.

"I do love you," I said. "Very much."

Stacy nodded. "I know. I love you too," she echoed—but in a tone that made her love seem utterly inconsequential. "Right now, I need a long walk to clear my head. Can you drop me at the airstrip?"

"I'll come with you," I offered. "It's safer that way."

My concern was grounded in experience. In Nuevo León, the only women who ventured out alone after dusk were prostitutes.

"I'll be fine," insisted Stacy. "Really."

"But I—"

"I've survived twenty-eight years without your protection," she snapped. "Now drop me off at the goddam airstrip, okay?"

So I did as commanded. We cruised through downtown Bontea— a shabby strip of bars and filling stations and more bars—then descended toward the coast plain. Our high beams proved no match for the pitch darkness, so it demanded all of my focus to avoid the jack rabbits and mule deer that periodically darted across the highway. When we finally arrived at the hangar, Stacy's anger appeared to have softened.

"I'll be absolutely fine. I promise," she said. "I have my phone."

She leaned across the gear shift and pecked me on the cheek.

"Don't wait up for me," she said. "I'm sure this too shall pass—that everything will make more sense in the morning. I'll see you in the lobby at eight, okay?"

I didn't feel at all okay. In fact, the fear crossed my mind that I might never see Stacy Sucram alive again—that I would be called the next morning to identify a naked body plucked from a ravine. But as Stacy's form faded into the shadows, I made no effort to chase after her. Long ago, I'd learned that women—at least the sort of women that I end up falling for—always get their way in the end.

※

I entered the motel lobby the next morning, fearing the worst. Instead, I found Stacy seated calmly in the breakfast alcove, snacking on a complimentary cheese danish. She had braided her hair into a ponytail that peeked from under her Boston Braves cap. On the chair beside her sat a bulging carpet bag. Stacy took a swig of coffee, wiped her lips on a napkin, and then greeted me with a ferocious hug. An equally fierce and passionate kiss ensued.

"What did I do to deserve that?" I asked.

"I told you I'd feel better in the morning," she said—her eyes practically twinkling. "Besides, I've made a decision."

"Have you?" I asked tentatively.

"Yes, I have, Jack Leppa," she announced. "I've decided not to wait for you to figure your life out. I'm going to make plans of my own. It's entirely up to you whether you want to be part of them."

"Fair enough," I said.

I kissed Stacy again. I wasn't sure what to make of her newly asserted independence—didn't know whether I felt liberated or threatened. I ran my lips along her neck and into her cleavage. She laughed as she pushed me away.

"Neither the time nor the place," said Stacy. "You shouldn't be thinking about anything except baby storks until we're on the ground in Texas."

"Slave driver," I quipped—slapping her playfully on the caboose.

We rode our separate vehicles out to the airstrip and left them in the hangar, keys beneath the floor mats, as we had arranged. The manager of the wildlife preserve and his nephew were to return them to Ciudad Victoria later that afternoon. Then we revved up the Messerschmitts and launched into the clear morning sky. To our west rose the unforgiving foothills of Nuevo León. On the eastern horizon, the white sun glistened off the Gulf of Mexico. Immediately below us, the town of Bontea rested like a concrete lily pad among the swamps and salt flats.

I was already several hundred meters above the airstrip when I noticed Stacy's phantom struggling to maintain altitude—lilting to the left, as though its weight were distributed unevenly. Eventually, my partner managed to level off and drew her plane up alongside my left flank. I threw her a puzzled look, but she just shrugged. Then she flashed me a thumbs up, grinning broadly, to reassure me that everything was in order.

"What was that?" I radioed.

"Carpet bag," she answered. "I knew I'd over-packed. Now turn that radio off, okay, before you scare away the baby storks."

"Yes, boss," I agreed.

I returned the radio to the dashboard and adjusted my goggles. The distinctive crimson tufts were easy to spot on the salt flats below. I circled at two hundred meters while Stacy initiated her descent. Like magic, when her Messerschmitt was only fifty feet or so above the sand bar, the birds below spread their majestic wings. One by one, as we'd practiced, the carmine-crested storks followed their 'mama duck' aloft. And then—without warning—Stacy's aircraft lurched to the left and went into freefall.

Her plane made impact about fifty meters up the flats from where she'd first collected the storks. Smoke rose from the aircraft's rear engine. It was only a matter of time, I knew, before the fuel stores caught fire. The rare birds, oblivious to the danger, settled again on the nearby sand.

I didn't have any other choice but to touch down on the same islet, hoping the creatures would scatter at my approach. Most did. But one of the birds got its wings tangled in the landing gear. I found myself racing toward Stacy across a landscape of mud and blood and feathers. And then the coarse sand turned to fine white powder: Stacy's Messerschmitt had left a trail of cocaine.

I reached Stacy's plane just as she scrambled down from the cockpit. Blood trickled down her forehead; an actual bone protruded through the flesh above her left wrist. All around us, the air smelled pungently of aviation fuel. I scooped up Stacy's tiny body in my arms and carried her along the sandbar, eventually sinking to my knees about two hundred feet from the burning plane. She had lost consciousness—and I focused all of my energy on transporting her back to my Messerschmitt, hoping against hope that I might yet dislodge the aircraft from the mud.

As I mustered my strength for a final effort, one of the surviving storks staggered toward us. A large gash crossed the bird's distorted face, bisecting an eye, so the creature appeared to be navigating entirely with the other. At first, the stork appeared content to watch us. But then it took a poke at Stacy's wounded wrist with its beak—and I punched the creature repeatedly in the head, until its neck cracked. Until that moment, I'd never realized that I was capable of such force.

EMUS FOREVER

CHERYL HAD AGREED to babysit a quartet of emus. The emus belonged to her sister, Layne, who also owned 500+ pristine acres along the Hudson south of Albany, and whose celebrated husband—my prospective brother-in-law, Adrian—had been asked to design a carbon-neutral ski resort in Chamonix. "Absolutely not," I said. Then: "We're city people." Then: "Emu allergies run in my family." Then: "Is Mr. Architecture too cheap to hire professionals?"

"I don't want him to hire professionals," said Cheryl. "I *want* to do it. I want *us* to do it. *Together*. Once you see the place, you'll fall in love."

We'd gone to Robustelli's to celebrate the anniversary of our blind date—our first year together, which my father quipped was always the shortest. I'd sozzled myself with cheesecake. "You can catch diseases from emus. Don't they carry bubonic plague in their fur?"

Cheryl laughed. "You're too much," she said. "They're *birds*. Like ostriches." She reached across the tablecloth and squeezed my hand. "You're thinking of alpacas."

She was right. I *had* been thinking of alpacas. Nevertheless . . .

"What's keeping you here anyway?" she asked. "You're always griping that math and Manhattan are incompatible. Why not do your conjecturing in the fresh air?"

My girlfriend was referring to the Hodge conjecture, a lingering problem in algebraic topography that had been the subject of my doctoral dissertation. Solving it would more or less have guaranteed tenure, as well as a six-figure reward from the Clay Institute. Cheryl, who taught pre-calculus at Brearley, got good mileage out of mocking my efforts.

"Griping? Is *that* what I do?" I replied. But I was grinning now too, because it was clear the matter had already been decided—that my protestations were merely for effect.

"When you're not grumbling or complaining," said Cheryl. "You need to have fun for a change. Maybe a hayride. Or some skinny-dipping . . ."

"I'll have you know my mother's mother *died* of emu allergies," I said. "Anaphylaxis. *From a fur coat.* And let me tell you—it was not the slightest bit emusing."

"You'll love it," said Cheryl. "Just don't let them kick you."

Six weeks later we drove up to Columbia County, valises piled high in the back of the well-used Oldsmobile I'd purchased off a dead colleague's son—a bargain struck by chance in the parking lot of the mortuary. (I also agreed to take the contents of Professor Abramowitz's office off the guy's hands, so in addition to Cheryl's easel and cartons of paperback novels, our trunk contained milk crates of vintage 78s and LPs: Perry Como, Johnny Mercer, Rosemary Clooney in the cast album of *The Stars are Singing*.) Layne welcomed us with a pointed glance at her watch, even though we'd hardly run twenty minutes late, and immediately led us through the orchard and over the footbridge to the emu compound. Didn't even offer us a drink. Or a thank you. She'd already loaded her Mercedes, shipped her boys away to baseball camp in the Berkshires. "I'm going to drive down to meet Adrian tonight," she announced. "That will give us twenty-four hours to paint the city crimson before we jet off to Mont Blanc." She sported one of those loose-fitting designer travel suits that looks casual, but probably cost more than my entire wardrobe—an absurd outfit for a woman under forty, especially a one-time sociology major from Vassar.

"So here's the deal," said Layne. "Emus are half-toddlers and half-teenagers. Your job is to keep them fed and to keep them out of trouble."

She plugged a combination into a padlock and unfastened the door to the birds' pen—a spacious, grassy enclosure with shaded stalls and mesh walls fifteen feet high. Its avian inhabitants huddled in the far corner, preening and grunting, under a white-blossomed tree that might, or might not, have been a hawthorn. Impressive creatures, I'll concede—even if the trajectories of their long necks and tapered beaks reminded me of antique fountain pens. "You'll have to feed them every morning, but don't worry if they aren't consuming much water," said Layne, strewing ratite fodder and cracked corn from a burlap sack. "They tend to binge drink. Like frat boys."

Cheryl stepped toward the birds, but Layne held her back. "Let me go first," she warned. "Gaudí is in a kickboxing mood this week. More toddler than teen."

The other three emus were named Saarinen, Frank Lloyd Wright and I. M. Pei—although Wright and Pei had turned out to be female. My renowned would-be brother-in-law, I thought. Pretentious fuck. The only purpose of pet emus, it struck me, was to tell people, other pretentious people at pretentious parties, that you owned them. Basically, a status symbol for leftist dilettantes, the progressive version of buying a Picasso or a thoroughbred.

"Do they have a curfew?" I asked.

Layne glowered at me. "You will *never*—I repeat, *never*—let the birds out of the enclosure," she said. "That's what the coyotes are waiting for . . ."

"Is that a warning," I whispered to Cheryl, "or a challenge?"

My girlfriend slapped my shoulder. Layne stooped to pet the nearest bird—Frank Lloyd Wright—who cozied up to her caress. "These are my babies, my extended family," she said. "I'm counting on you to treat them like you would my kids."

"Got that, Cheryl?" I said. "We have to find a baseball camp that takes emus."

Layne sighed and shook her head. "Where do you find these guys, sis?"

Then she told us how to contact the veterinarian—an authority on Casuariiformes affiliated with both Cornell and the Bronx Zoo—and, with an air kiss on either of Cheryl's cheeks, she vanished Alps-ward and left us alone with our brood.

Our first few days in the country proved uneventful. Cheryl set up her easel on the sundeck and captured bucolic scenes of the river below. She accompanied me to the farmer's market in Austerlitz one afternoon, and also on a guided tour of a Dutch colonial mansion, but she was perfectly content to paint and sip sweet tea, and when she grew tired of watercolors, to escape into the formal Italian garden to read her airport novel on a chaise lounge. Meanwhile, I installed myself in the oak-paneled library and knuckled down to my labors, surrounding myself with Chow groups and Kähler varieties in a veritable orgy of topological cohomology. We took turns tending to the emus: strewing the feed, filling the water troughs, conducting headcounts at daybreak and dusk. Not exactly rocket science. Twice Layne phoned to check up on us—once during a layover at Schiphol, next from a pay telephone in a lodge beneath the Matterhorn. A deaf-mute Guatemalan woman pushing sixty popped in every few days to launder the linens and scour the bathrooms, but otherwise we were largely abandoned to our solitary leisure. We could make love atop the Chippendale table in the dining room (which we did once)

or in the master bath's Jacuzzi, a tub almost the size of our entire kitchen on 95th Street. All that was asked of me was that I not stroll the grounds naked, an immodesty which, despite earlier prophesies of skinny-dipping, drew out the latent WASP in my girlfriend, and that I take care to keep my would-be in-laws' Australian fowl secured under lock and key.

Over dinner one night, Cheryl asked, "It's not so bad, is it?"

"I miss the pollution. All this fresh air can't be safe for my lungs," I said. "And without cabs honking outside the windows, I feel like I'm going deaf . . ."

Cheryl grinned. "I knew you'd like it."

I raised my champagne flute. "Emus forever, babe," I toasted.

"Emus forever," she echoed.

Our glasses clinked.

"Next time around, remind me to go to Vassar and major in sociology," I added. "And to minor in fucking architects."

So I confess I did appreciate the opulence. And the space. And the silence. How can a guy not enjoy twenty-foot ceilings and cordwood walls when he's used to getting up at three am to shout for the Portuguese dental students across the airshaft to turn down their television? Or relish watching porn on an 88-inch screen while swigging cognac straight from the decanter? At the same time, I acknowledge that I am something of a contrarian—maybe even a curmudgeon, or at least a curmudgeon-in-training—and by my fourth day of country living, I found myself growing frustrated with the crickets and orioles that greeted us each morning, with the dew that glazed my boot toes on the trek to count the emus. If I'd stayed in Manhattan, I'd have resented the cacophony of the city for imposing itself on my mathematical endeavors; since I was in self-imposed exile, I blamed the countryside for my struggles. I wasn't yet ready to concede the obvious: that my thick, almost middle-aged skull simply didn't contain enough gray matter to tackle the Hodge conjecture.

Not in the city; not in the boondocks. An emu had better odds against a coyote.

On day five, I set my notebooks aside before lunchtime and squandered the afternoon rambling the neighborhood on foot. Day six saw me visiting President Van Buren's estate in Kinderhook and touring a winery across the river near Saugerties. Cheryl preferred to sketch and catnap. "I'm avoiding any place I might run into an eleventh-grade girl," she said. "Besides, I'm making progress with my charcoals, and want to take advantage of the afternoon sun." She displayed little interest in my comings-and-goings, except to ask me to pick up a sack of quinoa and a jug of goat milk at the food coop in a nearby hamlet. "If you decide to have an affair," she called after me, "make sure you're home to feed the emus." That was day seven. After a stroll through an overpriced sculpture gallery in Beacon, and an agriculture lesson at the Catskills' only working yak farm, delivered by a college-age white girl sporting a traditional Nepalese *tongok*, I made a pit stop at a roadhouse along Route 23.

A chalked sign out front announced: "Every Hour is Happy Hour." Inside, the unfinished wooden tables stood largely empty: a thirty-something couple—probably no older than Cheryl and me—bickered near the dormant fireplace. Two grizzled men threw darts in the corner. Posters along the walls advertised European beers and bands whose names I didn't recognize. The bartender, a stocky girl with buckteeth, not *un*-cute, set an empty coaster in front of me. She had a jagged scar across her throat, as though she'd given birth to a goiter.

"What can I get you?" she asked.

I wasn't thirsty, just bored. "You don't have any cheap cognac, do you?"

She handed me a beer list. "I've got Guinness and a local IPA on tap," she said. "We also have a oatmeal lager special that's not on the menu."

I ordered a Guinness. After a week of top-shelf brandy, the brew tasted rather like cement, but that didn't stop me from downing two more pints. "You should probably cut me off," I said to the bartender, "Because I'm starting to have crazy ideas. Have you ever seen an emu drunk?"

She shrugged. "What's that?"

"Nothing. I was just thinking how funny it would be to bring home a six-pack for my emus," I said. "Not ha-ha funny. More conceptually amusing."

"For your *what?*"

"My emus. I've got a quartet of emus for pets."

The woman continued wiping down the bar. "You for real?" she asked. "My friend had an emu sweater once . . . or maybe that was angora . . ."

"Emus are birds," I explained. "Huge birds. Like ostriches."

"Sure, they're birds."

"I'm dead serious," I said. "Take a look at this . . ."

I switched on my phone and showed the woman—whose name I soon learned was Holly—a video of an emu fetching a Frisbee. Not one of *my* emus, but still. That proved enough to captivate the bartender. Pretentious cocktail parties apparently weren't the only places where emu possession came in handy.

"And you own *four* of those?"

"I don't exactly *own* them. I'm just looking after them for the summer. Babysitting or bird-sitting or whatever." And then—in a mildly inebriated and self-destructive impulse—I asked, "Do you want to meet them?"

I can't say what my intentions were. Or even if I had any intentions. I wasn't planning to cheat on Cheryl any more than a pebble plans to roll down the side of a mountain.

The invitation caught my new acquaintance off guard. "I don't know about that . . ."

"Come on," I said. "It will be fun. What time do you get off work?"

"Seven o'clock. But you're not messing with me, are you?" she asked. "I swear if this is just some twisted pick up line . . ."

"Cross my heart," I said. "I'm a math professor at Hunter."

I fished inside my wallet and handed her my university ID, as though my academic credentials were somehow proof against deceit—as though no algebraist had ever seduced a younger woman under false pretenses. And yet even as I mapped out our excursion in my head, I realized its futility. Cheryl was bound to object—to throw our guest off the property before she so much as glimpsed any birdlife.

"Here's the deal," I said. "My sister and I are looking after the emus for a couple of months. For rich friends of hers on vacation in Europe." I leaned forward, lowering my voice. "We're not allowed to have houseguests and Cheryl's a bit of a stickler, but if you meet me after sundown—maybe ten o'clock or so—I can sneak you out to the emu pen."

"This has to be a joke," said Holly. "Say, am I on camera?"

"No joke," I replied. "Who could possibly make this shit up?"

That was when the girl's eyes registered me for the first time—when she recognized me as a fellow human being, rather than a hops-dependent gratuity dispenser with an emu foursome. I could sense her mental gears in overdrive, puzzling whether I were a menace, or merely a well-heeled eccentric, or possibly even one of those lonely billionaires who tips a waitress college tuition on a ham sandwich. Her lips curved into a beavery smile.

"Okay, let's do it," said Holly. "But I'm photographing your ID and sending a copy to my mom just in case. She's a state trooper. If I'm not home by midnight . . ."

"If you're not home by midnight," I interjected, "I'm a dead man."

I didn't start with intentions, as I said, at least not conscious ones, but as I drove back toward Layne's, painstakingly tracing the yellow lines toward the river, I'll admit I started to entertain hopes. Vague, inchoate prospects. Alcohol-fueled possibilities. Not that any sane, red-blooded male could have found the big-boned bartender more attractive than Cheryl, but I suppose my week of enforced solitude had whetted my appetite for variety. Or maybe I was just a lecherous jerk. Who knows? The bottom line was that by the time I pulled onto my potential sister-in-law's gravel drive, I'd committed adultery extensively in my imagination.

Cheryl met me on the porch, gorgeous in her yellow sundress. Twilight had descended over the Hudson, casting long shadows through the millwork. A lone, mournful crow perched above us on the railing of the loggia. My girlfriend carried a pair of coffee mugs.

"Try this," said Cheryl. "Fresh apple cider."

She handed me a mug and I kissed her on the forehead. "You got a ride into town?"

"Better. It came to us," she said. "Door-to-door apple cider salesman."

"Beats vacuum cleaners and encyclopedias," I said.

Cheryl hugged me from behind, wrapping her arms around my flanks.

"You're late," she said, resting her chin on my shoulder. "Did you have a fun day?"

"More or less. I saw some over-hyped sculptures that looked like relics of the Stone Age and I turned down a chance to milk a yak," I said. "Oh, and my extramarital affair took longer than I anticipated."

"Did it now? And I thought speed was your strong suit."

"Touché. If you want to know the truth, I stopped for a beer."

Cheryl extricated herself from my body. "A beer?"

"Three beers, actually. At a local roadhouse."

My girlfriend stepped to the balustrade. For an instant, I feared I'd overplayed my hand—that she'd started to percolate suspicions. In the yard, a woodchuck yawned on hind legs.

"I wish we could live here," said Cheryl. "Year round."

"Emus forever," I replied. "Is that it?"

"Something like that," she answered. "Emus forever."

We enjoyed a cheerful dinner on the veranda: poached trout from a Native American cookbook recipe whose preparation had taken Cheryl much of the afternoon. Once the last sunlight vanished behind the hillscape, she lit a candelabra. We chatted comfortably about my visit to Van Buren's home, about the upcoming primary elections, about a distant cousin of Cheryl's who had traced their maternal lineage back to Washington Irving. Not once did our conversation drift toward delicate subjects: marriage, children. A warm romantic haze settled over us, and if not for my ten o'clock commitment to Holly Huber, I might easily have followed my girlfriend upstairs to the guest bedroom. "I'm a fool," I said. "I forgot to check on the emus."

"Can't you do it in the morning?" asked Cheryl.

"If *I'd* suggested that," I said, "You'd have cut my dick off."

Cheryl shrugged. "Well, don't take too long."

"How long can it take to count four emus?" I asked.

But from a year of experience, I knew that was more than long enough for a thirty-seven-year-old high school mathematics teacher to fall asleep.

The path to the emu compound proved challenging to navigate in the dark. A new moon offered little help; I nearly lost my balance on the iron footbridge, which would have meant a steep tumble into the dry streambed below. It was nearly ten minutes after the hour when I reached the service road, and I was beginning to doubt whether the bartender would actually show, when the fender of her white pickup appeared through the undergrowth. She'd changed into overalls with reflective bands at the knees and an orange parka, and, unlike yours truly, she'd possessed sense enough to bring along a flashlight. "Hey," she said. "I thought you were standing me up."

"Had to wait for my sister to conk out," I said.

I traversed the shallow swale between us, and I contemplating kissing her right there—emus be damned. She appeared chunkier in the overalls, approaching downright fat, but not in an unsightly way. The notion also crossed my mind that, had I been a serial killer, she'd have been largely helpless against the stun gun and galvanized steel wire that I'd have previously stashed behind a boulder. And if this girl could be so foolish, so cavalier with her very life, would my own hypothetical daughters be any wiser? Of course not, I thought. Another empirical argument against reckless procreation, although one I couldn't exactly share with Cheryl. "Follow me," I ordered, commandeering the flashlight, and I steered Holly along the woodchip trail that skirted the abandoned apiary, past the fenced patroon burial ground, until we arrived at the curtilage of the emu enclosure. I punched in the passcode. Gaudí greeted us with a hiss, his neck raised like a periscope. Across the pen, I spotted either I. M. Pei or Frank Lloyd Wright—it was hard to tell them apart—squatting on her tarsi.

"Wow," Holly exclaimed. "You weren't lying."

"Just don't get too close," I warned. "This fellow kicks."

We edged our way along the perimeter, across the knee-high grass.

"They're really rather miraculous creatures," I said. "At top speed, they can hit eighty miles per hour." I had no idea whether this were true, but it sounded impressive. "And they possess a world-class sense of smell. The French use them for hunting truffles."

Holly inched toward the sleeping bird. "Can you eat them?" she asked.

"Not these," I said. "My sister wouldn't approve."

That drew a giggle from my companion. A second bird approached the first—I believe the newcomer was Saarinen—and thrust forward its chest. From my Internet ramblings, I vaguely recalled this posture to be indicative of impending attack.

"Let's sit down a minute," I suggested.

We settled onto a rick of hay. I aimed the flashlight into the night sky, not wanting to disturb the emus, letting the beam cut through the heavens. A breeze rustled the undergrowth. The bartender said something about the stars, about an astronomy elective she'd taken in high school. Her index finger traced Orion's belt toward Betelgeuse, Bellatrix, Rigel. "Can I ask you an intrusive question?" I asked. "You don't have to answer if you don't want to . . ."

"Fire away."

I didn't answer verbally. Instead, I reached out and touched her neck, running my flesh along the scar—until her hand clasped mine. "Bar fight," she said. "Over a guy. You should see the other gal."

"Jesus Christ."

"I'm joking," said Holly. "I had a tumor as a kid. Benign. Nothing really . . ." She giggled again—without releasing my hand. "That's not what I thought you were going to ask."

"And what *did* you think I was going to ask?"

I could sense the warmth of Holly's body, her words like a taut string. She turned her head toward mine and I braced myself for the kiss—but there was no kiss, no warmth. Just silence leading to a longer silence, a tunnel without an opening at the distal end. And slowly the silence gave way to emus grunting, to the fluid nocturne of unseen flora and fauna.

"I'm sorry," she said abruptly. "Really, I am."

"What's there to be sorry for?"

"Look, I have a boyfriend. Sort of. In the Coast Guard." She stood up without warning. "I should really go home. But thank you for showing me the emus. Really."

Her sudden movement must have scared the birds. The enclosure resonated with scampering, followed by a scraping noise, and I lowered the flashlight just in time to see Gaudí bolt through the open gate into the wilderness.

We both froze in momentary shock; then I ran to block the escape route. The last thing I needed was a second emu on the loose. Holly followed me across the pen.

"Will it be okay?" she asked. "Should we call 9-1-1."

"He'll be fine," I lied. "Emus always find their way home eventually."

❊

I could have lived without seeing Holly Huber again. Gaudí the Emu was another matter entirely. The next morning, I woke before dawn—even though it was Cheryl's emu-feeding day—and tended to the breakfast needs of the remaining three birds. She came downstairs to find the chores a fait accompli and me preparing bloody marys.

"That was too sweet," said Cheryl. "Is there a catch?"

"No catch. I'm just bonding with my emus," I said. "I'm thinking we might buy a couple for our apartment. *Indoor* emus. Do you think they come in miniature? Like ponies? We could keep a whole flock of them in the guest room and sell the oil."

"I think you're nuts. But I'm glad you're adjusting."

"Crazier ideas have paid off," I said. "And there are no coyotes on the Upper West Side."

"Layne is right. Where *do* I find these guys?" replied Cheryl. "You have another Hudson Valley adventure planned for today?"

"I thought I'd head up to Albany," I lied. "See the capitol. Check on my tax dollars. Maybe take in a minor league baseball game."

Yet as soon as my girlfriend carried her palette down to the sundeck, I locked myself in the den and printed up hundreds of "MISS-

ING EMU" flyers. I offered a $2000 cash reward; I didn't have that kind of money handy, but I figured I'd deal with one problem at a time. At worst, I could always sell off some overpriced knickknack of Layne's and hope she didn't notice. The alternative was buying a replacement bird—but all I could find on the Internet were chicks, except one guy in Colorado trying to offload an entire fifty-head "mob," which I discovered was the technical collective noun for a heard of the creatures. Besides, even if I fooled Cheryl, that would just have bought me time; I harbored some doubts whether my in-laws to-be could recognize their own emus individually, but that wasn't a chance I wanted to risk. I never considered coming clean, not even a confession that omitted the busty bartender. Somehow, I sensed, an apology would lead to a higher stakes conversation—and I'd either end up chained for life or single.

By nine o'clock, I'd plastered every telephone pole and signboard between Clermont and Claverack. Then I parked the Oldsmobile opposite Layne's drive—to head off Cheryl, in the remote event that she decided to hitch a ride to the food coop or to explore the neighborhood on front. For the first time since our exile, I was grateful to be dating a homebody.

I'd anticipated a tedious wait. To pass the time, I'd brought along my notes on the Hodge conjecture, although I found myself too stressed to concentrate. Not that it mattered. I'd hardly reviewed my previous scribblings when the first call came in. From a housewife in Livingston who'd spotted something "emu-like" outside her kitchen window. *You'll have to come out to see for yourself*, she said. *It might only be a big pheasant. But it's something.* And I'd hardly jotted down her address when a bus driver in Gallatin phoned about a carcass on the Taconic Parkway. Both reports requiring investigation, both ultimately false alarms. Each an opportunity for Cheryl to escape the estate while I was otherwise engaged. By midday, the calls were coming in faster than I could possibly answer them. I was forced to triage, prioritizing reports of live birds, discounting anything with the words "goose" or "turkey" in the description.

I stopped for gas as the Exxon station on Shope Road. Just a random service station—a place I'd visited a dozen times before. When I ducked inside to buy a cup of coffee, the cashier beamed and said, "Say, you're the dude looking for the emu."

"Why? Have you seen him?" I inquired.

"Nah, I wish," said the cashier. "But you've certainly got people talking around here. You know you really shouldn't let those things out on their own."

※

My girlfriend hadn't left the property all day. She greeted me with a deep kiss on the lips, and I figured we were in for a frisky evening, when the house phone rang. Layne's number. It must have been approaching midnight in the Alps.

"I've got to answer it," said Cheryl.

As luck would have it, my own phone rang an instant later, and I took the call in the dining room. A community college student in Hager Falls, who'd been hiking with friends, had spotted what she believed to be emu droppings. She'd gone back and collected them in Tupperware. Did I want them? I had to get her off the phone quickly when Cheryl returned from the den.

"She's flying home early," said Cheryl. "One of the boys shattered his femur at a tournament. He's going to need surgery in Boston."

"Does that mean we need to clear out?" I asked.

Cheryl shook her head. "I don't think so. She'll probably just drop by to check on the birds and then head back to France." She poured herself a glass of sweet tea. "Who were you on the phone with?"

"Nobody," I said. "Just the college. About my grading forms."

Her expression tightened. "*On a Saturday? At midnight?*"

I'd entirely forgotten the day of the week. And the time. All days feel the same when your only responsibilities are summing Poincaré duals and searching for emus. "The department administrator was working from home . . ."

"Like hell she was," snapped Cheryl. "Do you want me to call her back?"

She reached for my phone. I had to retreat behind the dining table.

Then my girlfriend was leaning against the sideboard, sobbing. "I really believed you were just exploring the countryside," she cried. "Van Buren's home! How stupid could I be . . .?"

"I *was* at Van Buren's home," I insisted. "I still have the receipt."

My phone rang again. In hindsight, I realize I probably shouldn't have answered it—that, for any sane person, reassuring Cheryl would have been a higher priority. What did it even matter whether I found the damned emu if my relationship crumbled anyway? But, in the moment, I wasn't thinking too clearly; the goal of finding the missing bird had taken on a primacy of its own. So I answered, and found myself speaking with a beet farmer from Ancram Heights. He claimed to have the eloped Gaudí in the back of his truck and wanted to drop it off.

"You sure you've got it?" I asked. "Not a pheasant or a turkey . . ."

"Hard mistake to make," he said. "You sure you got $2000?"

I carried the phone onto the veranda, out of earshot of Cheryl.

"You'll get your money," I said. "Just bring me the emu. Does 9am work?"

"I'm not keeping this thing all night," said the farmer. "It's now or never. I'll be outside your door in the better part of an hour . . ."

When I returned to the house, Cheryl was no longer by the sideboard. She'd gone upstairs to the guest room and bolted the door behind her.

※

The last of the summer sun was still dancing in the poplars when the farmer's canopy truck lurched up the main drive. Fellow's name was MacDonald, of all things—but he wasn't old. Couldn't have been more than twenty-five. All business. He yanked a tarp off the back of the truck as though presenting an exotic meal. "Here's your emu, man. Looks like them coyotes had a field day with him, but that beak is definitely emu," he said. He pronounced the word "*kay-oat*" without an "e" on the end. But you couldn't really argue with the guy: the lump of tendons and talons and bloody feathers was most certainly Gaudí. I sensed tears welling behind my eyes, entirely unexpected, and drew the tarp back over the carcass in a pantomime of respect.

"So about that reward," said MacDonald. "You think you could manage cash?"

"The award was for a *live* emu," I said. "I thought that was obvious."

And if you're reading this, Cheryl, I realize you already know what happened next: the fisticuffs, the police report, the official call to Layne and Adrian in Chamonix. But what you probably don't know is how sorry I am, really, even after all these years. If I could do it over again, I wouldn't rendezvous with that bartender or take that phone call, and I'd find a way to be the best bird-daddy ever. The best husband and human-daddy too. I swear I would.

Emus forever, babe. Emus forever

THE SCHOOL OF ANECDOTAL MEDICINE

Y SCIATICA having resisted the cures of multiple neu-
rologists, a highly-touted female orthopedist, a professor of physiatry, a rather Parkinsonian osteopath and
even a chiropractor—desperate times being the breeding grounds of
quackery—I found myself one forlorn autumn afternoon in the office
of Dr. A. B. Majesterio of the School of Anecdotal Medicine. He did
not come, I concede, with the storied reputation of the orthopedist
or the august credentials of the physiatrist, but merely the second-
hand endorsement of my barber's sister, yet his address stood in an
upscale if sleepy neighborhood, only a few avenues from the river,
and the premises, adorned with pastel floral prints, proved reassur-
ingly benign. As for Majesterio, he was precisely what one might
expect in an anecdotalist: a hale, robust fellow in shirtsleeves and
an open collar whose specialty distinguished itself in his reassuring
voice and the panâche of his hand gestures. Beyond that, I can tell
you little of the man. His age I could not have pinpointed within
twenty years of fifty, while his ancestors might as easily have been
"Black Irish" as Veronese Jews or, to be fully candid, light-skinned
denizens of Mauritania. All I cared about was whether he possessed
the expertise to treat the intense pain jetting down my left leg.

"Mr. A——, the writer," Majesterio said. "We have been waiting for
you."

I confess he caught me off guard: I am an aviation engineer by profession, having retired many years ago after three decades at Sikorsky, and although I do take the blame for published biographies of Wiley Post and "Wrong Way" Corrigan, these were labors of love and not of commerce. I believe that afternoon to have been the first and final occasion upon which any human being has followed my name with a literary epithet. "Am I late?" I asked on instinct, defensively, although I knew myself to be several minutes early.

"Not at all, not at all," said the anecdotalist. He led me into his inner sanctum, a windowless den of mahogany paneling and rococo carpets, and we soon found ourselves seated face to face on a pair of gooseneck chairs. From the dimly illuminated chamber leached the sweet scent of pipe tobacco, of uncut, leather-bound pages. Majesterio's tone was soothing, almost mesmeric, when he asked. "Please tell me your story, Mr. A——. What seems to be the trouble?"

So I poured forth my tale of woe: the jolts of agony radiating from my hip to the sole of my foot, aggravated by an anticipatory dread that for nearly ten months had rendered the pleasures of gardening and golf beyond reach. I had visited eight esteemed practitioners of medical arts (if one included the chiropractor), but all they could agree upon, once their own proposed remedies failed, was that my condition appeared highly atypical. Yet as I divulged my medical saga, the nerve blocks and spinal manipulations, the tomographic scans and exploratory surgeries, my miseries sounded increasingly trivial. I had not been afflicted with a malignancy, after all, or injured in battle. Majesterio, for his part, expressed sympathy, on occasion, but otherwise allowed me to speak uninterrupted, which could not have been said for his allopathic rivals. "So there you have it," I concluded, ten minutes later, "At this point, I'm open to any ideas—good or otherwise."

"Indeed," said Majesterio. "I do have an idea. Only time will tell if it's a good one."

"I'll take my chances."

"I admire your attitude, Mr. A——," he said. "All remedies are a gamble, aren't they? But in your case, I'm reminded of a story I once heard from a colleague. If you were a medical man, his name would be familiar to you, as it has lent itself to several eponyms. Mayrhofer's paralysis and Mayrhofer-Tutt syndrome are the most well-known, but there are others. In any case, Dr. Mayrhofer—I assume he's long dead by now—was stationed at Subic Bay in the Philippines for several years between the wars. In a rare effort to generate good will among the local population, the navy at that time operated a free clinic, and Mayrhofer, as a junior medical officer, was assigned to staff this infirmary on alternate weekends. You must picture him there, far from his native Wisconsin, laboring in the stifling heat among the calamansi trees and the junglefowl. Are you able to see him in your mind's eye, Mr. A——?"

"More or less," I said.

"I can see him. Clear as day," said Majesterio. "And it was at this clinic that a patient came to Mayrhofer, a tagabantáy on a nearby coffee plantation, with an account much like yours. He had not visited multiple specialists, to be sure, or received a regional nerve block; his course of treatment to that date had consisted entirely of sambong poultices, which had proven fruitless. So too, alas, did the cures to be found in the navy's own pharmacopeia. In frustration, Mayrhofer considered invoking the services of a headshrinker, an authority on hypnosis who could claim some prior successes with victims of shellshock. Fortunately, the clinic had in its employ at that time a native medic from a neighboring district, a full-blooded Igorot old enough to have fought alongside Aguinaldo, who recalled a similar case from his village that had been successfully treated with cataplasms of milk from the giant bearded civet. And at a loss for other options, Mayrhofer commandeered an entire platoon to search the Luzon bush for this elusive creature. After two days of hard labor and rumblings of mutiny, they finally caught one. I give the man credit for his dedication."

The anecdotalist proved a compelling storyteller and I did find myself imagining this troop of sweltering seamen thrashing through the undergrowth—probably wondering which military god they had offended to be allotted this grueling mission.

"Mayrhofer did not have high expectations. But the tagabantáy suffered dreadfully, and his physician was not a man to go down without a fight," continued Majesterio. "So they milked the civet, and lacquered the plaster across the patient's flesh, and lo and behold, three weeks later, the tagabantáy was entirely pain-free." He allowed these words to sink in and then added, "I wish I could report a happy ending, but the man was later executed during the Japanese occupation."

With that revelation, Majesterio glanced at his wristwatch and rose unexpectedly.

"So there you have it," he said. "I'll see you in three weeks."

"I don't understand. What should I do?"

"I just told you," said Majesterio. "It's worth a try."

His meaning became clear to me. "You can't be serious," I objected. "How am I supposed to find a giant bearded civet?"

"You're not," Majesterio reassured me. "I believe they're extinct. Loss of habitat." He slid me a business-size envelope that I later discovered contained his bill. "You'll have to improvise, I'm afraid. We'll just hope for the best."

I did not have much confidence in Majesterio's plan, if one could even call it that, but a drowning man, as they say, will clutch at straw. Or civets, for that matter. Unfortunately, civet milk isn't easily found at the Stop and Shop. The best I could manage was the milk of the Asiatic linsang, a spotted, tree-dwelling cousin native to the evergreen forests of southern China—a creature about as closely related to the civet as human beings are to lemurs. I purchased a gallon of the costly nectar, on blind faith, from a grocer on Mott Street; had he sold me a cocktail of coconut powder and carpenter's glue, I wouldn't have been any the wiser. And then, for the next twenty-one days, I painted myself with the treacly, musk-scented substance.

The initial effects appeared promising, and on the second afternoon, I mustered the courage to wheel a tray of tulip bulbs to the base of the Japanese maple for planting. Yet these benefits proved to be placebic and all too fleeting. When I returned for my follow-up with the anecdotalist in late October, my muted hope had given way to outright despair.

Majesterio appeared as I had left him: blue Oxford loose at the collar, his voice as assuasive as ever. Soon enough, we once again settled into our stations. "I have been thinking of you often, Mr. A——," he said. "I have another idea."

"Don't you want to know how the first one turned out?"

"I already know," he replied. "Had it worked, you would not have returned."

He was right, of course, as much as I hated to admit it. Had my pain resolved, I'd have cancelled my follow-up and never laid eyes upon the fellow again. Why I'd kept the appointment at all remains a mystery to me.

"About a decade ago, I was having lunch at my club—not something I do often, you understand, but a man should drop in at his club a few times a year, I think, to make sure he's still welcome." Majesterio chuckled. I confess, as I have never belonged to a "club," unless one counts several professional associations wherein membership consists entirely of sending an annual check and receiving a quarterly newsletter, the humor was lost on me. "While I was there, I struck up a conversation with another member, who'd recently retired from the presidency of a major international health organization. This gentleman—you'll forgive my discretion, but some of our members can be exacting with regards to privacy—shared a curious episode from his early days in the public health service. He'd been charged with running a polio vaccination campaign in a recently in-dependent African nation—again, you must pardon my speaking in imprecise terms—but the local populace remained suspicious. Likely with good reason."

I found myself wondering which exotic mammal would be in-voked this time, whether I'd be expected to track down cheetah pelts or the horns of an oryx.

"So, to prove the safety of the shots, this gentleman gathered the elders of a major market village to watch as he injected himself. That did the trick. Over the next six months, in settlements across the Sa-hel, he jabbed a needle into his own thigh nearly two dozen times. The inactivated form of the virus, I'm glad to say."

"But I don't have polio," I interjected.

"Certainly not. You have sciatica," agreed Majesterio. "But so did this gentleman. Or he did, that is, until he started vaccinating him-self against polio. After that, nothing."

The anecdotalist waved a hand as though my pain might be brushed away as easily. Then he produced a prescription pad from his desk and wrote me twenty prescriptions for the inactivated polio vaccine. "I'm not sure your insurance will cover this," he said—and handed me both the prescriptions and another business-size enve-lope. I was rather shocked to discover that anecdotalists had the au-thority to write prescriptions in the state of New York.

"Is this even safe?" I asked.

"We'll find out," replied Majesterio.

His dark eyes honed upon me, almost weapons.

Then he grinned broadly and laughed. "A joke, Mr. A——," he said. "It's perfectly safe."

✳

Over the next twenty days, my stack of prescriptions thinned as I vis-ited pharmacies across five counties and two states. My cover story was marginally plausible: I'd been hired to inspect rural airfields in Pakistan—one of the few places on the planet where the paralytic virus still remained endemic. In extreme caution, my internist had suggested receiving a booster. Since I paid cash, none of these druggists knew that I was to receive not merely one additional injection, but a score. Yet whatever enigmatic property of the vaccine had cured the public health officer proved highly ineffective against my strain of sciatica. This time I didn't even enjoy a momentary if psychogenic reprieve. On several mornings in the week before Halloween, I made an effort to lay in the remaining tulip bulbs, as well as some Dutch master daffodils to fringe the peony hedge, but I'd hardly been at work for twenty minutes when sparks began to flare from my hip all the way to my heel. That's a thousand dollars I'll never see again, I berated myself, yet still I returned again in November to seek the wisdom of Dr. Majesterio.

"Highly atypical," said the anecdotalist. "But in a highly typical way."

"What do you mean by that?" I asked.

We were seated once more in his all-too-familiar gooseneck chairs like friendly adversaries in a never-ending chess match. He did not acknowledge my question.

"I had my piano tuned last week," said Majesterio. "And I thought to myself, that might be a solution to Mr. A——'s difficulties."

"Let me guess," I said. "Your piano tuner suffered from crippling sciatica until he heard a particular piece of music in the wrong key—let's say Brahms's sonata No. 3—and suddenly he found himself able to tap dance."

Majesterio smiled. "You have a writer's mind, Mr. A——. As for me, I know nothing about the lad except that he seemed skilled enough at his trade and that he charged $200 for less than an hour's labor."

"At least now he can afford to get vaccinated against polio," I said.

Again, Majesterio ignored me.

"There is a sketch in an essay by the English critic, Lytton Strachey, in which—as I recall—he discusses the case of a retainer of his father who was injured while hoisting a piano in Mayfair and developed intractable lumbago. Being of a certain liberal mindset, the man's employer, Sir Richard, called upon the services of the most skilled specialists on Harley Street. Gowers, Hughlings Jackson, Macewen—none could silence the servant's pain. The essay plays his agony up dramatically, emphasizing the domestic's extreme torments. Keep in mind that you couldn't just walk into your druggist back then and purchase a bottle of ibuprofen."

Only morphine and cocaine, I thought—but kept this to myself.

"The fellow was hardly able to leave his bedchamber. He lost his appetite. He developed a nagging catarrh and a hacking cough. If Strachey is to be believed, the fellow even considered taking his own life. All on account of his lumbago. But then, as fortune would have it, Sir Richard's cook fell into possession of an excess quantity of persimmon preserves. How exactly this came to pass, I no longer remember. What I do recall is that the preserves were ultimately served as a cobbler—and Strachey's younger sister took it upon herself to deliver a portion to the ailing workman. Seeing the positive effect on his spirits, she served him another portion the following morning, and then another. The man's skin turned orange, but he did begin to recover. And after three weeks, he was able to walk pain-free. It's a heartwarming tale. Highly out of character for its author, I might add."

"Persimmons," I said. "Do you know what variety of persimmons?"

"That detail, I fear, has been lost to the ages," said Majesterio. "You may have to experiment."

❋

I resolved to give the anecdotalist's methods one more chance. Despite extensive efforts, including a visit to the reference desk at the public library, I was unable to locate the Strachey essay to which he referred, but resigned to my destiny, and against my better judgment, I combed the city for persimmons of all shapes and sizes: I sampled squat fuyus and angular tamopans, cloying saijos and astringent tanenashis. I consumed persimmons for breakfast, persimmons for supper, persimmons while waiting in line at the bank. If I didn't exactly turn orange, by evening each day, my fingers and clothes were stained with juices. All, I fear, to no avail. Unlike the injured piano hoister, I appeared to possess a persimmon immunity.

And then the strangest incident occurred. I had determined, pain or no pain, to lay in what remained of my unplanted fall bulbs. The soil had already turned stubborn, as it does in mid-November, warning that first frost lurks only nights away. So I descended the stairs to the garage—lowering my good leg, then trailing with its partner—and set about loading an assortment of crocuses, hyacinths and other early blossoms into my cart. Somehow, in doing so, I dislodged a nest of wasps that had taken refuge from the chill.

Paper wasps—I later learned—grow highly aggressive in the weeks preceding their winter die-off. Raging, I suppose, against the dying of the light. Who can say I'd be any less enraged under similar circumstances? In this case, however, I found myself the victim of their righteous anger. I vaguely recall dialing 911 and sharing my address. And next I knew, I'd lost nearly forty-eight hours and I woke to the eternal incandescence of the step-down unit at the county hospital. All told, I'd received somewhere in the neighborhood of fifty stings. My right arm remained bandaged to the shoulder; my chest and neck were patched with gauze. Another day elapsed before I was back on my feet again, able to use the toilet on my own. And that was when the insight grasped me: my sciatica was gone.

For the first few hours, I dared not move my leg, afraid that the pain might return—maybe with more gusto than ever. But no!

Somehow—as least, this is the best explanation I've been able to muster—the anti-inflammatory agents that had suppressed the wasp venom had also pacified my nerves. Or maybe that notion was entirely off-base. Who could truly say? Whatever the reason, that was the last I ever felt of the pain, and now, nearly six years later, I can report with confidence that I am cured.

My story might have ended there. Needless to say, I did not return to see Dr. Majesterio, nor did I give the anecdotalist much further consideration. My life returned to the simple pleasures of late middle age: cocktails on the 19th hole, forsythia and rhododendrons in summer. With time, I took up an interest in breeding daylilies and met a retired chemistry professor who enjoyed a similar pursuit. I am pleased to report we have been seeing each other for several years and are quite happy. My sciatica retreated into the past, a dull ache of memory. That was that.

So I confess I was entirely unprepared for my final encounter with Dr. A. B. Majesterio. It was a promising day in early May, and I'd agreed to join two fellow lily breeders for lunch at a French bistro near the river. To my surprise, returning from the restroom, I caught sight of a man of indeterminate age and ethnicity ensconced at a corner table. He remained entirely unchanged: shirtsleeves, open collar, dark eyes as piercing as ever. With him sat a much younger woman, rather a looker. The notion that the anecdotalist was married—that there might be additional generations of Majesterios scampering about—left me feeling betrayed. That his bride might be half his age shattered my image of the man even further. I decided to avoid noticing him.

"Why if it isn't, Mr. A——, the writer," he cried. "As I live and breathe."

That forced me to acknowledge him. "Dr. Majesterio," I said.

"So good to see you," he replied. "And this is my niece, G——. I am pleased to say that she is following in my professional footsteps."

"You must be proud."

"How could I not be? And you? I trust the sugar plums did the trick. Or were they apricots? It has been a while . . ."

"Persimmons," I said. "Variety unknown."

I considered telling him about the wasps. In the end, I chose not to. My case was atypical, after all, even if in a typical manner. And besides, I had no wish to undermine the fellow's accomplishments in front of his niece. So I returned to my lunch companions, and he to his, each of us a mystery to the other, and each with his own story to tell.

Jacob M. Appel is currently Professor of Psychiatry and Medical Education at the Icahn School of Medicine at Mount Sinai in New York City, where he is Director of Ethics Education in Psychiatry, Associate Director of the Academy for Medicine and the Humanities, and Medical Director of the Mental Health Clinic at the East Harlem Health Outreach Program. Jacob is the author of five literary novels, ten short story collections, two volumes of poems, an essay collection, a cozy mystery, a thriller, and a compendium of dilemmas in medical ethics. He is Vice President and Treasurer of the National Book Critics Circle, co-chair of the Group for the Advancement of Psychiatry's Committee on Psychiatry & Law, and a Councilor of the New York County Psychiatric Society and of the American Academy of Psychiatry & Law. More at: www.jacobmappel.com

www.ingramcontent.com/pod-product-compliance
Lightning Source LLC
Chambersburg PA
CBHW031945010726
47493CB00007B/2081